AFTER THE END

ALSO BY AMY PLUM

Die for Me

Until I Die

If I Should Die

Die for Her: A Die for Me Digital Novella

AFTER THE END

AMY PLUM

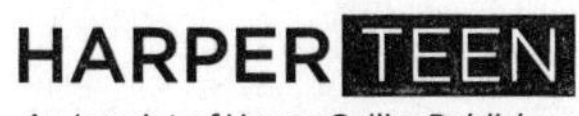

An Imprint of HarperCollins*Publishers*

HarperTeen is an imprint of HarperCollins Publishers.

After the End

www.epicreads.com

Library of Congress Control Number: 2013958340

ISBN 978-0-06-222560-3 (trade bdg.)

Typography by Ray Shappell

14 15 16 17 18 LP/RRDH 10 9 8 7 6 5 4 3 2 1

❖

First Edition

For Maximilien. Love. Courage. Joy.

"IT TOOK THE VIEW OF THE EARTH FROM SPACE . . . to let us sense a planet on which living things, the air, the oceans, and the rocks all combine in one as Gaia. The name of the super-organism, Gaia, is not a synonym for the biosphere. . . . Just as the shell is part of a snail, so the rocks, the air, and the oceans are a part of Gaia. Gaia, as we shall see, has continuity with the past back to the origins of life, and extends into the future as long as life persists."

—James Lovelock, *The Ages of Gaia*

". . . IN ADDITION TO OUR IMMEDIATE CONSCIOUSNESS, which is of a thoroughly personal nature and which we believe to be the only empirical psyche . . . there exists a second psychic system of a collective, universal, and impersonal nature which is identical in all individuals. This collective unconscious does not develop individually but is inherited. It consists of pre-existent forms . . . which give definite form to certain psychic contents."

—C. G. Jung, *The Archetypes and the Collective Unconsciousness*

1

JUNEAU

I CROUCH LOW TO THE GROUND, PRESSING MY back to the ancient spruce tree, and raise my crossbow in one hand. Keeping my eye on the precious shard of mirror embedded in my weapon, I inch it out from behind the tree. In the reflection, I spot something moving behind a cedar across the snowy clearing.

From the cracking of branches to my right, I sense that another foe lurks nearby. I can't see him. Can't see his inevitable scars and pockmarks—damage from the nuclear radiation. But I know he's there. I'll have to take my chances. You have to be tough to survive an apocalypse.

I leap from behind the tree, duck as I see a missile hurtling toward me from a low scrub of holly bush, and simultaneously shoot in front of me. I hit the ground and roll, leaping back to my feet.

"I hit you!" yells a voice from the bushes. I hear a rustling of leaves, and then my friend Nome pops out, her hair glowing like burnished gold against the green and red holly.

"No you didn't!" I yell back, but then I look down to where she's pointing. Gooseberry pulp drips off the sleeve of my buckskin parka. "It's just my arm. It wouldn't have been lethal," I say, flicking off the fruit sludge. But I know that though it wouldn't have killed me on the spot, I would have been injured. And any injury would slow me down. Nome's gooseberry would have meant my eventual death in the case of a true attack on our village.

Kenai steps from behind the cedar with a moose antler in his hand. He has painted an evil face on the wide part of the horn, and my arrow protrudes from its forehead.

"Bull's-eye," he says, and begins to make gurgling sounds as his homemade brigand suffers a painful and drawn-out demise. Trust Kenai to lighten a heavy moment.

The antler's death throes are interrupted by Nikiski, who runs up with his hands in the air. "Cease-fire," he yells, and then grins widely to show two missing front teeth. "Juneau, Whit wants you to come see him in the school. Something about hunting. Something about being low on meat. And Dennis wants you two"—Nikiski gestures to Kenai and Nome—"to drop by the library for something about a project he wants you to do."

"Thank you for that precise and informative message," Kenai

says, ruffling Nikiski's hair with his hand as he walks past the boy toward the village. "Battle officially over," he calls behind him. "Brigand slain, but Junebug injured. Ten points to Nome."

Nome lets out a whoop and then, shoving her slingshot inside her parka, jogs over to me. When she sees my expression, her playful mood deflates. "It's okay, Juneau. Like you said, it wouldn't have been lethal."

I'm silent. She sighs deeply as we begin walking toward the village. "Juneau, you can't be perfect. You're going to be clan Sage, not our sole protector."

"I'd rather be prepared to do both," I respond.

"You're seventeen, Juneau. And you're already carrying the weight of the clan on your shoulders."

I don't respond. But inside, I acknowledge it: I'm just a teenager now, but one day the well-being of a few dozen people will be in my hands. It's a heavy burden—one I know I must carry. Why else would I have been given my gift?

We crest the hill. Before us crouches the Great Ice Bear: Mount Denali, scraping its sugar-white pelt against the sky. And between its foothills and the forest are nestled twenty yurts. The light-colored skins stretched across the roofs and sides of the yurts make them almost invisible against the snow—a necessary camouflage.

It's been thirty years since the war. My parents and fifteen others escaped in the very last hours, after the first firestorm of nuclear explosions triggered the aftermath . . . the creeping death of radiation and famine and genocide. They came here to

Alaska's unspoiled territory, far from any city that would have been targeted for destruction.

Although little was left in the wake of the Final War, it would be foolish to think we were the only survivors. Over the decades, during their rare scouting trips, the elders have found evidence. Abandoned cars run on the scarce drops of fuel that remained after the oil fields burned. Human trails left just beyond the boundaries of our territory. Sounds from the air of a lone renegade flying machine.

But there haven't been any new signs found for a long time. Only a handful of close calls since I was born—seventeen years ago. The only deaths have been accidents: one by bear attack, and then my own mother's death when her sled broke through lake ice.

These are the cautionary tales we are brought up with. Instead of the bogeyman (who terrified my mom as a child), our nightmares are populated with armed brigands roaming the land to plunder what is left. Merciless survivors of the apocalypse, bent upon taking what our clan has worked so hard to preserve: clean food and water and immunity from the radiation and disease that will, in the end, finish off the outside world.

A rebirth. That is what the clan hopes for. What Whit teaches us will happen. But it could take centuries. Millennia. Our goal is survival.

"See you later," I say to Nome as we arrive, and jog ahead of her toward the school yurt. Once through the door flap, it takes a minute for my eyes to adjust from the blinding reflection of sun on snow to the soft light filtering through the open crown of the yurt and the glow of the schoolroom's fire.

I brush off my moccasins and leave them with my crossbow next to the door. If Whit's teaching the younger children, it means he's explaining the Yara. Which before long will be my job. When I was five—just after my mother's death—Whit tested me and found I was able to Conjure. Besides him and my mother, I am the only one of my tribe capable.

In three years I will undergo the Rite, and will then take his place as clan Sage, as my mother should have if she were still alive. So recently Whit's left more and more of the clan Readings to me and has begun to show me how he Conjures, being careful what he shows me, since I can duplicate his results with ease.

"Why don't you join us, Juneau?" Whit asks. The children are seated in a half circle around him. Nikiski's there—he must have sprinted back—and next to him are Tanaina, Wasilla, and Healy, ready to hear Whit's lesson, one he repeats for all age groups several times a year. I've heard it so many times, I could recite it by heart.

I sit down next to Whit as he pours a layer of ground mica on the floor. The firelight reflects in it, making it sparkle. The young children watch, their attention caught and held by the glistening powder.

Whit etches a large circle with his finger. "This is the earth. Everything in it is a part of the same organism: you, me, the dogs, the ground, the air." He takes Healy's hand and blows a puff of air on it, demonstrating wind, causing the four-year-old to giggle in delight. “We live inside a superorganism, and everything within it is connected by a powerful force.”

“The Yara,” the children shout in unison.

Whit pulls a mock-surprised expression and asks, “Have you heard this story before?”

“Yes!” the children yell, laughing gleefully. Whit smiles and unconsciously smooths down the solitary strand of gray hair in his black mane. It’s the one sign of his aging before he found the Yara. Proof that he is the oldest in the clan.

“You’re right,” he concedes. “The Yara is the current that moves through all things. It’s what allows us to Read.” Inside the circle representing the earth, Whit draws concentric smaller circles. “Can you tell me what kinds of things have the Yara flowing through them?” He points to the outermost circle.

Tanaina lifts her hand and blurts out, “People!”

Whit nods and points to the next circle in.

“Animals,” Wasilla says, and then adds, “Plants,” as Whit moves to the next circle.

Placing his finger on the innermost circle, he says, “Even the elements—fire, water, air, earth—they all have the Yara running through them.

“Since you are close to the Yara, you can use it to connect with all the other members of earth’s superorganism.” Whit draws lines from the outer “human” circle to those inside. “Even rocks have a memory of what has happened around them. If you can ever get them to talk!” The children laugh again, knowing that speaking rocks are one of Whit’s jokes, even though there is a measure of truth behind it.

"Okay. Today's lesson is over," Whit says. The children let loose, tapping their fingers in the mica powder and wiping it on their faces like war paint. Everybody piles outside, and Whit and I head toward his yurt.

"Did Nikiski give you my message?" he asks.

"In his own way," I say, grinning. "Something about meat?"

"Yes. We're running low," he says. "I thought you could handle it, since the rest of the hunters are needed for the clearing of our summer encampment." Whit's mouth quirks up into a smile. "I didn't think you'd mind going on your own."

My mentor knows me as well as my father does. Besides Ketchikan and Cordova, I'm the best hunter in the clan. And I relish time spent on my own.

We arrive at Whit's yurt. Beside the door sits a lightweight sled with a mountain of supplies strapped to it and a pair of snowshoes draped across the top.

"I Read the skull for you," he says. "You'll find caribou in the south field tomorrow. Get a good night's sleep and you can be down there first thing in the morning."

I nod. "I'll start at daybreak."

"And be careful not to—"

"—cross the boundary. I know, Whit. I'll be careful," I promise.

"All right then. I'm off," he says, and gathers up his pack from atop his sled.

My father appears from behind the neighboring yurt.

"Sneaking away again, Whit?" he teases.

"I hate long good-byes," Whit responds with a smile. "And I'll only be gone two weeks." He turns and straps the sled's rope across his chest, and disappears down a path in the woods.

"I still don't understand why Whit won't take dogs on his retreats," I say.

My father puts a hand on my shoulder and walks with me back toward our home. "He has his own way of doing things," he replies.

We reach the main encampment. The smell of dinners cooking and warm puffs of smoke exiting the crowns of the yurts makes my stomach rumble.

Dad and I push through the door flaps to see Beckett and Neruda lying lazily by the fire, keeping watch over the steaming stew pot.

"So how is my warrior princess?" he asks, as I hang my crossbow from a side beam and begin shucking off my moccasins and parka. "Did Whit say he was sending you hunting?" he asks.

"I leave tomorrow morning," I respond, as he begins ladling out bowls of moose stew. He hands me a bowl and spoon, and I join him in front of the fire. I blow on a steaming spoonful of meat and take a bite. Nestled in the warmth and security of our yurt, I think for the thousandth time of how lucky we are. Dad and I have each other. We have a good life, while the world outside our boundaries is nothing but radioactive waste, bands of marauding brigands, and for anyone else who might have survived World War III, an existence filled with misery and despair.

2

MILES

"AS I HAVE EXPLAINED, I CAUGHT YOUR SON cheating on his final exam." Ms. Cochran, my English teacher, makes a face like she smells something rotten as she holds up my minuscule rolled-up crib sheet. I force myself to keep a neutral expression in front of my dad and the principal, but shrink down into my chair.

"Since when was cheating on a test grounds for expulsion?" my dad exclaims.

Mr. Riggs, the principal, glances at the open file on the desk in front of him and runs his finger down the page. "When a student has had two previous suspensions for bringing alcohol and drugs onto school grounds."

My dad clears his throat. "Well, perhaps we can talk further about it, like we did on those occasions," he says, glancing at Ms.

Cochran. If she wasn't here, the conversation would already have turned to donations my dad's company could give to the school, but judging from the dark look on Mr. Riggs's face, I doubt that would work this time.

"Yes, well, I know that there have been mitigating circumstances, but we can't keep making your son an exception to the rule. Billingston Academy has a strict three-strikes-and-you're-out rule, and I'm afraid I'm going to have to enforce it in your son's case."

A few days later Dad gets a call from the Yale admissions office saying that my enrollment is on hold until they receive some proof that I am "receiving help for my behavioral issues." And that's when Dad comes up with his mail-room plan.

3

JUNEAU

MY ARROW FLIES TRUE AND THE GREAT BULL CARibou slumps to the ground. I sling my crossbow over my shoulder, and the virgin snow crunches under my moccasins as I sprint across the field to kneel by the beast's heaving side. "Thank you," I say as I draw my knife from my belt. I pet the bristly fur of his muzzle and look him straight in his huge glassy eye. And then I slit his throat.

Some of our hunters go into a whole long prayer to the spirit of the animal when they kill. But Whit once told me that respectful treatment and a thank-you equaled all the lofty words in the world. I have to say I agree.

As I clean my knife in the snow, I whistle for Beckett and Neruda to bring the sled over. But they're already on their way, their wriggling bodies bursting with excitement as they bound through the icy drifts. I sling the leather straps over the top of the beast and push the iron dowels underneath its body to pull the straps around.

This bull must weigh two hundred pounds—twice my weight—but with the help of my puller, the dogs and I manage to shuffle him over and onto the sled within minutes, the undulating crimson line he leaves in the snow as bright as a ribbon on a wreath of white lilies.

I am securing the caribou with hemp ropes when I hear something strange: a loud flapping noise, like the beat of a thousand eagles' wings synchronized into multiple steady pulses.

I've heard this sound before, but only from the safety of an emergency shelter. It's a flying machine. Which only means one thing: brigands. My heart skips a beat, and I freeze, scanning the sky.

Why didn't Whit foresee this and hide the clan? They must not be coming close enough to us to be any danger. But in my mind, close enough to hear is close enough to hide. My stomach twists as I think of what I would do if I were the Sage.

The burden of being Whit's successor is already beginning to weigh upon me. Like him, I will protect the clan. Predict storms or natural catastrophes. Conjure healthy crops and Read where food can be found in the lean years. Read when predators or even brigands are near and Conjure camouflage to hide the village.

I can't see where the noise is coming from. Before me looms Mount Denali. The noise of the flying machine echoes off its foothills and is quickly absorbed by the snow-drenched valley sprawling at its feet. I hope it isn't behind the mountain, where my village is. Surely not. Whit would have Read it.

A talon of worry scrapes at my belly. I rush to detach the huskies from the puller and clip them back to the sled. "Hike!" I yell, and we begin racing toward Denali, toward home. The noise has stopped. The machine must be gone. It was probably far away, and the valley's echoes made it sound close, I tell myself, but I don't cut the huskies' pace.

Ten minutes pass and all I can hear is the hiss of my sled's blades through the snow as we fly over the open field toward the track leading around the base of the mountain. The cold wind burns my cheeks, and I tighten the strings of my coat's fur collar around my face.

We still have another twenty minutes before we reach the foothills. I was almost to the boundary when I found the bull caribou I had Read in my vision. It's a good thing the animal stopped when it did, because I would never venture outside. Even a kill this size wouldn't be worth the risk.

Suddenly, out of the silence comes the flapping sound again, closer and louder than before, confirming that I'm going in the right direction. But the source of the noise is still invisible. The mechanical rhythm of the eagle wings seems to hover and then becomes more distant. *It's got to be behind the mountain,* I think, and my worry blooms into panic.

I pull hard on the dogs' reins, and they come to an abrupt stop. Jumping off the sled, I use my mittened hand to clear the snow, scooping it away until I have a patch of wet ground. Jerking my pendant on its leather thong over my head, I pull my mitten off with my teeth and press my fire opal, still warm from my skin, between my palm and the sodden grass. I close my eyes and picture my father in my mind, and the earth speaks to me.

My mind is frozen by my father's ice-cold panic. Petrified by his fear. As I feel his emotions, bile rises up my esophagus and burns my throat. I leap up, spitting and wiping my damp hand on my parka.

We must go faster, I think. Pulling my knife from my belt, I cut the caribou free. "Hike!" I yell. The dogs hear the fear in my voice and run like they never have before. The deer shifts and then slides off the back of the sled onto the ground, and, freed of its weight, we are off like an arrow across the snow.

Almost an hour later we finally pull over the hill into my village's valley. My throat has been clenched so tightly that it's been hard to breathe, but upon seeing the yurts safe and sound, smoke puffing out of the chimney holes, my breath spills out of me. I feel dizzy as oxygen floods my brain.

But as I survey the scene more carefully I see no movement in the camp. I lift my fingers to my lips and whistle the note that everyone knows is mine. The one that always wins me cries of "It's Juneau! She's back!" from the children who run to see what I have brought from a hunt. But this time I am greeted by silence. And then I notice the disorder of the camp.

Tools and weapons are scattered around the ground. The clothes drying on the line have all been blown to the mouth of the woods and are hanging in the trees, flapping around like flags. Baskets are overturned, grain and beans spilled over the hard-packed ground. The sides of the two closest yurts have been ripped from their posts, and the canvases are snapping back and forth in the breeze. It looks like a great wind has passed through.

Beckett and Neruda begin to growl, the fur on their backs bristling. I unclip them, and they race for our yurt. They disappear through the flaps and are back out a second later, puffing and barking frantically. As they begin sniffing around the empty camp, I plunge through our entrance to see my father's desk knocked upside down and his books and papers scattered over the floor.

He's gone. My heart stops, and then as I look down at the ground it slams hard against my ribs, forcing a cry from my throat. In the soft dirt floor, in my father's careful block lettering, is written: JUNEAU, RUN!

4

MILES

WELCOME TO WEEK TWO OF MY OWN PRIVATE hell.

As I push the mail cart through the swinging double doors, I move from fragranced air and mood music into the mail room's sweat/glue combo stench and bad-eighties-hair rock.

"Hey, Junior," says Steve, a fortysomething burnout with a ponytail. "What's up with the uniform?"

I look down at the regulation company yellow short-sleeved shirt that I'm wearing over a pair of jeans and shrug.

"I gave you blue slacks," he says. "You're supposed to wear them."

"Yeah, but you see, Steve, there's this thing called a washing machine. And sometimes you're supposed to put your clothes in there so you don't smell bad. Since you only gave me one pair of 'slacks'"—I can't even say that word without flinching—"I don't have a spare."

"Dude, that's what weekends are for. I wear my uniform during the week, and then wash it on the weekend."

From the permanent sweat marks under his pits, I have my doubts as to the frequency of his laundry habits. But I just stand there and stare at him, unblinking, until he looks away and starts fiddling with the radio dial. "Your dad said I'm supposed to treat you like everyone else," he says, not looking at me, "and that means wearing your uniform."

"Yes, sir," I say, avoiding sarcasm in my tone but meaning it with all my heart.

I should be in school getting ready for graduation. Partying my ass off like the rest of my classmates. If it weren't for Ms. Cochran, I would be coasting through the last six weeks of high school and easily into my spot at Yale.

And if it weren't for my dad, I'd be at home watching Comedy Central. "Working in the mail room, you'll be getting to know the business from the ground up," he said. "Prove you're responsible and I'll make sure they let you into Yale for second semester. But until then, you work forty hours a week, minimum wage, no screwing around."

His motivation is as transparent as glass. He wants me to see what life will look like if I don't "shape up." That, unless I change, I will be doomed to become Steve, spending my days sorting envelopes and wallowing in self-importance from bossing around lowly mail-room staff.

There's got to be another way to prove myself to Dad instead of being stuck here for the next nine months. A few more weeks in this hellhole and my brain will explode. Or I'll kill Steve. I imagine wrapping his hair around his neck and pulling hard. Death by ponytail. It could happen.

5

JUNEAU

THE DOGS ARE HOWLING. I STUMBLE OUT OF OUR yurt and toward their sound. They are in Nome's yurt, standing above a mass of fur and blood. Her huskies. They've been shot. I choke back tears: I knew these dogs as well as I know my own.

We have one rifle among the clan, and it is only used on the very rare occasion of a bear attack. Our few bullets are dispensed sparingly. But the casings scattered on the floor around me are not from our gun. Flying machines? Guns? These brigands are terrifyingly well-equipped.

I run out of Nome's yurt and into Kenai's. Empty. There is another heap of bloody fur behind that yurt, and at the mouth of the woods I see more dead huskies. But no people. I check all twenty yurts, saving Whit's for last.

Our Sage's fire is out, his hearth cold. I stand there, confused, until I remember that he left yesterday for his retreat. The cave on the far side of Denali where he goes a few times a year to "refresh his brain," as he calls it. He has never taken me, but I know where it is. With all the exploring that Nome, Kenai, and I have done, there isn't an inch of our territory that I haven't seen.

My heart pinches as I think of my best friends and where they might be right now. What unknown danger are they, my father, and the rest of my clan facing? If they're even still alive. I shake my head and refuse to allow that thought to fix itself in my mind.

I've got to get to Whit. Even though he didn't foresee this attack, maybe he'll know what happened. I take my big pack from my shelf in the back of Whit's yurt. The one I use on our daylong lessons, when we travel into the woods to search for the plants and minerals used for the Rite.

Juneau, run! My father's words shake me back into action, and I sweep bags of dried herbs, vials of plant extracts, powders, and precious stones off Whit's shelves into my pack. I don't know what he will need, so I take a bit of everything. I grab a stack of his treasured books off his desk and shove them in with the rest.

I whistle and the dogs come running. "Good boys," I say as they sit in front of the sled, waiting for me to clip them on. I secure the pack to the sled, and then, glancing back at my home, I tell the dogs to wait and push my way through the flaps.

I see the fire and am tempted to Read it. But I can't ignore the words on the ground and choose to wait until I reach Whit. And although I know that the fire will burn itself out, I take the pail of melted snow water and throw it onto the embers.

I pick up the framed photograph of my parents that sits on my nightstand. It was taken the month before our clan's emigration. A month before the war. My mother and father stand in front of their house in Seattle. Mother's head rests on my father's shoulder, and he has both arms around her.

In the picture she looks just like me. Long, straight black hair, courtesy of her Chinese mother, wide-set full-moon eyes and high cheekbones from her American dad. Dad said that if she hadn't drowned when I was still a young child, we would look like twins now.

In this old photo, my father looks exactly the same as today, except for one difference: He is happier. More carefree. "The calm before the storm," Father says when he refers to those days.

I slip the picture out of its frame and carefully slide it into my coat pocket. And before I leave the yurt, I bend down and brush out my father's message, erasing everything but the letter "J." If he comes back, he will know I have seen it.

I steer the dogs toward the woods. The moment we hit the trees, I hear the flying machine again. The chopping winglike noise coming from far away, barely audible but getting louder by the second. The brigands are returning, I realize with terror.

It takes great effort to push my fear aside. *Stay calm*, I think, and bring the huskies to a stop. I glance back at our camp and hesitate a second before leaping off the sled and running back toward the clearing. Breaking a low branch off a tree, I use it as a broom to sweep away the sled's tracks, following my own footsteps well back into the trees. I look back at my handiwork—no one could see that we had been there or how we had left.

"Hike!" I yell, and we are off, streaking across the wooded path as fast as a hawk at hunt. And just in time. The noise is almost on top of us. Although I'm grateful for the thick tree cover, it prevents me from seeing what is flying overhead. All I get is a glimpse of metal shining through the branches.

We cover a distance that should have taken an hour in almost half the time. I don't even have to tell the dogs how fast to go. They feel my fear and fly.

Whit's cave is empty when we arrive. Not only is it empty, but from the cobwebs and the dank smell, it's clear that there hasn't been a fire here for months. I try to ignore the sharp sting of disappointment, the lump in my throat. Pulling the sled into the mouth of the cave to hide it from outside view, I stand trembling as the huskies clean themselves and scamper around.

I recall the mechanical *chop chop chop* of the flying machine's wings, and it triggers a memory of reading an article in our school's encyclopedia: Encyclopaedia Britannica, 15th Edition, printed in 1983, the year before World War III. "The EB," we call it while quoting it dozens of times a day. Like all the clan children, I am so wildly curious about the world outside ours—a world now extinct—that I've practically memorized the whole thirty-volume series.

But the specific memory about the flying machines stays out of reach. I gather a bunch of kindling from Whit's stack and pile it in the middle of the cave floor, on a spot already black from a hundred former fires. I place only two logs on it. I won't be staying here long enough to need a roaring fire for warmth.

Once the flames catch and the dogs drape themselves close to the fire, I empty my pack. Placing the books to one side, I fish through the bags and rocks and bundles of leaves until I find what I'm looking for—Whit's firepowder—and pour some into my hand.

One of the first things Whit taught me was how to connect to the Yara. In order to Read—to make your will known to the Yara and receive an answer, if the Yara decides to grant you one—you must go through nature. We use animal bones to locate prey. Firepowder helps provide a good visual connection through fires, since you can't actually touch them. But I use my opal for most other things. Whit says these objects are conduits, helping the information move back and forth.

I settle myself on the floor in front of the blaze. Bowing my head, I exhale and try to relax. To let the panic and terror of the day fall away from me. I open my eyes and stare into the flames and feel my heart slow and my breath become shallow. I toss the powder onto the fire.

"Father." My lips move. The word comes out. But I know it isn't the sound that matters. It's focusing on who he is that directs the elements. That communicates to the Yara my desire to see him.

As images of my father appear in my mind, I do as Whit has taught me—looking just above and to the right of the flames—and see something forming in the fire's glowing aura. I'm inside a flying machine, members of my clan sitting all around with their hands attached behind their backs. My heart lurches as I see Nome sitting next to her mother, sobbing, but unable to wipe her tears. The view must be through my father's eyes. Out the windows there are four other flying machines: two in front and one on either side.

As I study them, it comes back to me: "choppers" was the colloquial word listed in the EB; the chopping sound comes from their spinning blades cutting through the air. Helicopters, I remember. But the machines in the fire are much bigger than those in the picture I remember from the EB. And from the size of the vehicles in the flames, there would be plenty of room for the entire clan onboard. The image is right there in front of me, but my brain can't accept what it is saying: that there is a brigand troop large and organized enough, with working vehicles and fuel, to sweep in and take my clan.

I wish the Yara would show me more. Give me an idea of where my father is headed or even show me his face. But as Whit often reminds me, the Yara doesn't always give you what you want. You take what it offers you.

I try to think of what the brigands could be after. It doesn't make sense. They took my people. Not our resources. Besides the slaughter of our dogs, who were probably defending their masters, the camp was left untouched. Whatever they wanted, it seemed like they hadn't gotten it. Because they came back. And if all they wanted was my clan, then the only reason they would come back would be to find its missing members: Whit and me.

I close my eyes and change my focus to Whit. I speak his name and picture him in my mind. Boyish face with high cheekbones. Eyes staring off into space, as if he sees a whole world that others can't.

And in the flames I see what he sees. Pressed against either side of him stand two massive men in camouflage, who hold him by the arms. They must be in league with the brigands who kidnapped my clan, I think, and then focus harder. Whit is being led somewhere by the men, and there is water beside them. A lake? No. My heart races. The ocean. Far from our territory. Three days' journey by dogsled, my father has said. Three days away from everything I have ever known. But that's where I am going. What other choice do I have?

6

MILES

"WHAT DO YOU MEAN HE'S DISAPPEARED?" MY dad roars into the phone.

I'm in front of the TV eating a massive plateful of homemade lasagna that Mrs. Kirby left in the oven. I lean back in my chair and look through the open door into Dad's office. As usual, he's eating his dinner at his desk in front of his laptop, both home phone and cell phone within easy reach.

"I thought we had a deal!" My dad is turning puce. Which is strange for him. As is the yelling. He's usually one of those stone-faced guys who scares the shit out of everyone by acting so calm. I grab the remote and turn the sound down so I can listen to his freak-out.

"I didn't send you all the way from Los Angeles to Anchorage just to have this deal slip through my fingers. I knew I should have gone myself." Dad runs his hand through his hair and stands up to pace around the room. Glancing my way, he sees me watching him. He stomps over to the door and slams it, shutting me out.

I feel my face burn, and lift the remote to up the sound, blocking out my dad's now-muffled yelling. I don't know why I let him get to me. I should be used to being shut out by now.

7

JUNEAU

WE RACE ACROSS THE FROZEN TUNDRA, CHASING the ghosts in the fire and listening for the danger from the sky. Now that we have left the woods, there is no cover. It is mid-April. In just a month the snow will be gone and the landscape will transform overnight from the brown and white of tundra and snow to the green and purple of thick grasses and wildflowers. But for now, we are a moving target against the crystalline fields veined with frozen streams.

I don't yet know which path we'll take to the ocean, but it doesn't matter. I have a stop to make before I leave clan territory.

Beckett and Neruda slow as we near the emergency shelter. They've been here before and sense where we are going. They stop at the boulder marking the edge of our clan's boundary, and

I leap off the sled to clear the snow from an indentation at the base of the boulder. Shoving my mittens into my pockets, I scrabble with my fingertips to dig out the edge of the loose sod. I feel the tarp and, grasping it with both hands, pull it back to expose the trapdoor.

Whit made the door spring-activated so even the smallest of the children could access the shelter if necessary. All it takes is a light pull on the ring and the heavy plank swings upward, revealing a wooden staircase descending into the dark. I walk down a few steps and then detach the lantern from its hook under the cave ceiling. Using my flint, I light the wick, although I don't really need its glow: I know this place by heart. Nome, Kenai, and I check it once a month, year-round, to make sure that scavengers haven't discovered our stores. We restock the dried meats and make sure the worms haven't gotten the rest.

We are taught where this shelter is as soon as we can drive a dogsled. "Just in case," our parents tell us. We all know what the unspoken "case" is. Attack by brigands. Discovery by survivors of the war. The shelter has hidden us the handful of times that Whit has Read brigands nearby. It's been an integral part of our security since the beginning.

What we never planned on was an abduction of the entire clan. So there is no one here to meet me. No one to wait for. Only supplies to gather before I flee.

I take one of the empty bags and fill it with enough provisions for the dogs and me. Three . . . no, four days of food, unhooking dried meat and fish from where they hang from hooks in the ceiling, well out of reach of rodents. Dried beans that can be hydrated in melted snow. A cooking pot. My sled already holds survival basics in case I get trapped while hunting: furs and a tiny caribou-skin pup tent. But for three days in the outdoors, I take one of the winter tents: its white-cured leather will be invisible against the snow.

And finally, in case I am captured, I bring insurance. Something valuable I can use to negotiate with brigands.

I make three trips between the shelter and the sled before I am finally ready. *Ready for what?* I think, realizing I have no idea where I'm going.

Until I get a sign of where my clan was taken, the best I can do is try to find Whit. His captors have got to be part of the same group of brigands. I peer up at the sun—already far to the west—and then at the shadow the boulder casts in the snow. I have at least three hours until sundown. In midsummer we have twenty hours of functional light, as compared to the short five-hour days of winter. I know the earth's calendar like I know my own body's. Today I can travel a good distance before the sun sets.

There is no time to lose. The temperature will drop with sunset, and although I have my arsenal against the cold, I will need every advantage I can get in a new terrain. "Hike!" I yell to the dogs. Unnecessarily. They are already running and we are once again off across the white expanse, heading south. Across the boundary. Out of the protection of my clan and into the wild.

* * *

We run for an hour before I attempt to Read.

Serenity. Your connection with the earth. A quiet spirit is essential. I hear Whit's words in my mind, complete with his clipped, practical tone.

Serenity. Not quite my frame of mind at the moment. Panic, maybe. Insecurity . . . fear, definitely. It's going to be a far stretch for me to reach serenity anytime soon.

I have no choice. The only thing directing me is my general knowledge that the ocean is south. I'm going to need more than that, or I could lose precious hours: Whit was already at the ocean when I saw him in present-time. And my clan was taken by air. I am moving at a snail's pace compared to them. They might not even be in Alaska anymore. They might not even be alive. Reality slams me like a pickax.

Stop! I reprove myself, clenching my fists against the sled rail. In the distance, I spot a flock of Canada geese flying toward us in a perfect V. They're flying north, returning to Alaska in their spring migration. I adjust our trajectory slightly to align with their path so that we're pointing due south, and then yell, "Easy!"

The dogs slow down, and at "Whoa," they come to a stop. I step off the sled and lean down to wipe the snow from the ground. Pulling my opal over my head, I press it to the earth. I think of my father and get nothing in response.

Fear courses through me. This has never happened. Does it mean he's dead, I wonder, or just too far away?

I change the image in my mind to Whit and feel a sudden surge of anxiety. The fact that Whit is horribly worried shouldn't be surprising, but I respond with my own fear. I jump back onto the sled and yell, "Hike," and we are off, sprinting southward to the sea.

There are fifteen hours of daylight, and that is how long we run each day, resting enough to eat four meals, and stopping at twilight to pitch camp. The first two nights I sit outside in the darkness, watching the stars. On the third, I am rewarded with the aurora borealis. Its colorful lights shimmer like silk banners.

I have felt the earth a dozen times a day and cannot connect with my father. No emotions resonate through my fingertips as I press the sodden dirt with my opal. But now I stand under the aurora stock-still with my arms raised and my opal clenched in one hand and Read the wind. I ask if my father is still alive, and suddenly, in the middle of the barren tundra, the smell of a campfire reaches my nose along with the odor of cooking meat. And I know that, wherever he is, my father is alive and being fed. I fold my arms across my chest, hugging myself, and am dizzy with relief. I smile as I watch the colors above me explode in pulses of blue and green. I return to the tent feeling comforted. And for the first time since I left our territory, buried deep under furs in my tent between the two huskies, I sleep well. I sleep deeply.

8

MILES

I'M DROPPING OFF SOME LETTERS WITH MY DAD'S secretary when I hear him yelling again.

"I don't know why she's so important, but she is! Apparently the whole deal hangs on her. . . . I don't care what you tell your men! Say that she's an industrial spy with information on the drug I want. That's near enough to the truth. Just get as many people onto the street as you can!"

Dad's secretary looks up at me and rolls her eyes.

"What's going on?" I ask.

"He's been agitated for the last few days. I guess some deal he really wants is falling apart." She picks up her coffee mug and heads for the break room.

Dad has lowered his voice, so I scoot closer to his door.

"My informant says she's probably coming from Alaska by

boat," he says. "Could be landing anywhere along the western seaboard. Everyone and their mother will be after this girl. We have to get her before our competitors do. Hell, I'd comb the streets myself, but you're the security expert, so I'm trusting you to find her."

A manhunt, I think. *Now this sounds interesting.*

9

JUNEAU

ON THE THIRD DAY I BEGIN NOTICING EVIDENCE of brigands. Until now, the huskies and I have managed to elude any signs of life. Yesterday we came within sight of a paved road. I avoided it, steering the dogs away and putting a sight-blocking ridge between us and that relic of a dead civilization.

But today, as we near the coast, we are forced to cross one road, and then another. Seeing no sign of humanity, I resign myself to following along it at a distance. After a while a small structure comes into view—a type of complex built in glass and wood with two plinth-like machines standing in front of it. I immediately recognize what it is from the photos in our books: a gas station—this one obviously abandoned. A fuel reserve would have been cached beneath the pumps and used to fill cars with gasoline. Although the sight fills me with a sort of excited horror, I can't help but smile. It's my first real glimpse of the world outside the one where I've spent my entire life.

The sides of the building are plastered with weathered artwork—advertisements, I remind myself, rolling the word around in my mouth like honeycomb candy—that are half falling off and rusted through.

The dogs pay no attention to the place as we speed by, and once it has disappeared from my vision, I breathe my relief. I have seen the outside world and nothing bad has happened.

As we pass a couple of other abandoned buildings—one with a burned-out wheel-less car parked eternally outside—my confidence grows. Brigands aren't hiding behind every corner, as I have always imagined. Maybe the ones who kidnapped my clan are the sole survivors. Maybe I will be able to not only find my clan but somehow set them free.

As this flash of hope pierces like a sunbeam through my mind's dark clouds, I see something else on the horizon. Something moving. Coming along the road toward us, just a speck in the distance but growing larger by the second. "Whoa!" I yell, and steer the dogs off the road behind one of the patches of fir trees that has begun to regularly punctuate the treeless expanse of tundra.

The dogs flop flat on the ground, panting, and I spread the white skin tent over the sled, making us invisible against the snow. I huddle behind and watch as the car grows larger by the moment. It resembles one of the army vehicles from the EB—like a Jeep but twice as big, and bright red like a field poppy.

My heart skips a beat. The car is brand-new. Not thirty years old. Not rusted out or cobbled together from spare parts like the brigand vehicles that Kenai draws to illustrate Nome's wild stories.

This car looks like it was built recently. But I know that's impossible. How could a car factory exist in a dying world? Unless the brigands have organized themselves. But even so . . .

The car speeds past our hiding place, and I get a glimpse of its passengers: a man drives and a woman sits next to him. They're laughing. And behind them in the backseat is a child.

They don't look like desperate survivors of an apocalypse; they look like a happy family.

I crouch, stunned, as the car disappears into the distance. After a minute, I shake myself out of my confusion and force myself to move, pulling the tent off the sled, stowing it, and directing the huskies to run. I don't have time to waste.

As the sled lurches forward, I automatically reach for my fire opal. I feel lost, but my amulet reminds me that no matter what strange things I find in this new world, the Yara will be there to guide me. And a grain of comfort settles in my heart.

We are almost to the coast. I can feel the change in the air and smell it in the wild, briny gusts of wind. The dogs' pace quickens as they speed toward this unknown factor. They've never been outside our territory either, being the third generation of dogs raised in our clan. But from the joyful wiggle in their strides, I suspect that knowledge of the sea is embedded deep inside their psyche.

We reach the top of the ridge, and I leap off the sled to view the magnificent vista spread before us. The ocean in all its wide wild grandeur. The stories I heard and photos I studied didn't do it justice. Its wind-whipped waves extend all the way to the horizon, going on forever, while shrieking white birds dip and dive over its surface. Tears spring to my eyes, and I feel the thrill of discovery course through my veins.

Then my gaze lowers and the world slams to a stop. I manage to keep my knees locked for a moment but then crumple to the ground. I can't breathe. I can't think. I can't do anything but kneel in the snow and look at the impossible.

Beneath me lies a city. It is not in ruins. It isn't decimated by war and poisoned by radiation. It is a thriving city with massive glass buildings glistening in the late-afternoon sun. People—not dangerous brigands, but normal-looking people—are walking down its streets. Cars that look brand-new—more rounded than the ones in the EB—are driving down the roads and are parked along their sides. This is not a postapocalyptic wasteland. Where am I? What is going on?

My throat clenches so tightly that I cough and then gasp in the cold air. My body is numb with shock and my mind a jumble—thoughts stumbling and tripping and then stopping altogether. I sit. And watch. And try to understand.

10

MILES

I JUMP BACK FROM THE DOOR AS DAD COMES stomping out of his office. "Son, were you waiting to see me?" he asks distractedly.

"Nope, just dropping off the mail," I say, and hold up a couple of envelopes as proof.

"I'm leaving in a few hours for that weekend conference in Denver that I couldn't get out of," he says, already walking away. "And after that, there's some business elsewhere I have to take care of, so I'm not sure when I'll be back. But I'll be checking in with you, and I asked Mrs. Kirby to stay at the house."

"But, Dad!" I protest. "I'm eighteen freaking years old. I don't need a babysitter." As soon as the words leave my mouth, I feel about eight.

Dad turns and gives me the eye. "It is precisely because you are eighteen years old that you need a chaperone. I've got enough on my plate at the moment. I don't need you getting into any more trouble."

"Thanks for the vote of confidence," I say, but he's already gone.

11

JUNEAU

WE SPEND THE NIGHT ON THE TOP OF THE RIDGE, watching, waiting. I want to understand this city before I set foot in it. The sleeping dogs heat the tent with their warm breath, and I lay half-in, half-out with the tent flaps tucked in around me to keep in the warmth. I am not cold. There is a flame burning inside me since my clan disappeared, and this new mystery has made it burn hotter.

I chew on a piece of venison jerky as I watch the city. Near the waterfront a forest of tall buildings crowd together, growing sparser and shorter as they spread outward from the city center. On the edges of the town are groups of houses dotted with small parks and supply centers. I try to remember what they're called . . . *shops*.

During the few hours before dusk, a number of cars leave the city and head toward the outskirts. I watch as some drive directly to the houses and others stop first at the shops. The people—tiny as ants from my vantage point—emerge with rolling metal carts full of supplies, pile them into the cars and, once home, transfer them into the houses.

My mind struggles with what my eyes are seeing. People—regular people—are going to work and then coming home to their families. Children play happily in front of their houses, bundled in brightly colored snowsuits. There seems to be plentiful fuel (I count at least ten gas stations), and supplies appear to be abundant.

I try to push my emotions aside—confusion, shock, fear—and use every ounce of rationale I possess. I cannot let myself panic. If I can't keep a cool head, I might not be able to find my people. And the thought of being alone in the world is one that I've had to repeatedly dismiss. The idea is too frightening to consider. I have to remain focused on my goal: finding Whit. Then—together—we will find our clan.

Too many questions are darting through my head. How can this one city have escaped the nuclear catastrophe of World War III? Could it have completely rebuilt itself in three short decades? And if this city survived, did others, too? I watch boats enter and leave the port. They have to be going somewhere.

What I'm seeing is an impossibility: a thriving metropolitan civilization only three days away from our village. I pull my fire opal from my neck and hold it in my palm against the ground.

Still no connection with my father. And the wind is giving me nothing at all.

I push away a rising sense of alarm. I've never been far from my father—my clan—for more than a day or two on the odd camping trip with my friends. And those times, I enjoyed the solitude, knowing everyone was safe and sound in their yurts. Unlike now. I breathe deeply and try to shed the alarming thoughts crowding in on me.

I change my focus to Whit. I imagine that face I know as well as my father's, and the Yara shows me his emotions. Fear. Confusion. If I can't feel my father and I can feel Whit, maybe it means he's still nearby.

Although the tiny people below don't look threatening, I don't want to draw attention to myself. I'd rather watch them like I do my prey when hunting. Observe their patterns. Understand them before making a move. I don't dare light a fire here on the ridge, else I would use the firepowder to ask the Yara where Whit is. I must wait until tomorrow to use a less conspicuous way of Reading his location.

I scoot back into the tent, securing the flaps tightly behind me, and settle between my layers of furs, listening to the sound of the huskies' sleeping puffs and the alien sound of civilization in the distance.

The sun has just risen. The city sleeps. I have hidden the sled and bulkier supplies on the outskirts of the city, taking only one large rucksack that I carry strapped across my back. Beckett and

Neruda walk protectively on either side of me as we cross through the outlying housing areas.

As we approach the city center, more and more shops appear until we are walking along a broad road lined with businesses on either side. I hear a noise and freeze as a car approaches us from behind. The dogs' fur bristles and they nudge in closer to me as a man steps out of the car and walks up to one of the shop doors. He takes something out of his pocket and begins wiggling it in the door handle.

Opening the door, he stomps the snow off his boots, glancing briefly up and down the street before stepping inside. Catching sight of me, he smiles politely, nods his head, and calls, "Morning!" And then he disappears into the shop. I remain frozen for another ten seconds, and when he doesn't come back out with a loaded gun or other deadly weapon, I breathe out my relief in a cloud of warm air.

In my seventeen years I have known only forty-six people. The same people, every day, each of whom I know everything about. And I just saw a man who I will never speak to and will never know. I walk past the shop and see him inside bustling around and—poof—I continue walking and he no longer exists to me. I can hear Dennis teasingly chiding me in school. "Juneau, give us all a break and save the existentialism for our philosophy discussion group."

A few minutes later, a woman with white hair steps out of a doorway, and once again I am petrified with alarm. Her face is wrinkled, and although I've seen pictures of old people before, this is the first time I've witnessed one with my own eyes. I feel like I'm looking at an alien—someone from a world away. My spine tingles with the newness of the experience.

She turns and catches my gaze but, after casting a curious glance at me and the dogs, ignores us as she goes along her way. I spy a fenced-off area of grass and trees, make a beeline for it, and take refuge on a bench. I sit there with the dogs as the city comes alive. Until I can watch people come and go without my heart racing.

A man sits down on a bench across from me, sets down a steaming white cup next to him, and pulls out a newspaper. I tell the dogs to stay, and I walk over. He looks at me, and his eyebrows shoot up in surprise. I can tell I look odd to him. No one else I've seen is dressed in furs and skins. "Can I help you?" he asks.

"Where are we?"

He looks around us and back at me. "In a park," he says, shrugging.

"I know we're in a park," I say, "but what city is this?"

"Anchorage," he responds. He narrows his eyes like he thinks it's a trick question, and then his expression changes to concern. "Are you lost?" he asks.

"No," I say, and whistle for the dogs, who flank me in seconds flat. We begin to leave the park, but I hesitate. When I turn back around, I see the man is still watching me, and I have to ask.

"Tell me—how did this city escape the war?"

"What war?" he asks, intrigued.

"World War III. The Last War. The War of 1984," I reply, identifying it in every way I know.

He opens his mouth and out spill the words that, since last night, I have suspected were true. "There hasn't been a World War III," he says, "knock on wood," and he raps his knuckle against the park bench.

I feel a wave of nausea wash over me. I have to sit down. My face and palms feel clammy, and I think I'm going to throw up. I return to my park bench and put my head between my knees until the nausea passes. I see the man leave, throwing a worried look my way before pushing through the metal gate and disappearing. I try to reason through what he told me.

There was no war. I still can't believe we were so close to this city, yet we knew nothing. How could my father and the other elders have been so mistaken?

There's no way they could know what happened, I realize. They've been isolating themselves for thirty years.

I push these thoughts aside. I have to find my clan. Even if their kidnappers aren't brigands, they took my people and killed our animals. And I still have to find Whit. I need a clear sign to know what to do.

And suddenly the right person comes along. Someone whose thoughts are free of the restrictions of reality. Whose mind is open enough to access the collective unconscious shared by all humans past, present, and future.

She is an old woman dressed in a coat of rags. She pushes her way through the iron gate, dragging behind her a metal cart piled high with strange objects: old shoes, stacks of paper, aluminum cans laced on a string that clatter as they drag behind her.

She crosses the park and, seeing me, approaches. Beckett and Neruda glue themselves to either leg but don't growl. She stops at the other end of my bench and slowly lowers herself to sit. Stowing her cart next to her, she pats it lovingly, like it is a baby in a carriage instead of a mountain of garbage. Then, turning, she looks vaguely in my direction. Her expression is glazed-over. Opaque.

"The men—they put a movie camera inside my television and watched everything I did," she says matter-of-factly. "They even put a camera in my shower."

I ignore her disheveled appearance and paranoid speech and see her for what she is. A gift from the Yara. "Can I hold your hand?" I ask. She hesitates, and suspicion flashes across her face. Leaning forward, she holds my gaze in hers. Then, finding what she is looking for, she gives a satisfied nod and pulls her right glove off. Removing my mittens, I take her gnarled, chapped hand in my own and hold my opal in the other.

"Thank you," I say, "for being my connection to the Yara. I need to ask you some questions. Very important questions. Are you willing to answer them for me?"

"Of course, dear." The woman's eyes begin to look more focused, and a serene expression settles upon her face.

"I am looking for a friend. His name is Whittier Graves. I am picturing him in my mind right now. Can you see him?"

The old lady closes her eyes abruptly and then, opening them slowly, focuses on a spot in midair to the left of my head. "I see your friend," she says.

"Where is he?"

"He is on a boat. Leaving our harbor." She lifts her free hand and gives a distracted wave toward the invisible boat floating over my shoulder.

"What!" I exclaim, and then quickly control my emotions before I pass the shock on to my oracle. "When did he get on the boat?" I ask, my heart pounding painfully, but my voice as steady as I can manage.

"Moments ago."

"Was he alone?" I ask, my already-cold face turning numb with fear.

"No, he was with a group of big men. Bad men. Two went with him and the others stayed."

I fight to stay calm. "Do you know where his boat is going?" I ask. This is asking a lot of the woman. Using her to see the present and recent past is well within the bounds of realistic expectations. But from the oracle-reading exercises that Whit used to practice with me, I know this question verges on divination. The woman has to see into the future or even tap into Whit's subconscious to give me an answer. The response I get will be cryptic at best. I focus on her, ready to catch every vital word.

The woman's face crinkles in concentration. "Say it another way," she responds after a few seconds.

I consider that, and finally ask, "Where must I go to find Whit and my clan?"

"You must go to your source," she answers immediately.

"My source?" I ask, confused. "Denali?"

"No." She shakes her head, frustrated by my incomprehension. "No, before that."

"But I was born in Denali," I respond.

Her frown deepens. "Aren't you listening? You have to take a boat." She is getting upset, and I know that her link with the Yara is fading if not already gone. I have so many questions I still want to ask. I flail around for the most important.

"Can you see my father? Do you know if he's okay?"

"I have no idea what you are talking about," she says stubbornly, and tugs back the hand I am holding.

Disappointed, I take her glove and fit it carefully back over her fingers. She has returned to the mad world in her mind. She blinks, as if surprised, and I clasp her gloved hand until she is oriented.

"Thank you for your help," I say, standing. The dogs are at my side in a flash.

"They're watching me. They know everything I'm thinking," the lady says.

"Tell them to go away, and maybe they'll leave you alone," I respond.

"Now that's an idea," she says, her lips forming a surprised smile. Her smile broadens as her mind recedes into some pleasant memory, so that when the dogs and I leave her, she looks almost happy.

12

MILES

IT LIES THERE ON HIS DESK LIKE AN INVITATION: The notepad with my dad's writing:

> The girl is the key. No drug without her. Possibly still in Alaska, but coming by boat to the continent. Around 17. Shortish: 5'5". Long black hair. Two huskies. Gold starburst in one eye.

What's a gold starburst? I wonder.

I push the notebook back to where it was when I found it. And then I get the hell out of there before Dad comes back.

13

JUNEAU

IF I HAVE TO TAKE A BOAT, I WILL NEED MONEY. Currency. "The root of all evil," Dennis called it in our history class. He claimed that it was the cause of World War III. That capitalism and greed set the whole thing off, beginning with a war over oil and ending with the destruction of the environment. Although he was wrong about the war, everything I have read and heard about the world confirmed that money has always caused corruption. Now I have to find some money of my own. Just the thought of it makes me feel compromised.

I consider stowing away on a boat for about a second, like a character in one of our books. Then I realize that's way too eighteenth century. What am I going to do—hide in an empty ale keg? No, there's no way around it. I'm going to have to buy a ticket. I saw something on the way into town that may prove useful: a sign in a shop window.

I have to turn toward the harbor to remember which direction to go in. The buildings are confusing me. If I were standing in the middle of a mountain field, I could find my way. But with glass buildings reflecting one another every way I turn, I have to concentrate. I glance at the sun and then the water, and head north-northwest.

In ten minutes we are there. CA$H FOR GOLD, the sign reads. The window display holds a treasure trove of fragile-looking rings and necklaces. I swallow my fear and stare at the door for a moment. There is no handle. But there is a small sign on one side that reads PUSH. I push, and with a whoosh of warm air, the dogs and I are inside the building and blinking in the artificial light.

"How can you help me?" comes a voice from the far side of the room. I blink again, and then focus on a small man standing behind a cupboard made of glass. His eyebrows are gray, but his hair is raven black and looks strangely crooked. He is wearing a pelt on his head, I realize, and try not to stare. He rubs his hands together and plasters on a large smile.

I walk forward and force myself to speak to this stranger. "I saw the sign. Cash for gold."

"That's right, young lady," he says, looking me up and down.

My buckskin trousers and fur-lined parka are very different from his clothing, which is made of shiny woven material. I push my hood back and sweep my long hair out of the back of my coat to fall around my face, using it as a curtain between us.

He stares oddly at my eyes and clears his throat. "What can I do you for?" he asks, with a joking smile.

I am having a hard time understanding him—both from his strange expressions and the fact that he speaks through his nose—so instead of talking, I lay my pack on the floor and crouch to dig inside. My fingers find the bag holding my brigand insurance. The objects I was told to use if I needed to negotiate with them.

I pull it out and, after opening the drawstrings, choose carefully and set a stone on the glass in front of the man. I watch his face attentively as he flinches in surprise and then draws a blank expression over his features. A term my father uses when we play cards pops into my mind: he is using a "poker face."

"Well, now, what do we have here?" the man asks. He picks up the stone and fits a black spyglass type of lens to one eye. "A gold nugget"—he pulls a measuring stick out from beneath the counter—"measuring almost two inches." He weighs it in his hand and then places it on a metal contraption, squinting as he reads numbers off a little screen. "Weighs a hundred twenty-five grams." He peers at it again through the lens. "Low to medium quality, I would say. Well, little missy, today's your lucky day, because I have just the buyer for this sort of nugget, and I can offer you the top-notch price of five hundred dollars."

There is something wrong with his face. I lay a hand across Neruda's head, my thumb pressing one of his temples and my middle finger the other. I grasp my opal as I crouch down to whisper into his ear, "How do you feel about this man?"

The man chuckles nervously. "Do you always consult your dog for your business decisions?" he jibes, and a bead of sweat forms on his brow just below the black pelt.

I stare at him and feel the tingle as I connect to Neruda's thoughts. Animals don't think in words. It is my dog's primal instincts that I Read, and Neruda's instincts tell me the man cannot be trusted. My dog sees him as an inferior pack member that must be expelled to ensure the security of the others.

I stand and hold my palm out. "My nugget," I insist, and wait.

The man's hand trembles slightly. "Let's not be hasty, girlie. I'll check my charts and see if I can do any better on that offer."

I pluck my nugget from his fingers before he has a chance to pull his arm away, and turn his scales around toward me. Placing the gold atop the scales as I saw him do, I read aloud from a shiny strip near the base. "Two hundred grams, not a hundred twenty-five."

I nod toward a sign I saw when I entered the store. "That says you pay forty dollars per gram of gold. According to your chart, you should be offering me eight thousand dollars for this nugget." I slip the stone back into its bag.

"Now just wait a minute here, missy. You have no idea what standards the pricing is based on. A gold nugget is not as valuable as gold dust, which is what is melted down to make this high-quality jewelry." He waves his hand to display the ugly jewelry inside the case.

His eyes tell me that he is lying. That my nugget is rare, and that he desperately wants it. I think of Whit's satisfaction whenever one of us finds a nugget in the Denali riverbeds. "That may serve us well someday," he says before ordering us to take it to the shelter and stash it with the rest. Unlike plentiful opals and semiprecious stones, the gold nuggets are hard to come by, and this man's excitement confirms their value.

"I saw another 'cash for gold' sign by the waterfront," I say, and nestle the bag into my rucksack.

"Stop!" he shrieks. Sweat courses down the sides of his face. "Okay, I'll give you seven thousand," he says, pain audible in his tone, "as well as some valuable information."

I hesitate. "What kind of information?"

"Someone is looking for you," he responds.

We stare at each other in silence for a minute before I fish the bag back out of my rucksack. He ogles it and licks his lips.

"Talk," I say.

He walks back to where a red plastic apparatus is attached to a wall. *Telephone*, I think, as I recall the picture of a similar one in the EB.

The man pulls a card off a board stuck full of scraps of paper and slaps it down on the counter in front of me. On it is printed a ten-digit number, and scribbled in pencil in one corner is "Girl w/star."

"They were big guys. Dressed in camo," the man says. "Came in here yesterday saying they would pay top dollar for information on your whereabouts."

My chest clenches painfully. The man's description sounds like Whit's captors, the big men I saw in the fire holding his arms. Why are they looking for me? "What does this mean?" I ask, pointing to the scribbled words.

"They described you as a teenage girl, long black hair, probably accompanied by two huskies." He hesitates and studies my face suspiciously. "And what looks like a gold starburst in one eye."

My starburst. The same as the rest of the clan children. The sign that we are in close union with nature. Yara-Readers. Our parents tell us it is something to be proud of—an inheritance from the earth. But now it marks me as someone to pursue.

And how do these men know what I look like anyway? I could ask the same about how they found my clan. Or how they knew I wasn't with the rest of the group. But the knowledge that they may actually recognize me chills me to the bone.

I slip the card into my rucksack, pull the nugget back out of the bag, and place it on the counter. The man makes a grabbing motion, but I keep my hand on it. "Count the money out for me first," I command, and he darts to the back of the room, disappearing through a doorway and then emerging with a handful of paper money.

He begins counting it, and I watch the numbers on each bill as he does, totaling them in my head until he reaches seven thousand. He pushes the stack across the counter toward me, not even looking at my face. His eyes are only for the nugget.

I withdraw my hand, and he plucks up the gold and pushes it under the counter. I have no doubt that the value of my piece is much more than what he has given me. I only hope that it is enough to obtain a boat ticket to wherever it is I am supposed to go.

I turn to leave, and the dogs leap to their feet, rushing before me to the door. They are as uncomfortable as I am in this artificial space with this artificial man.

"A word of advice, girlie," the man calls as I open the door and gulp in the frosty outdoor air. I glance back at him, and his face has changed. He got what he wanted and his greed is satisfied, so he is happy. "Take out that weird contact lens, cut the hair, and lose the dogs."

I nod at him and let Beckett and Neruda run outside. "And if I were you," he yells, as I shut the door behind me, "I would get as far as you can—as fast as you can—out of town."

I decide to take his advice. At least what I understood of it. Whit's captors are sure to be watching the harbor, so it will be my last stop. Before that, I have a lot to do.

The woman in Beulah's Hair Emporium takes one look at the huskies and calls, "It's cold outside, so the dogs can come in, but they have to stay by the door. We have sanitation regulations, you know."

I flick my finger, and they immediately drop to lie next to each other under a potted tree. "Wow, you've got yourself some obedient dogs there," Beulah (I suppose) says, and instructing me to hang my coat on a rack, leads me to a chair. "What would you like, dear?"

I point to one of the giant hairstyle photos hanging on the wall.

Beulah gapes at me. "Oh, honey, you can't mean that. You have such beautiful long hair." I stare back at her, determined.

A half hour later the dogs and I leave. My hair looks just like the boy's in the picture.

On the same street as Beulah's Hair Emporium is a large, bright clothes store called the Gap. I leave the dogs at the door and follow the MEN'S DEPARTMENT signs. The artificial light and mirrors make me dizzy, but I deep-breathe and walk downstairs to an underground floor. The stale air makes it feel like a spot-lit tomb.

I leave twenty minutes later wearing all-new clothes, a baseball cap, and a black parka. My new synthetic backpack bulges with five shirts, a red "hoodie," three sweaters, and three pairs of jeans. After buying some hiking boots at a shop next door, I drape my bulky fur parka and hand-stitched leather rucksack over a garbage can outside and hope that someone like the old lady in the park will find it.

Then the dogs and I head to our final destination together.

"These are beautiful huskies. Can't say I've seen their exact markings anywhere on the sled-dog circuits. Where did you buy them?"

The woman ruffles Beckett's fur with her fingers and peers up from where she crouches on one knee in front of him.

"My family's been raising them for a few generations."

"What's your family's name?"

"Will you take care of my dogs for me?" I cross my arms over my chest. My heart hurts so much, it feels like it's bleeding.

She stands. "Our boarding fees are five hundred dollars per month for one dog. For two it's nine hundred. I take care of these dogs like they're my own kids."

"That's what the woman at Beulah's said." My voice cracks. I can tell that Beckett and Neruda like her and, from that alone, I know she can be trusted.

"How long do you plan on leaving them?" she asks, her tone softening as she sees my emotion.

I clear my throat. I won't cry in front of this stranger. "I don't know. But I will be back for them." I dig through my backpack, count the money quickly, and place it in her hand. "Here's three thousand dollars."

"That's a lot of cash to be carrying . . . ," the woman begins to say, and then gasps when she sees what I place in her hand on top of the money.

"And that's insurance," I continue. "In case I don't make it back in three months. I want to know that these dogs will be well cared for and stay with you for the rest of their lives."

"I can't take that!" The woman's face is white with shock.

"Trade it for cash if the money runs out. Otherwise, you can return it to me when I come back for the dogs." I sink to my knees between Beckett and Neruda and pull their furry heads toward me. I can't stop the tears now; they are streaming down my face. "Good-bye, friends," I whisper.

And then, standing, I turn and walk out of the kennel, leaving its astonished director holding a gold nugget more than double the size of what I sold to the gold dealer.

* * *

The harbor's ticket office is a small boxlike building with windows that look like mirrors from the outside but that are see-through on the inside. Above a counter hangs a board listing destinations, dates, and times. For the last few hours I have pushed from my mind every thought but those that facilitate my departure. But now, seeing three dozen cities listed on the departures board, my shock returns in full force. All those cities that we thought were destroyed in the war still exist.

I imagine how astonished my father must have been a few days ago when he discovered that the war never happened. All the protective measures we took to avoid brigands were in vain. Our isolationist mentality kept us from discovering that an outside world still existed.

The flame in my chest burns brighter. Once I'm reunited with my clan, we will discover together what's actually happened to the world during the last three decades. But right now I have to find them.

I scan the names of the cities as I consider which could possibly be the answer to my oracle's cryptic clue, "You must go to your source." And then I see it. Seattle. That's where my parents came from. Where they lived before I was born. It is my source, in a manner of speaking. And there's a boat leaving for the city today.

"How much is a ticket to Seattle?" I ask the teenage boy behind the counter. I keep my eyes lowered. The startled reactions of the salespeople and the woman at the kennels when they saw me up close have confirmed to me that my starburst is not a common occurrence in the outside world. No one I've come across has eyes like mine, and Whit's captors even used it to describe me.

"Round-trip that'll be one thousand ninety-four dollars," the boy says, "two thousand if you want a private cabin."

"I only need to go one way," I say, digging into my pack for money. "How long does it take?"

"Four days, eight hours," he responds. "When do you want to leave?"

"Today."

"You're in luck. We have a boat embarking in a half hour," he says, pointing to a shiny blue-and-white ship at the far end of the harbor. A thrill passes through me as I realize that I will actually be riding on a boat. A few days ago, I wouldn't have even expected to see one. I feel like I'm in a dream—like I've suddenly been popped into some sort of strange new world.

A long line of people pull rolling suitcases up the boat's lowered gangplank. I hoist my pack onto my back and shove the ticket the boy gives me into my parka pocket. "Have a good trip," he says in a voice that indicates he couldn't care less whether my trip is good or not.

I am three steps away from the ticket office when I see the men. They are dressed the same as the ones who held Whit in the fire-Reading vision. And they are seated yards away from the loading ferry.

Slowly, I back up behind the edge of the ticket office, careful not to draw their attention. Once I'm out of sight, I poke my head out to watch them and am paralyzed by fear. They are checking out every passenger who gets on the boat. Carefully.

I reach automatically for my dogs. It takes a second for me to remember that I no longer have Beckett and Neruda for protection, and at that thought I'm struck breathless by grief. They couldn't help against these men anyway, I tell myself, remembering the bloody masses of fur throughout our village. I suck the cold air into my lungs and accept the fact that from now on, I am truly on my own.

I peer into the mirrored window beside me. I look like an adolescent boy. It's only when I speak that I give myself away. Even so, I wonder how quickly it will take these men to figure out that the adolescent boy boarding the ferry by himself is actually the girl they're searching for. *Not long,* I think.

I remove the baseball cap and run my fingers through my spiky hair. It is short—really short—but it's still black. And it's not like I was able to change my height—I'm still five foot five and fine-boned. From where they're sitting, they'll be too far away to notice my eyes. But if they come within a few feet of me, they're sure to see the starburst.

My neck muscles tense as my fear is replaced with anger. At myself. For being naive enough to believe that I could fool my pursuers with these weak attempts at a transformation.

Transformation. The word plants a seed of inspiration in my mind, which springs into a fully formed idea. I plunge my hand into the backpack and rummage around until my fingers touch a soft lump of fur. I pull it from the pack to see Whit's rabbits'-feet amulet: one foot white and another brown, bound together by a thin copper wire. The snowshoe hare in its winter and summer incarnations. I think back to the day when he taught me about transformation.

"An animal that changes color with the season. Nature's metamorphosis. Can you get any more magical than that?" Whit said as he instructed me to bind the two feet together. "Camouflage is one of nature's most crafty defenses," he continued. "A temporary form of metamorphosis. Watch what the Yara allows, Juneau." And taking the rabbit feet between his fingers he suddenly—and startlingly—changed color. His skin turned a dark earthen color like the yurt around him, and his hair transformed from black to chestnut brown. Even his hazel eyes morphed into a deep chocolate color. Then, setting the furry amulet down on the table, he instantly changed back.

"This is the amulet I use when I camouflage the yurts from brigands. You'll need to know how. Try it," he said, handing me the amulet, and showed me how to use it by visualizing the rabbit's seasonal transformation.

That is the only Conjuring I have done by myself. Whit demonstrated things for me but was waiting until I turned twenty and underwent the Rite before letting me Conjure on my own.

Whit had explained that because Conjuring actually has an effect on nature, unlike Reading, it shouldn't be used lightly.

But now I have no choice. I have to try. I hold the furry amulet between my fingers and open myself to the Yara. As usual, I feel the tingling the second my mind taps into the stream of nature's consciousness, and begin picturing a snowshoe hare in summer with rusty brown fur and mahogany eyes.

I speed time up, flashing through a few months, and watch the animal forage for soft flower buds in the browning tundra grasses. I watch its fur begin its transformation just before winter's first snowfall, and soon its pelt is pure white, except for the black tufts tipping its ears.

I switch my focus to my image in the mirrored glass and watch, astonished, as my body begins to take on the colors of the snowy harbor around me. My suntanned skin fades to milky white. My black hair transforms to a pearl-white blond. And as I lean toward the mirror I see that my eyes match those of the rabbit whose feet I hold: dark brown, almost black. No starburst in sight.

Size, I think. *Make me bigger. Taller.* But my shape in the reflection stays the same. This is the extent of the Conjuring. Now I must make it last long enough to get me safely past the men and into the boat.

I swing the pack onto my back and stride purposefully toward the boat, adding what I imagine to be a boyish gait to my steps. My stomach twists itself in knots as I near the men, but I keep my gaze steadfastly on the ferry and try to ignore them.

I near the base of the gangplank. My palm has coated the rabbits' feet in sweat, and my heart hammers painfully in my chest. I feel the men's eyes on me, studying my face as I wait my turn behind an elderly couple wearing fur-lined cowboy hats. My throat clenches as I see one of the men get up and walk toward me until he stands only a couple of feet away.

I can't help myself: I look his way. As soon as his eyes meet mine, the aggressive hunch of his shoulders relaxes. He crosses his arms and nods at me, and then turns to go back to his partner. I am so numb with fear that I can barely move forward when the couple in front of me steps onto the boat. But I manage to hand my ticket to the woman at the door, and climbing into the artificially lit room beyond, I slump onto the first bench I see. Dropping the amulet, I feel my rabbit-invoked disguise disappear, and I become myself again.

14

MILES

I GET HOME TO FIND AN EMPTY HOUSE. THERE'S A note on the kitchen counter.

> *Miles, I've got a family emergency.*
> *Left you a casserole for tonight and will*
> *stop by tomorrow to check on you.*
> *Give me a call if you need anything.*
> *Mrs. Kirby*

I finally have a weekend alone . . . no, make that a long weekend, since on Monday the office is closed for a holiday. Three days to myself. I load my plate with chicken casserole and settle in front of the TV. I notice a light on in Dad's office and go to turn it off, only to see that it's the glow from his computer screen.

When I touch the mouse, his screen saver disappears to show his open email account. Several unread messages sit in his in-box, and the subject of the last one is *Re: the girl.*

I click on it and read the two-sentence message it holds. *Source says she's taken a boat from Anchorage to Seattle. Sending men there.*

I mark it as unread so Dad won't know I saw it. It'll come up on his cell phone anyway.

I turn the screen off and go back to the couch. And sit motionless for about five minutes. Because an idea's forming in my head that's too crazy to entertain. But maybe Dad won't find out. If I keep checking in with Mrs. Kirby by phone, I could be gone for the whole weekend, and back to work on Tuesday without anyone knowing.

This could actually work. I mean, they're looking for a teenage girl. Who better to find her than another teenager?

And then my rational mind kicks in. I check the distance on my iPhone—it's a nineteen-hour drive from L.A. And Seattle's a big city. And I'm not only grounded, I'm on lockdown—only allowed to leave the house to go to work and back.

But if I can pull this off, Dad will be so impressed that he might excuse me from the whole mail-room torture scheme. He might even pull strings to get me into Yale in the fall. And with that thought, I'm decided.

I scarf down the casserole and then throw some clothes in a suitcase. I don't need much. I'll only be gone for three days.

15

JUNEAU

I HAVE BEEN HIDING IN MY ROOM—MY "CABIN"—since we embarked two days ago. As soon as we launched, I found the ship's self-service dining area and stocked up on enough bread, fruit, and plastic-wrapped sandwiches to last me a few days. I haven't ventured out since then.

I have never felt loneliness before. Even the time I got snowed in overnight on a hunting trip, I knew my father and clan were waiting for me, and actually enjoyed the time alone. Not now. I want to be home in my yurt with my father and dogs, knowing that Kenai's and Nome's families are within shouting distance. I hate this room where everything is made of plastic, on a boat in the middle of an unending ocean, among complete strangers.

I glance over at the photo of my parents, which is propped atop a tiny table. It is surrounded by the remaining supplies from the emergency shelter and the pile of things I brought from Whit's yurt: feathers, fur, stones, powders, dried plants, and books. The objects are familiar. Soothing.

I return to the book I am reading on the history of the Gaia Movement of the 1960s. It's about how earth is a superorganism, which I know was one of the theories that led Whit to the discovery of the Yara and the tapping of its powers. Normally I'm not allowed to browse freely through his books—he has me on a learning schedule and is very strict about revealing things in "the right order." So this book is new to me, and I am greedily gobbling up every tidbit of new information.

I set the book down on my bunk to get a bottle of water, and when I come back, the pages have flipped to the front. I begin turning back to my place, but I see something that makes me hesitate. I go back to the copyright page.

The book was published in 2002.

I stare at the number. And then I drop the book, recoiling as if it had transformed into a rattlesnake. I stumble to my feet and back up as far as I can, wedging myself into a corner of the room.

My head spins and I feel like I'm going to keel over. Unthinkable thoughts careen inside my mind. The elders said they escaped just before war broke out in the spring of 1984. Yet Whit had a book published in 2002.

Suddenly, I remember the expression on my father's face whenever I asked him about the war. About his and my mother's flight to safety. He never looked me in the eye when he told me that story. I always thought it was because the memories disturbed him. But that wasn't why.

It was because there was no war.

He knew. They all knew, and someone—probably Whit—had even gone off-territory to get this book. The elders lied to us. Whit lied to us. My father . . . lied to me.

For the last twenty-four hours, my heart has known what my mind couldn't admit. They knew.

I sink to the floor. Putting my head between my knees, I wrap my arms around my folded legs and rock back and forth. My mouth is dry and metallic tasting.

If the fundamental elements of my life—who I am, why and where my clan lived as we did . . . are all lies, then what can I believe? I have no idea what is truth and what is fiction. I have been brainwashed my entire childhood.

I'm all I've got now. I can't trust anyone.

16

MILES

HOW DO YOU SEARCH AN ENTIRE CITY FOR SOMEone you've never seen? You try to get into their head and think of where they would go. Considering she's a teenage girl, my first thought is shopping. But when I arrive in Seattle Saturday night, the stores are already closing.

My second thought is to check the city's popular hangout spots. My internet search of Seattle told me to go to Capitol Hill, Belltown, and here, Pioneer Square, where I am sitting on the steps, eating a sandwich. For an hour, I watch people come and go, and don't see anyone who fits the description on Dad's notepad.

I drive north to Capitol Hill and begin combing the streets, looking for a girl with two huskies. *How hard can that be?* I think. But as I walk I begin to get an idea of the scale of the city and start to realize how stupid my plan is. It would be like trying to spot a friend at the Super Bowl without having a clue where their seat is. How in the world am I going to find one girl in the middle of this enormous city? I am well and truly fucked.

17

JUNEAU

THE DAY I ARRIVE IN SEATTLE, I WANDER FOR hours watching the city, trying to understand how it works: the cars and the different-colored lights that show them when to stop or go, the people dressed in the same dark colors, walking swiftly and looking worried, as if they are all about to miss something important. I move past them, unremarkable in my boy's clothes, cap pulled low over my eyes so that people won't stare at them.

I stalk the city like an animal until I understand its rhythm and can walk through its streets as invisible as I am when I hunt my prey. Once I am able to navigate with confidence, I decide to try to reproduce my most successful Reading so far and set out to find another oracle.

"Look, it's Crazy Frankie," I hear a little boy say to his mother. She shushes him and walks quickly away. I look to where he was pointing and see him sitting against a building on a street corner: a broken man, wizened skin like moose-hide leather left for months in the sun. A hat sits in front of him with coins inside, and empty metal cans with BEER printed on them are scattered around him.

I approach. His odor is pungent. Rancid. "May I sit next to you?" I ask, and he looks up at me with watery red eyes.

"Sure," he says, and knocks a few of the cans out of the way. I ignore the stares of the passersby who look at us oddly.

"Can I ask you some questions?" I ask.

"Well, why not? Shoot away!" he says, and I reach for his hand. His fingers are caked with grime; his fingernails outlined in dirt. I grasp my opal with my free hand and look him straight in the eyes. "Do you mind being my oracle?" I ask. "There is some information I need to know."

"Well, I can sure as hell try," he says with a shattered-glass voice. And as the tingling of the Yara connection moves through me to him, his breathing grows calm and his eyes clear.

"I am picturing my father in my mind. Could you tell me how I can find him?"

The man sits silently for a moment, looking at a space above my head. "You can't do it alone," he says finally. "You must find someone to take you on your journey."

"Who?" I ask. "How will I find them?"

Frankie leans his head to one side like he's thinking, and then says, "You will know who he is because his name will take you far."

My heart drops. It's a riddle. I don't know why I'm so disappointed. I can't expect a clear answer from a divination. "Can you tell me anything else about this person?"

"Yes," responds Frankie. "You must be completely honest with him. Tell him everything he wants to know. But whatever you do, don't trust him. He needs you as much as you need him."

I push a little further. "Once I find the person you're talking about, where do we go to find my father?"

"South . . . southeast. A place that is the exact opposite of here," Frankie says, and an image forms in my mind of a barren landscape with cactus and strange rock formations.

He's given me more than I was hoping for. "Thank you," I say.

"One more thing," the man says, and I can feel our link weakening and see the watery haze start to return to his eyes. "When you find the one who will accompany you, don't let him use his cell phone."

"What's a cell phone?" I ask, releasing his hand and letting our connection break. He leans his head back against the wall and begins chuckling.

"Thank you for helping me," I say, and fishing in my bag, pull out a few bills and place them carefully in his hat.

He picks up the money and looks up at me, surprised. "Hey, missy, that's way too much," he says as I walk away.

"It's not, believe me," I say, and set out to find a place to sleep for the night.

18

MILES

I'VE BEEN WANDERING FOR HOURS WITH NO LUCK, feeling like the biggest fool on earth. I want to give up, but remember the look on my father's face when he said I needed to prove myself to him. That'll never happen in the mail room. I've got to find this girl.

I try to think like a detective would. If you're new to a city, you most likely go to touristy areas. I walk up a road with several restaurant terraces and sit down on a street bench to watch the people passing by.

At least I got out of the house for the weekend. When I told Mrs. Kirby I would be fine on my own, she actually sounded relieved. And I answered Dad's *Is everything okay?* text this morning with: *Just watching TV in my jail cell. Don't worry, I'm fine.*

I finally get up and begin following signs for Pike Place

Market, the one spot in Seattle that I've actually heard of. Across the street a rowdy crowd sits at tables outside a sports bar. I doubt this girl will be in that group. I sigh. This is worse than finding a needle in a haystack.

"Hey, Starry Eyes, baby! Come back, I was just kidding!" someone yells.

I'm suddenly on high alert, my eyes scanning the crowd across the street. I home in on a group of college-age guys wearing identical Greek letter T-shirts and drinking pints of beer. It was one of them who shouted "starry eyes." But walking away from them is what looks like a small-built boy with a kind of fuzzy crew cut.

Wait, no. It's a girl.

I jog across the street toward the frat boys, watching as the girl stops at another table, leans in, and talks with them.

"Hey, what'd that girl ask you for?" I ask the first table.

One of the guys looks me up and down and then, satisfied that my button-down and jeans meet his dress code or something, says, "You don't want her, man. She's crazy."

"You've got that right," the guy next to him says, and laughing, they lift their mugs to clink in agreement.

"What do you mean, crazy?" I ask.

"Chick's been showing up every night, wandering around asking everyone their name," another guy says. He shakes his head and wipes the foam off his mouth with the back of his hand.

"And what about that creepy star-shaped contact lens?" the first guy says. "Weird, right?"

Star-shaped contact lens? Excitement rises in my chest. I walk away from their table. "You're welcome!" one of the frat boys calls after me, and his friends laugh.

The girl is watching something across the street, and I turn to see what she's looking at. My heart stops in my chest. It's two of Dad's security guards from work, and they're staring straight at her.

A car speeds by, forcing them to wait before they jog across the road. I look back at the girl, but she's gone, and Dad's guards are looking around like *Where'd she go?*

I take a quick right onto the next road, and then I see the girl dart out of an alleyway a block away. She moves so smooth and fast it looks like she's gliding.

I spend the next hour trailing her around town while I run over Dad's description in my mind: starburst eye, long black hair, probably traveling with two huskies. Looks like she lost the dogs and the hairdo sometime during the last week, but according to the frat boys, she kept the weird contact lens. She doesn't seem like an "industrial spy" who everyone's dying to get his hands on. She looks more like a lost little boy.

As I watch her, I realize there's something wrong with her. She flinches at the smallest provocation. A street cleaner goes by and she looks ready to climb the nearest tree to escape. She stands outside the Apple store and stares at the window for so long, it looks like she's planning a major electronics heist. You'd think she was seeing everything for the first time. Like she's Tarzan or something—raised by wolves in the deepest, darkest forest. And then there's the fact that she keeps stopping people and asking their names.

I follow her as she roams the streets until well after dark and watch as she finally walks into a guesthouse with a sign outside reading CATCHING DEW GUESTHOUSE: NO VACANCIES. I jog back to where I parked my car, hoping she doesn't leave while I'm moving it. Once parked in front of the guesthouse, I settle in and keep an eye on the front door. That's when my phone rings. Dad's yelling before I even have a chance to talk.

". . . called the home phone and when you didn't answer, I got Mrs. Kirby on the line. She went straight over to the house and then called to tell me you weren't there. Now you better have a good reason to—"

"I found her," I say, cutting him off.

"You found her? What the hell's that supposed to mean?" my dad asks, confused.

"I'm in Seattle, and I think I found the girl you're looking for."

Dad is silent for a whole thirty seconds, and I wait to hear whether he's going to start yelling again or if he'll take me seriously.

"Where are you?" he asks, his tone clipped. Unreadable.

"I'm parked in front of a guesthouse I saw her go into," I say.

"Where? Give me an address."

Within minutes, one of Dad's company Saabs comes down the street and parks a few places away. I stay in my car and watch as one of the men I saw earlier today walks up to my window and taps on it.

I roll the window down and stare at him. "Your father says for you to check into a hotel and then drive straight back to

L.A. in the morning," he says.

"Got it," I say, and roll the window up in his face. I make no move to leave. He shakes his head and walks back to his car.

The guards and I spend the night in our cars. Finally, around 10:00 a.m., one of them goes into the guesthouse and comes back out at a jog. "She's gone," he calls to his partner, and throws me a scowl as they speed off.

Dad calls five minutes later and commands me to head home. Now I'm in a bind: if I go home without the girl, Dad will definitely kill me. I have to find her before his security team does and somehow convince her to come back to L.A. with me. I rest my head on the steering wheel and experience a moment of pure panic. What have I gotten myself into?

I breathe deeply and reason with myself. What worse can happen? I'm already grounded. I'm already going to be kept out of Yale until Dad feels like greasing some palms. I can't think of a fate worse than the mail room, although I'm sure Dad could. *I have to do this,* I think, and start the car.

Three hours later I finally spot her, crouched down outside an ultramodern glass building, talking to a street person. Just then it starts pouring down rain. The girl stands, pulls her hood over her head, and sprints into the building.

I turn the car around, park in the building's parking lot, and make a dash to the door she disappeared through. I just hope she's still here. If she's not, I'm going to seriously consider admitting failure and going home.

19

JUNEAU

I HAVE SEARCHED THE STREETS OF SEATTLE FOR several days, looking for the person my oracle spoke of, without the foggiest notion of what he looks like. Yesterday I felt he was near, but I had to run from my pursuers before I could spot him.

Used to being the hunter, I am now the hunted. Men are chasing me—they aren't dressed like Whit's captors, so I have no idea who they are. I just know I have to continue looking for the person I'm supposed to meet while keeping the men at bay. It would help if I knew what he looked like instead of just trusting my hunter's instinct that he is following me.

But the second he walks into the library, I know it is him.

I am sitting at my usual table: the one I use whenever the rain drives me off the streets, reading magazines and newspapers to familiarize myself with the events of the last thirty years.

I keep my head down, scanning the pages of a *Time* magazine while I see him glance my way and take a seat at the end of my table. Only when he pretends to be reading a book do I allow myself a peek.

I study his features carefully. His light-brown hair is the color of fireweed honey tossed about in a scramble of loose curls. He has a long, straight nose and lips that look like they're hiding a joke. Or a secret.

He glances my way and sees me staring at him. I can't tell if his eyes are blue or green. I rise, walk to his end of the table, and sit down directly across from him. He watches me, his face reddening with surprise.

"What's your name?" I whisper. The page-padded hush of the room swallows my voice, but he hears me.

He hesitates, looks uncertain, and then focuses on my left eye. Clearing his throat, he whispers, "Miles."

It's the answer I've been waiting for. I nod and study him for another few seconds. And then I rise to my feet. "Come on," I say. I swing my backpack over my shoulder and stand next to him, waiting.

He sits there looking dumbfounded. "What? Where?"

I extend my hand. He looks at it warily—like it's an inanimate object. Like it's one of those mystery boxes Kenai loves to make: you never know if it holds a piece of blueberry cake or a coil-spring snake that will smack you in the face.

The boy doesn't take my hand. Instead, he follows me out of the library into the parking lot. It's still raining. I pull up my hood and let the rain drizzle down my jacket, while Miles huddles beneath the building's overhang.

"Which one's yours?" I ask.

"The Beamer." Miles points to a silvery-blue car that looks brand-new, and then wraps his arms back around himself. It isn't very cold, but his shirt is too light for the weather. *Doesn't come prepared,* I think, continuing the mental assessment I had begun the moment I saw him.

I walk to his car and stand next to the passenger side. "What are you doing?" Miles calls.

"Waiting for you," I respond. "And getting wet."

He gives me an incredulous look. When I don't move, he leaves his dry spot and jogs through the rain toward me, pressing something on his keys as he runs. I hear the locks click and I open the door, slide in, and stash my backpack in the rear seat. Miles bundles into the car and turns to gape at me. "What are you doing?" he repeats.

"I could ask you the same thing," I respond. "You were looking for me. And now you've found me. I'll tell you what I'm doing if you tell me what you already know about me."

His jaw snaps shut and his eyes grow wide. Green eyes. I can tell now. They're the dark blue-green-black of a Denali lake at dusk. The thing about lake water is it's opaque. You never know what's hidden underneath.

"What I know about you? Nothing!" he says.

I stay silent, crossing my arms as I wait. He sees that I won't talk until he does.

"Seriously," he claims. "All I know is that some people are looking for you. And the locals think you're crazy because you go around asking people's names." He pauses, looking sorry that he said that last part. Understandable. It's not the kind of thing you would want to mention when sitting in an enclosed space with said crazy person.

Tactless, I add to my list, and ask, "Do you?"

"Do I what?" he asks, looking cornered.

"Think I'm crazy?"

"Um, I would have to say . . . at this moment . . . yes," he admits.

I chew my lip and look out the window at the parking lot. No question about it—I'm sure Miles is the one Frankie foresaw.

I look back at him and raise my eyebrows impatiently.

"What?" he asks, looking defensive.

"Let's go," I say.

"Go where?"

"To find my clan."

His features flip through a series of comical expressions: incomprehension, doubt, surprise, and finally exasperation.

"Where . . . where do we have to go to find your . . . clan?"

I lean forward to peer at the point where the sun hides under the rain clouds to get my bearing. "It looked kind of desertlike. Kind of Wild West. It's in that direction," I say, pointing southeast.

"Whoa," he says, holding his hands up in a defensive gesture. "Listen here. I don't have any clue what you're talking about. And

I haven't said I'm taking you anywhere. Much less to the Wild West."

"Then tell me why you were following me." I look at him.

He stares back at me as long as he can before shifting his gaze away. I just sit and watch him, waiting for him to come around. Finally he sighs and says, "Okay, I'll give you a lift. But I was headed south, actually. To California. We've got a lot of Wild West there. You could ride there with me and then go look for your clan. But I'll need to make a stop and pick up some . . . stuff first. Clothes. You know."

"What's in the suitcase behind the seat?" I ask.

"Um . . . clothes," Miles says, fidgeting. "Yeah, I forgot about that. But I could take you to your hotel if you need to get . . . supplies." He rearranges his face into a helpful smile and then lifts his eyebrows in a way that I think is meant to charm me.

Nome would be eating this up, I think. She had actually gone through the EB and ranked the photos of every scientist, politician—anything male—from one to ten, based on "charisma," as she called it. I can never think of John F. Kennedy without the number 7.5 popping into my head.

But I feel only amusement watching Miles. I have a goal, and he is the one who will help me. My interest ends there. "I don't need to go back to the guesthouse," I say. "I've been here seven days and paid up front for the week. Plus, I have everything I need in my pack. Let's go."

"So you have money?"

"Some."

"Well, then, why didn't you rent a car and drive yourself?" he asks curiously.

"I don't know how to drive."

He raises a skeptical eyebrow. "You could take a bus."

"You're supposed to take me. And California's due south. I'm going southeast."

Miles clenches his jaw in frustration. He digs his fingers into his temples and squeezes his eyes shut. And then, opening them again, he glares at me. *Doesn't like to take orders,* I think, noting that tidbit on my checklist, and then add, *Is used to getting what he wants.*

"Why in the world would you trust me to take you anywhere?" he asks. "I could be dangerous. I could be psycho. You don't know me from Adam."

I turn to him. "Actually, I don't trust you. Frankie told me not to, but he also said I had to be honest with you."

"Who the hell is Frankie?" A note of hysteria creeps into Miles's voice.

"Frankie is the guy who sits and drinks beer on the corner of Pike and Pine. People call him Crazy Frankie."

"You take advice from an insane alcoholic?" Miles's face is dead serious now.

Be completely honest, I hear the voice in my head. I exhale and brace myself. "He was my oracle," I respond. "And he told me to go with you. Therefore, whether or not you are dangerous or psycho—which I don't think you are—"

"Thanks," Miles interjects drily.

"—you are driving me."

"How does this Crazy Frankie even know who I am?"

"He doesn't," I respond. "He told me to go with the person whose name will take me far."

Miles stares at me, all semblance of coolness gone. He looks scared.

"You are psychotic," Miles says, eyes wide. Tearing his gaze from mine, he sits for an entire minute staring straight ahead at the parking lot. *He needs you as much as you need him,* Frankie had said. I wait.

Finally, shaking his head in despair, Miles turns the key in the ignition. "Okay. I'll take you at least part of the way on your crazy road trip." He reaches for something on the dashboard. "But first I have to make a call."

I get to the contraption first. "Is this your cellular phone?" I ask.

"Yeah," he says.

Clasping it in my hand, I close my eyes and contact the Yara. I've been waiting for a week for this to happen. I'm ready. A little spark flies out the side of the phone, and its screen goes dead.

"What the—" Miles yells.

"Frankie also told me not to let you use your phone," I reply. "Now let's go."

20

MILES

MY BRAIN HURTS. I AM SO FAR OUT OF MY COMfort zone that I might as well be in the Amazon, swimming with piranhas. This girl somehow just broke my phone and now she's telling me to drive her to Mount Rainier. And I'm actually arguing with her over directions, like we're some geriatric married couple.

"You pointed south a minute ago. The mountain is due east," I say, stopping the car at the edge of the parking lot. "You have no idea where you're going, do you?"

She wraps her arms around her chest and says defiantly, "Actually, I pointed southeast. Our destination is in that direction."

"And you know that because Crazy Frankie told you," I state incredulously.

"I don't think he's actually crazy," she says.

Oh my God, I'm driving a psychopath. "So if the wino told you to go southeast, why are we heading due east?"

"Because. As I said, we have to go to that mountain first," she insists, nodding in the direction of Mount Rainier.

I just sit and stare at her for a minute until I remember how valuable this girl is to Dad and the fact that my name is, at this very moment, written in his bad books in bold capital letters. The last thing I want is for her to get out of my car and find someone else named Taxi or Greyhound Bus and ditch me.

"You are taking me," she says, as if I have no choice in the matter. Man, does she have me pegged: I need her as much as she needs me.

"Seat belt," I say. She looks confused. "If I'm taking you, you have to wear your seat belt." Still no reaction. I yank on mine, demonstrating what a seat belt is, and she fiddles with hers until she finally gets it attached.

I mash my foot on the accelerator and go. We drive in silence for a few minutes, which is good, because I have to get my bearings. I search for road signs, finally see one for MOUNT RAINIER NATIONAL PARK, and follow it east out of town.

We drive over long bridges spanning large bodies of water, and past ugly urban sprawl until mountains appear in the distance, one capped with snow. We've been on the road a good twenty minutes before I notice that the girl is holding on to the dashboard with both hands.

"What?" I ask.

"What, what?" she responds.

"What are you doing? Why are you pushing on the dashboard like that?"

"You're going kind of fast," she says, in an accusatory voice.

"Fast? I'm only going fifty. That's not even the speed limit!"

"It feels fast to me," she mutters.

"Listen, if you're going to criticize my driving," I begin, and then I remember . . . I'm arguing with a crazy person. "Just stop doing that," I say, glancing at her death grip on the glove compartment. "It's making me nervous."

She frowns and lets go, but moves her hands to the edges of the seat on either side of her legs and clutches tight. I decide to ignore her completely until I'm on the highway going out of town, at which point I speed up to sixty and relax. We pass a sign saying 54 MILES TO MOUNT RAINIER, and I see the girl's eyes flick from the sign to the speedometer and back as she calculates how long it will take us to get there. She looks at the sun, or at least where the faint shape of the sun glows from underneath the rain clouds, and then at the dashboard clock, and finally lays her head back against the headrest and relaxes. And when I say relaxes, I only mean she doesn't look like she's going to explode or spontaneously leap out of the speeding car.

I wish she'd take off that contact lens. It freaks me out. One of the goth girls at school has scary yellow cat-eye lenses. Definitely not my scene—the artsy goth posers. And thinking of school reminds me that, however weird she is, Cat-eyes will be attending graduation next month, and I won't. I step on the accelerator, and the engine roars as I take the car to ninety miles per hour.

And when I see the girl's fingers grip tightly around the edge of her seat, I smile.

We drive the next hour without speaking. As we approach the mountains, city-appropriate sedans are gradually replaced by massive pickup trucks and semis stacked with logs. One-story identical wooden houses are lined up side by side like a countrified version of Monopoly.

After a little while, I turn the radio on—my music is on my dead phone—and all I can find is country. I keep it on—it's better than sitting in silence with the odd boy-girl.

I can't help but glance at her every once in a while; she could be part Asian, with high cheekbones and thick black hair. Her clothes look straight from the men's section of Old Navy. Her hairstyle is truly ugly: It looks like she got a bad crew cut, and now that it's growing out, she's spiking it to make herself look taller. Or fiercer.

She's small. I'd say five-five was a pretty close estimate. When she's quiet, she looks her size. But when she talks, she somehow gains a few inches . . . becomes bigger than herself. When she first got in the car, I thought, *If she's insane and freaks out in my car, I can take her,* but now I'm not so sure. There's this energy . . . and anger . . . jam-packed into every inch of her.

Dad said that calling her an industrial spy was "near enough to the truth." When I first saw her, I couldn't imagine her being involved in anything spy-related. But now that she's sitting inches away from me, I totally can. She seems dangerous.

As if reading my thoughts, she glances over at me, and when our eyes meet, she glowers. "Where are you from?" she asks.

I hesitate, and then decide it can't hurt for her to know where I live. "L.A.," I say.

She just stares at me. "Where is . . . Ellay?" she asks finally.

"Los Angeles. It's in—" I say.

"Oh, yes. California," she interrupts, and then to herself mumbles, "Most populous U.S. city after New York City; however, not the capital of California, which is"—she pauses and thinks a second—"Sacramento. Or at least, it was in 1983."

Freak.

I turn off onto a two-lane road, and we pass a group of hunters dressed in brown camouflage, carrying guns. I hate guns. Dad tried to take me hunting once. I spent the whole time in the lodge playing video games, refusing to go out on the hunting range and embarrassing him in front of his friends.

"What is your whole name?" she asks, continuing her interrogation.

Uh-oh. Now we're in tricky territory. Everyone's heard of Blackwell Pharmaceutical. My last name is usually a status symbol, but right now it's probably better not to flaunt it.

"Why would I tell you my last name when you haven't even told me your first?" I lob back.

"My name is Juneau," she says.

"Like the goddess . . . what, queen of Olympus?" I ask.

"No, like the capital of Alaska," she responds.

Bingo! I think, remembering that Dad had mentioned that the girl was coming by boat from Anchorage.

Juneau points to a National Forest road map posted by the side of the road. "Stop here," she says, and clicking off her seat belt, gets out of the car before I've come to a complete stop. She stumbles slightly as I slam on the brakes, and then, catching her balance, walks to the sign as normally as if she bails out of moving cars all the time.

The girl's on drugs. That's got to be it. Whatever secret drug Dad's trying to get his hands on, she's probably already taking it by the truckload. Unless it's an antipsychotic pill, in which case she could use a few.

She studies the map for a few minutes, and then walks back to the car, gets in, and says, "Okay. Drive." Like I'm her chauffeur or something.

"Would you mind telling me where we're going?" I ask, masking my sarcasm to avoid another nasty scowl. The girl—Juneau—scares me, and it's just not worth getting her riled up.

"Up there," she says, pointing halfway up the mountainside.

I can't help it. I begin speaking to her as if she were a toddler. Or deranged, which she is. "As you can see, it is now seven p.m.," I say, gesturing to the dashboard clock as if I were a game show host and it was a brand-new car. "There are no restaurants anywhere nearby. And the sign for 'accommodation' was back a ways, pointing in another direction. So if we want to, say, eat dinner—or sleep anywhere besides here in this car—we have to turn around and go somewhere else."

"That way." She points up the mountain.

I squeeze my hands into fists. But I think of the look on Dad's face if I manage to get her back to L.A., and ask with clenched teeth, "Would you like to close the car door then so I can drive?"

"Oh yeah," she says, as if it hadn't occurred to her. She leans over and slams the door shut, and we're off.

I'm lying here in a tent, pretending to be asleep but actually fearing for my life as I watch a bunny murderer have a conversation with our campfire.

Here's how it went down. Halfway up Mt. Rainier, Juneau orders me to go off-road down this dirt track. Once we're way past where anyone—say, rescuers—could actually find us, she tells me to stop. It's getting dark, and it's like we're in a scene from one of those documentaries where oblivious backpackers set up camp near a bear cave or a wolf den or on top of a killer scorpion nest and are taught their lesson for thoughtlessly encroaching upon nature. And just when I'm thinking this, Juneau gets her pack out of the backseat, pulls a nylon bag out, and starts setting up a freaking tent.

"What are you doing?" My voice shoots up an octave, like I've been breathing helium.

She looks over at me and says simply, "What's it look like?"

"We're not sleeping here tonight! This isn't even a legal campsite!" I squeak.

"We have to. I wasn't able to Read nature in Seattle. The city made me too anxious. I saw a postcard of this mountain and knew it would be the perfect place to Read. It kind of looks like home," she responds. And just like that, she goes back to unwrapping the nylon tent and sticking folding metal poles through it. I stand like an idiot while she brushes twigs and rocks away from a flat bit of ground and then pulls the tent over to it and starts banging pins into the earth to anchor it.

She turns to me. "If you want to help, you can get a fire going before it's too dark to see."

"A fire? I'm pretty sure that's illegal in the middle of a national park. And why do we need a fire?" I ask. "It's not even cold out."

"For dinner," she says, and out of her pack she takes two carved and painted dowel-looking things, clicks them into grooves to fit together, and grabs a bundle of little pointed arrow-stick thingies, and I'll be damned if she's not walking off into the forest holding a mini-crossbow.

I don't even try to make a fire. I go back to the car and for a half hour I fiddle with my iPhone, trying to turn it back on, but it's completely shot. I'm wondering what she could have done to break it when I look up and see Juneau stride into the clearing, holding a dead rabbit by the hind legs.

Not even looking my way, she sits down on a rock and takes a huge bowie knife out of her pack and starts peeling the fur off. I can't watch. I feel sick.

By the time I turn back around, she's made a fire and has set up a kind of makeshift spit by driving two branches into the ground on either side of the flames. Then, ever so casually, as if she were tying her shoes or something, she shoves a third stick through the raw, red-skinned rabbit's mouth and out its other end, and I have to walk off into the woods by myself because I think I'm going to puke.

By the time I get back, the thing on the spit actually looks like meat and smells appetizing enough to make my mouth water. I stand there and watch her as she roasts some mushrooms and leaves in a little pan over the flames, using the juice dripping from the meat to cook them.

"I get it that foraging is the hip new thing for you back-to-nature types, but you do realize there is a McDonald's about a half hour down the road?"

For a moment it looks like she doesn't recognize me. Then she nonchalantly cuts a sliver of cooked leg off something that was cute and fluffy and hopping around about an hour ago. She holds it grimly up on the end of the knife, like a dare. I shudder, but pick the meat off the knifepoint and pop it in my mouth. Oh my God, it's really good.

She sees my expression and smiles. "Saw the McDonald's sign on the way. But I tried it in Seattle, and frankly, that stuff's nasty."

21

JUNEAU

HE IS QUITE LIKELY THE STUPIDEST BOY I HAVE ever met.

No, strike that. Not stupid. He actually seems smart enough. He has a good vocabulary when he makes an effort to use it. And I can tell he listens to every word I say and stores it away for later. Why?

Like Frankie said, he's got an ulterior motive. Miles needs me as much as I need him. He's got secrets. But so do I. Even though my oracle told me to be honest with him, that doesn't mean I have to tell him my whole life story—not unless he asks. So I won't expect him to do the same.

I change my assessment from stupid to naive. It's clear he's lived a sheltered life. And not just sheltered in the fact that he hasn't been brought up in the wilderness like I have. He has lived what Dennis would call "a fortunate life, unfortunately for the rest of the world." The blissfully ignorant spawn of the rich.

After wandering the streets of Seattle for a week, the difference between rich and poor is obvious to me. Compared to those I met who were living rough, Miles's studiedly casual clothes, educated speech, and flippantly confident way he carries himself all point to money that he hasn't had to earn himself.

I glance back at the flames and wonder if he didn't know how to build a fire or if he was just too lazy to be bothered. I don't understand why Frankie said he was necessary. He seems like the last person on earth I would actually need right now. If Miles couldn't drive, he would be complete deadweight.

He actually insisted on sleeping in the car until I informed him that the scented skull and crossbones hanging from the rearview mirror and bags of chips and cookies stashed in the backseat were likely to attract bears, and that a bear could easily peel a car door off with its claws.

It's the first time I've seen him move fast. He ripped the little fragrant skull off the mirror, scooped the bags out of the backseat, and set off at top speed into the woods with them, returning ten minutes later empty-handed. And although he left the windows down to air the car out, he didn't hesitate to bunk down in the tent when I told him it was safer.

I wait impatiently for him to fall asleep. Finally, when I haven't seen him move for a while, I fish the bag of firepowder out of my pack. Carefully measuring out a small silvery handful, I throw the powdered mica mixture onto the flames. "Dad," I say, and visualizing my father's face, stare just up and to the right of the licking flames.

Nothing happens, and a thread of worry pulls tight in my chest. Like I said to Miles, besides Reading my oracle, I couldn't Read a thing in Seattle. And I don't know if it had anything to do with being in a city. Thankfully, I was able to perform that minor Conjure and make fire in his cell phone. But it feels like something is changing, either in me, or in my connection to the Yara.

I actually started feeling the change during those tortuous five days on the boat to Seattle. A black fog of doubt settling over everything I know. If the elders lied about the war, could the Yara just be another of their fictions? But something even deeper in me reassures me that the Yara exists. It's just my connection to it that feels like it is slipping away.

I banish those thoughts from my mind and concentrate on the fire. It takes a while, but finally an image appears. It's exactly as I saw it in the vision: an arid landscape with cacti in the foreground and rock formations in the distance. Although it is nighttime, the moon glows brightly, illuminating the scene.

I see a group of small buildings made of clay or dirt. I remember seeing something similar in the EB—in an article on Native Americans—and try to remember in which part of America they were located. Surrounding the group of buildings is a high fence topped with barbed wire. It stretches into the distance before hitting a corner and continuing on as far as I can see in another direction. A perimeter fence. My people are being kept in captivity.

As I watch, my father emerges from one of the huts, arms wrapped around himself. He walks a little ways, and then stops and looks up at the moon. His expression is wistful. Worried. I know he's thinking about me. I wonder if the reason he came out was because he somehow felt me Read him.

I have been thinking about my father and the whole clan so much over the last couple of weeks that, now that I see him, I am bombarded with a volley of conflicting feelings. One part of me wants to throw myself on him and hug him tight and not let go.

Another part wants to scream. To shake him. To ask why he lied to me. Why, since Whit began training me when I was five, the clan Sage perpetuated the lies. Why the adults misled the children. Why they brainwashed us to think that an outside world didn't exist and to hide like cornered rabbits from a danger that was never there. Because of this conspiracy of lies kept by the adults—the family—I always trusted, my whole life has been a farce.

My eyes sting, and I brush away an angry tear. I fumble around in the pack until my fingers find my fire opal. Pulling it out, I hold it in my palm and grind it against the ground. "Dad," I say. Nothing. He is too far away for me to Read his emotions. Or maybe I'm just too furious to connect to the Yara.

I wonder for the hundredth time how much of what I learned was part of the web of lies my father and the other clan elders spun around us, and how much was true. Their betrayal still hurts so fiercely that it burns a hole in my chest, but at least I know I still have the Yara. Other than that, I'm not sure what I believe anymore. I am unanchored. Adrift in this new world.

I turn my focus back to my father, whose figure stands immobile in the desert scene. "I'm okay, Dad," I say, although I know he can't hear me. I swallow the lump in my throat. "And I'm coming to get you."

22

MILES

SHE TALKS IN HER SLEEP. SHE MENTIONS A COUPLE of writers—Beckett and Neruda—and some other names I don't recognize, just kind of mumbling like people do in their sleep. She talks about "brigands," like she's afraid of them. Then she says something about her dad, and in a tortured voice she moans, "Why?"

And she looks so vulnerable—so normal—for a second, despite her tragic haircut, that I actually feel like hugging her. Telling her things will be okay, even though I don't know exactly what's going on with her.

And then I remember that she is not only the top-priority focus of my father's manhunt but is dangerous and most likely mentally unstable. I stay on my side of the tent.

23

JUNEAU

MY SLEEP IS PLAGUED BY NIGHTMARES. EVERY night the same image appears: brigands descending on my clan's encampment. Dressed in torn leather and blood-matted furs, their eyes glowing green with radiation. Using an assortment of handmade weapons as well as high-tech guns, they swarm my village, killing first the dogs, who rush out to protect us, and then my clan. I stand there in the midst of the slaughter, paralyzed. Unable to react. And then I hear my father's voice calling to me: "Use the Yara, Juneau. Use your gifts."

I awake as the sun begins to rise, the stench of burning yurts still stinging my nose until I sit up and breathe in the pure mountain air. Through the mosquito net I see the dew-kissed world around us turn rosy pink in the blush of daybreak. There was no war. There are no brigands. I remind myself that an apocalyptic world war never happened. But that image is such an integral part of me that this new world seems like the tall tale—a fairy-tale world, wrapped loosely like colorful paper around the burned-out husk of a postwar planet.

I glance over at Miles. His lips are slightly parted, and his breath is slow. I force the scary images out of my mind and remind myself that this is my world now. It's just me and this boy, who I apparently need in order to complete my quest. Once again, I wonder why Frankie told me to find him. Wouldn't I be better off on my own?

His curls tumble across his forehead, and his chin is slightly lifted. I wonder how old he is. Probably the same as me, I guess. Seventeen. Maybe eighteen. I let myself see him as Nome would for a moment: he would definitely rate a 10 in her book. Considering that John F. Kennedy is a 7.5. *Oh, Nome,* I think. *I hope you're safe.* I turn my thoughts back from my best friend to the boy sleeping beside me.

What was he doing following me around? What is it that he needs from me? When I asked him, he wouldn't answer. My only other option is to Read him, and I've never Read anyone against their will. I force that thought away and prepare myself. There are some things I must do before we leave. I slip quietly out of the tent, careful not to wake him.

Last night after Reading the fire, I consulted the wind. A fresh breeze was blowing. I raised my arms and clutched my opal in one hand. It was a long time before I felt my connection with the Yara, and when I visualized my clan, I received nothing in return.

My frustration cut sharp, like a knife on flesh. What is wrong with me? Am I losing my connection? I changed my request and whispered, "Whit." And after a moment, the smoke of a far-off campfire tickled my nostrils. I turned in a circle, trying to figure out which direction it was coming from, but got nothing else. Whit must be outdoors as well. Maybe he is near. Perhaps his captors are transporting him to where our clan is being held. Or maybe he escaped and is looking for me. He should be able to find me by Reading. In fact, if he had been free to, he could have probably found me in the streets of Seattle.

As I think of him, a feeling of uncertainty—of mistrust—creeps its way into my mind, but I do my best to ignore it. Yes, Whit was probably the one who traveled out into the world as recently as a few years ago—when he bought the book. But all the clan elders had to have been in on the deception. He isn't any guiltier than the rest of them. They all lied, not just him.

But he was the one who was supposed to be revealing truth to you, something nags. *Revealing truth while simultaneously feeding you lies.* The sting of betrayal returns, and I banish it into a far corner of my mind to deal with later.

The burden of responsibility I used to feel when Whit talked to me about being his successor weighs heavily on me now. I can't be sidetracked by childish emotions. I am responsible for my clan. Besides Whit, I am the only one who isn't imprisoned. I must think of him as my ally and not let petty feelings get in the way. I will be strong.

But how to contact Whit? He must be outside a city if he's

near a campfire. If only I could get a message to him. I wish he had shown me more Conjuring. The few simple tasks he did aren't going to help me now: camouflage through metamorphosis. Keeping ice from melting so our meat stocks wouldn't go bad. Creating intense heat to liquefy a solid, like we used to repair our decades-old metal sled runners and wheels. *Or to fry a cell phone,* I think, and smile.

I know I'm better than Whit at Reading. Even he admitted that "the student had surpassed the teacher," and attributed it to my being raised so close to the Yara my entire life. But as far as Conjuring, I don't even know yet what is possible.

Just as I am mulling over my options, a raven the size of a large cat alights on the ground in front of me. It cocks its head to one side, regarding me suspiciously, and then walks straight up and squawks loudly, ruffling its feathers. Something is tied to its leg. A message from Whit.

"Thank you," I say, and detach the piece of paper from the raven's claw. Unfolding it, I see Whit's spindly writing.

Juneau, I can Read you are near and that you are okay. Time is of the essence—help me find you. Write a note saying where you are, and the raven will bring your message back to me. After that, STAY PUT and I will come get *you. My fire-Reading showed you camping in woods with a boy. Whatever you do, do not trust him. Your friend, Whit*

Your friend? Those two words trip off every alarm in my body. Whit has never referred to himself as my friend before. My mentor, yes. Clan Sage, maybe. Either he suspects I am doubting him and wants to remind me that he is trustworthy, or he was forced to write the note and used those words to alert me.

I click my tongue in the universal human-to-animal sound for "come here," and the raven takes a step closer. I relax, slow my breathing, and reach out to touch him, sharing my calmness with him. He allows me to pick him up, adjusting his wings for comfort as I pull him close to my chest to touch my opal and close my eyes. "Show me what you saw," I whisper. Like last night, I have to wait a while before the connection arrives. But after a moment I feel the tingling buzz as I connect with the Yara, and the raven becomes very still as it lets me sift through its memory.

I see Whit. He is with the two soldier-like men who I saw him with when I fire-Read in his cave. They hulk over him, watching him write the note. *They are making him find me for them,* I think. My suspicion is confirmed. Whit's being forced to act as their pawn.

I see him hesitate and pat the pocket of his jacket. He takes out a telephone. The two men wander off, leaving him alone as he talks into it. After a moment he puts his fingers to his lips to do the loud whistle I've seen him do a million times. And then, tying the note to the raven's leg, he releases it and it takes flight.

My view becomes aerial. The bird looks down as it flies away, and I watch as Whit climbs into the driver's seat of an army-green military-looking vehicle (the word "Jeep" is written in large letters across the back) while the two men jump into the passenger side and backseat. Whit waits until they close the doors and then drives off.

Stunned, I let go of the bird and our connection is broken. My blood feels like ice in my veins. Whit is no prisoner.

Is he working with the men who took my clan? Or could they even be working for him? I am so shocked I don't know what to think. Nothing makes sense anymore. The pain of the betrayal rushes back, and there is nothing I can do now to dull it.

Through the open tent flaps, I see Miles sit up. He rubs his hair back to front, causing it to stick up in all directions. Whit says I can't trust him. That's not exactly new information: Frankie already warned me he wasn't trustworthy.

But it's clear now that Miles isn't the only one I have to watch out for. My father deceived me. My very own mentor is out to get me. I am the only person I can trust. I have never felt so alone.

24

MILES

WHEN I WAKE UP, SHE IS TALKING TO A BIRD.

That shouldn't faze me, but I'm not quite awake yet, and a wave of alarm rocks me before I remember that hanging with a crazy person is a means to an end. The end being the look on my father's face when I finally do something right.

I take my time crawling out of the tent, hoping that the reality fairy will wave her wand and things will suddenly be normal when I look back up. But no, when I stand, Juneau is staring at me, as if she's waiting for me to say something ground shattering.

"What?" I ask.

"We have to go," Juneau says. "Now."

"No flame-broiled roadkill for breakfast?" I joke. She acts like she doesn't hear and starts stuffing her pack with the cooking gear.

"Someone's coming after us. We'll eat on the road," she says in that I'm-the-boss-of-you way that's really starting to get under my skin.

"Ah," I say, raising an eyebrow purely for my own sake, since she isn't looking at me anymore. "Would these pursuers happen to be government agents? Or maybe aliens? No, wait. Angry rangers who keep tabs on the park's bunny population."

"You can take the tent down if you want to help," she states simply. And although I really couldn't be bothered to join in as a willing partner of her paranoia, the way that she says it—like it's a challenge she doesn't think I'm up to—makes me turn around and start yanking tent pins out of the ground.

"You might want to take the bedding out first," she says.

"Yeah, I was about to do that," I mutter, and pull out the blow-up camping pillows and paper-thin thermal blankets. By the time I've figured out how to take the folding rods apart, she has everything packed and in the car and comes around to help me. "Have you ever camped before?" she asks, but not in the mean way I was expecting.

"No," I admit as I shove the final rod into its bag. "Does it show?"

She looks up and gives me this quirky little lips-pressed-together smile, and I can't help but smile back, which makes her laugh through her nose.

And for one second I am actually enjoying myself, even though my back is paralyzed from sleeping on the hard ground and I am standing in the middle of an illegal campsite, grinning at a paranoid schizophrenic. She actually seems halfway normal. Nice, even. The thought rockets through my mind and ricochets around once or twice before I catch it and twist the life out of it. *This girl is a means to an end,* I tell myself. *All that should matter to you is getting her to California.* And forcing the smile off my face, I start the car.

Juneau throws the tent bag in the back and jumps in beside me. With a squawk, the bird flies in too and settles on the backseat and stares at me, daring me to react.

"What's that?" I ask, gesturing at the bird as Juneau pulls her door shut.

"The raven's coming with us," she says.

My eyes widen in disbelief, and I try to control my voice, reminding myself that she's the crazy one, not me. "And why, may I ask, is the raven coming with us?"

"Because if the guy who sent him to spy on us calls him back, it won't be very hard for them to find us."

My brain starts hurting again. I stare at the bird incredulously. It just eyes me for a second and then casually begins picking something out of its wing. I look back at Juneau, and the star-decorated contact lens makes me shudder from its weirdness. I don't think she even took it out last night.

I can't believe I thought she was normal for even a second—I must have Stockholm syndrome or something. I put the car into gear, turn it around, and head back down the dirt road we drove in on.

"So where to?" I ask in what I hope is a calm tone as we pull up to the paved road. She has me trained now. I watch her check the position of the sun and glance up and down the road in both directions.

"This road runs north-south," she says. "Do you think there's a way for us to get onto something heading southeast?"

"Well, if you can jump-start my iPhone, I could use the GPS to find the way," I say. She stares at me like I'm speaking Chinese. I remember the L.A. mix-up and ask, "What part of what I just said did you not understand?"

"Jump-start. iPhone. GPS," she responds.

I pick one. "Global Positioning System," I explain. She shakes her head. I can tell by this tiny muscle that clenches in her jaw that it's costing her to admit she doesn't know what something is. "Where are you from that doesn't have GPS?" I ask, hoping she'll say something about Alaska, or tell me more about who she is.

"No time to talk," she says. "Take that road. I'll explain on the way."

Joy. I pull the car out onto the pavement and begin driving south. "I guess that means you can't jump-start my iPhone," I prod after a few minutes.

She doesn't look at me but stares straight out the window and then down at the speedometer, looking anxious. I step on the gas and she relaxes slightly. "Alaska," she replies.

It takes me a second to realize that she's one conversation back, but I catch up and say, "They've got to have GPS in Alaska. With all that wide-open wilderness and . . . tundra, or whatever they have there."

She considers that for a second. "I've been living in a tiny community outside the major cities. When you described me as 'back to nature' before, you pretty much hit it on the head. It was just nature and us."

"But I bet you've seen on TV—" I begin to say.

"We didn't have TV," she cuts in. "Or electricity, for that matter."

"And you lived there for . . ."

"My whole life," she replies.

While I try to wrap my brain around this, it occurs to me that, in this light, she suddenly doesn't seem quite as crazy. If she was raised in some kind of hippie commune out in the middle of nowhere, no wonder she was freaking out in Seattle. I see her fiddle with the window, trying to fit her fingernails through the top of the glass as if she thinks she can push it down with sheer force.

"It's the button next to the door handle," I say, and she wiggles the control back and forth for a second until her window goes down and she leans her head to the side so the cold morning air hits her in the face.

"What? You don't have cars either?" I ask, remembering the way that she leaped out while the car was still moving yesterday and forgot to close the door after she got back in.

She shakes her head.

I look at her incredulously. "How did you get around?"

"Dogsled," she replies matter-of-factly. "Of course, our sleds were fitted with wheels when there wasn't snow on the ground."

"Of course," I respond, one eyebrow cocked. She looks at me to see if I'm making fun of her, but I grin my goodwill and she does her lips-closed smile back.

She actually doesn't look half-bad when she's not scowling. I mean, that haircut still makes her look like a deranged pixie. But that's definitely an improvement from evil elf girl, shoving skewers through dead animals' body cavities.

"So why did you leave?" I ask tentatively. "I mean, now that we've established that it wasn't an insatiable craving for Big Macs," I add to lighten the mood.

Juneau leans her head back against the headrest, as if speaking more than a few words at a time is exhausting. She talks less than any girl I know. Uncomfortable silences don't faze her. In fact, I'm not even sure she knows what uncomfortable is. She's like a robot. Or an old person.

She sighs deeply. "When I said I was looking for my father, it's because he went missing. Actually, not just him, but it seems my whole clan was abducted."

"What? Why?" I ask, although as I say it I think, *Wait a minute, Miles. It's just more paranoia-speak*. But she looks so sincere that I decide to swallow my doubt for just a few minutes. Even if she is spouting a load of crap, it's obvious that she believes what she's saying.

"I honestly have no idea," she responds. "If I hadn't been out hunting, I would have been taken too." Her eyes flit to the backseat, and I see that she has placed the loaded crossbow within arm's reach. I decide to ignore the fact that I am driving with an oversize crow and a dangerous weapon behind me and take advantage of the fact that she's actually talking to press her further.

"And so you think the guys who took your father are the same ones who are following you? And they"—I can't believe I'm about to say this—"sent the bird to spy on you?" I peer into the rearview mirror and see that the bird is treating my balled-up T-shirt from yesterday like a nest.

"Them . . . and my old mentor," she says in almost a whisper.

"Your mentor?" I say, genuinely surprised, because I have no idea who she's talking about.

Her face scrunches up like, if she were the kind of girl who cried, she would be blubbering about now. But she's not the kind of girl who cries, thank God, so she just grinds her teeth and looks back out the window, focusing on a tiny shack with an enormous American flag in its garden, whipping and snapping in the wind. Cows lie sprawled out underneath, fast asleep like they had been whooping it up all night at some crazy bovine Fourth of July party.

Juneau's eyes take in the landscape. Her mind is somewhere else. And all of a sudden it dawns on me. There could actually be people after her. Hell, I was after her. So were Dad's goons before she shook them. If Dad's trying to track her down so urgently, his competitors must be after the prize too.

That realization shakes me. I mean, it's not like we're in a Hollywood film where people will do anything for the chance to get their hands on a new drug. We're not talking international espionage.

Or are we? Dad said that calling her an industrial spy was close enough to the truth. She's obviously got valuable information.

This is getting complicated. When I thought she was a total nut, it was easy—I didn't believe a word she said. But now that what she's saying is starting to make sense, I have no clue what to believe.

25

JUNEAU

WE DRIVE MORE THAN AN HOUR, DOWN WINDING mountain roads and past sprawling barns topped with so much moss you can't tell what color their roofs were originally. Mountains fold in the distance like puffy mounds of rising dough. We pass rusted-out buses and trailers grouped for eternity—or until someone cares enough to tow them away—around a burned-out campfire.

The landscape is both magical and menacing. For every abandoned grocery store advertising beer and wine, fishing tackle, and "Xmas tree permits," we pass a crystal lake that looks like it has sat unspoiled by man since the dawn of time. As we drive along white-capped rivers, logging trucks roar by, stacked high with enormous stripped trees.

I am reminded of Denali, and my heart aches for what once

was. For my life shrouded in a fiction. Why did I feel safer in a postapocalyptic world than in this functioning, civilized world?

Because I knew what to expect, I answer. I don't know this place where friends are the bad guys and even this boy sitting next to me can't be trusted. The rules are different. I have faced bears, wolves, snakes, and ice storms. *And for the first time in my life, I'm truly scared,* I admit.

Survival. That's all that's important. My own survival, and that of my father and clan. I will do anything to guarantee it. *And I will use whoever I need to achieve it,* I think, glancing at Miles, who is concentrating on the sharp turns. I formulate plans in my mind, but most fall one way or another into the "not allowed by Whit" category. I remember him driving off with those army-looking guys and feel my heart turn to stone. To hell with his rules. I'll make my own rules now.

Miles slows down as we approach an old, battered building with a Coke sign hanging out front. MAMA'S DINER AND GROCERY is stenciled in black letters in the space beneath the red swirls. Besides some empty forest ranger stations, this is the first place that's had its lights on since we came down from our mountain camp.

"Do you think it's open?" I ask.

"There's a truck parked around back," Miles says, pointing to a rusted-out pickup truck with a paint job matching the decrepit state of the store. We step out of the car. Miles hesitates before shutting his door. "Is the bird staying in the car?" he asks.

I lean down to peer in the window. The raven looks pretty

content with the pile of dirty clothes it is nestled in. "It should stay with us until we're farther away," I respond.

Miles shuts his door softly, as if the raven is a baby he's trying not to wake. He clears his throat and looks uncomfortable. "Did it tell you that?"

I stop walking and stare at him. "Did the bird . . . tell me . . . it wanted to stay?" I clarify, watching him carefully.

He nods sheepishly. "It's just that I saw you talking to it this morning, and . . ." He trails off.

"I don't know what things are like in L.A.," I say slowly, "but where I'm from, birds don't talk." I walk away from him, shaking my head. I can't figure this boy out.

The uneven planks creak loudly as I step up onto the porch. I open a dirty screen with a big rip in the netting and give a little shove to the wooden door inside. It swings open, ringing a bell that hangs on a hook above the lintel.

The brightly lit space is spotlessly clean, with groceries stacked on shelves against one wall and one lone table with four chairs in the middle of the room. A woman wearing a red-checked apron matching the tablecloth and napkins bustles in through a door in the back.

"I'm Mama," she announces, wiping her hands on a towel that she folds neatly and places on the counter beside an antique cash register. Beside the register sits a large handwritten sign: NO MORE CHARGING GROCERIES UNTIL YOUR TAB IS PAID.

Planting a fist on one hip, the woman cocks her head to one side and stares curiously at my eyes. Miles steps through the door behind me. She turns to him and says, "You kids are up bright and early this morning."

Mama looks exactly like an illustration of Mrs. Santa in one of the books in our library: plump body, rosy cheeks, and snowy hair piled up on top of her head. From the outside of the shop and the pickup truck, I was expecting the owner to be a mountain man with no teeth, but seeing Mama, the cozy interior makes sense.

As if reading my mind, she chirps, "My mother always told me it's the inside that counts. Plus, if we do up the front of the store, we'll attract more undesirables."

I lift an eyebrow.

"Tourists, I mean," she says with a laugh. "Now, what can I get for you?"

"Breakfast to go. And a map," I say.

"Are you sure you don't want to stay and eat?" she asks, nodding toward the lone table.

"We're in a hurry," I explain.

"I have some fresh blueberry muffins. Picked the blueberries myself out back," she says proudly.

"That sounds great," Miles pipes in. "And some coffee?"

While the woman gets our breakfast together, I slide a United States atlas out of the magazine rack and flip to the page showing the Pacific Northwest. Studying it, I find a major road that heads southeast all the way to Utah, and wave Miles over. "We should get on that," I say, tracing the red line with my finger.

"Or we could go due south," he says, drawing a line down

the coast to California, "and then head west to hook up with Route 66."

"I don't want to go to California," I say, giving him a look that I hope will shut him up. "California isn't southeast, and we're going southeast."

Miles puts his hands up in an "I surrender" gesture. "Fine," he says, and leans in to look closer. "Highway 82," he says. "We have to go through a town called Yakima."

"You're about a half hour from Yakima," the woman says, emerging from the back room with two paper bags. Placing them on the counter, she says, "You taking that atlas?" I nod. She presses a couple of buttons on the cash register, and it springs open with a *cha-ching.* "That'll be eighteen ninety-five."

Miles is staring at me and I am wondering why, and then I jump as I emerge from this kind of lapse-of-memory daze and remember that I am no longer living in a share-everything extended family, but in a currency-based society where we have to actually pay for what we take.

Before I can do anything, Miles shakes his head and, digging in his pocket, spills a handful of bills and change on the counter. Sorting through them, he gives some to the woman, shoves the rest into his jeans, and mumbles something about not only having to chauffeur me across the state but foot the bill as well.

Thanking Mama, we head outside. "You know, your friends were driving in the other direction," the woman says with a mischievous glint in her eye.

I freeze halfway out the door. "What friends?" I ask. My words come out in a rasp, since my throat feels like someone has grabbed it and is squeezing hard.

"The men who stopped by here about a half hour ago. Two in combat fatigues. The third with black sticky-uppy hair. Last guy asked me to call him if his friend with the star-shaped contact lens stopped by. Said you kept missing each other." She holds up a piece of paper with a phone number on it.

"Please don't call him," I gasp.

She smiles and, crumpling the piece of paper, tosses it in a white wicker trash can with a red bow on the front. "They didn't look terribly friendly, to be honest," she says, crossing her arms. "And besides, who am I to stand in the way of young love?" And with that, she picks up a cloth and begins wiping down the already spotless counter.

In a flash, we're back in the car, slamming the doors behind us and pulling on seat belts. As Miles turns the key, he looks at me with the weirdest expression on his face.

"What?" I ask.

"There *are* people after you," he says.

My eyes narrow. "Did you think I was making it all up?"

He suddenly looks defensive. There's a strange glint in his eye. A scared glint.

"You think I'm crazy," I say, unable to stop a grin from spreading across my lips. Miles looks away. "Ha!" I laugh and shake my head in wonder. Tell people the truth and they'll think you're crazy. *Maybe, with my story, that's actually better than him believing every word I say,* I think.

Miles thinks I'm laughing at him and in a heartbeat goes from scared to pissed off. Red-faced, he steps on the accelerator and spins out into the road. I am tempted to hold on to the dashboard but know he will go even faster if I do, so I brace my legs and focus on keeping our coffees from spilling.

We're heading at top speed toward Yakima, and I'm hand-feeding the bird crumbs of my blueberry muffin. Miles hasn't touched his food, although he gulped down the coffee in a couple of swigs. I take a few sips of mine and then, grimacing, stow it under the seat. I'm used to chicory—this drink is too flavorless for me.

"The guys who are following you . . . are they dangerous?" Miles asks finally.

"Well, normally I would say that Whit wouldn't hurt a flea. But from what Poe here told me—"

"Poe?" Miles interrupts.

"The raven," I say.

"You named the bird?" Miles asks, his voice tinged with a note of hysteria.

Yet another reason for him to think I'm crazy, I think, and wonder again if that's not actually a good thing. "Back in Alaska, we named all our animals after literary figures. It was something our teacher Dennis started, so I was thinking that with Edgar Allan Poe's poem about the raven—"

"Yes, thank you . . . I got the reference!" he snaps. His face is flushed red, but he does this deep-breathing thing and calms down a little. "Okay, first of all, we're not keeping the bird. So don't name it. I am not driving you to wherever it is we're going with a wild animal in my backseat."

"He's not wild," I protest.

"Has it shit on my shirt yet?" Miles asks, his nose wrinkling like he doesn't really want to know the answer.

"Birds don't shit while they're sitting down. They would be sitting in their excrement, and if you haven't noticed—which of course you haven't, you"—I can't think of an insult that fits the bill—"city boy, birds are clean." I don't know why I'm getting all defensive about Poe, but I can't help correcting Miles's glaring misconception.

"Secondly," Miles continues, ignoring my argument, "a little while ago, you confirmed my long-held belief that birds don't talk. Yet you just said that Poe"—he pauses—"I can't believe I just called it that . . . this bird told you something."

"I shouldn't have said 'told.' I should have said 'showed.'"

"Because that makes a difference?"

I just sit there for a moment, steaming from Miles's sarcasm and regretting having followed Frankie's advice and telling Miles the truth. But the moment passes when he says, "And thirdly, who is Whit?"

I have to tell him. Oracles are never wrong—only our interpretations of their prophecies, I remember Whit saying.

"Whittier Graves is my mentor. And I know that he is after me with these thugs, or whatever they are, because Whit sent me a note tied to Poe's leg, and I"—how to explain it?—"tapped into Poe's memory to see what he saw. But this is not Narnia.

No talking animals. Poe isn't sitting back there listening to everything we say and mulling it over in his little raven brain. However, if he flies back to Whit, which he might do if Whit calls him, Whit could use the same technique I did to see where we are."

Miles is quiet for a whole three minutes, pressing his lips tightly together and tapping nervously on the steering wheel. "Okay, I get a few things out of what you just told me," he says finally. "The least troubling of which is that the bird stays with us."

"Until we're farther away from Whit," I reassure him.

"Not that that's not troubling," Miles corrects himself. "It's just the least troubling. Because the next item on my list of concerns is that you claim this Whit guy, who was once your mentor but is now chasing you, can control where the bird goes."

I nod. "Yes."

"Okay," Miles says. "So the raven's like one of those homing pigeons? I assume it's Whit's trained messenger and not some wild bird he snatched out of the woods."

"Actually, Whit—"

Miles holds up his hand to stop me. "But the most troubling thing you said was that you tapped into the memory of the bird to see something. Now, I was not raised in a hippie commune in backwoods Alaska. But most people I know would have a hard time believing that you weren't . . . I don't know . . . crazy."

He presses his index finger to his temple and opens his eyes wide. *Now I've done it,* I think. He's scared. "Or on drugs," he continues. "Wait, no . . . I have another theory. You were brainwashed by your hippie cult into thinking you have magical powers. In your head you're like a cross between . . . I don't know . . . Superpower-Flower-Child and Harry Potter." That's it. I'm not sure what he's talking about exactly, but it's clear he has shifted into sarcasm overdrive.

I won't let this boy get to me. Why do I care what he thinks? "So I'm crazy, a druggie, or a cult member?" I ask as we crest a hill to see a sparkling city spread like a starry blanket beneath us in the broad valley below. "Well, you're free to just drop me off here in Yakima."

This shakes Miles out of his rant. He's silent as we drive into the city center. I have obviously made my point. I've reminded him that he needs me as much as I need him, like Crazy Frankie said. But I still have no idea why.

26

MILES

I HAVE TO GET TO A PHONE. TO CALL MY DAD. Have him take her off my hands. I can't stand this much longer. I'm in way over my head. It's one thing playing driver for a schizo teen who thinks she's being chased by dangerous people. It's a whole other thing when said dangerous people are actually chasing said teen and, by proxy, me.

But I can't get away from her. She had me pull up to a woman pushing a baby carriage so she could ask where a supermarket was. (She called it a "food shop," but whatever.) And once we had walked into Walmart Supercenter, she insisted that I accompany her every step of the way while she crammed a cart with food: canned stew, beans, and vegetables; liters of water; a sack of potatoes, a sack of apples; and, yes, a small pouch of birdseed.

She went all out on the flashlights, buying three jumbo ones along with a mountain of batteries. "I saw batteries in Seattle," she whispered to me as if they were a state secret. I wonder what they would have thought of her pack of size-D Duracells back in hippie camp.

It looked like she was preparing for a monthlong wilderness survival trip from all the staples she was stocking up on. But that was just the beginning. Then we hit the junk food aisles.

She transformed from a middle-aged nature mom into an eight-year-old girl with a serious sugar deficiency in the time it took to fill the rest of the cart with Pop-Tarts, Cap'n Crunch, and cheese puffs. This was followed by a meltdown in the chocolate aisle. The hippies obviously didn't grow their own cocoa beans back in Alaska, because I've never seen anyone load up on so many candy bars in my life.

At the checkout, Juneau digs in her bag and pulls out a leather pouch with money in it. Seriously—a leather pouch tied together with a cord. Like Grizzly Adams, but with major cash. I'm talking a fat wad of bills. She pulls it out and starts counting really slowly in front of the checkout lady, turning each bill over a couple of times and squinting at them like they're Japanese yen.

The clerk stares at the money kind of scared, like she's afraid Juneau's running a teenage counterfeiting operation. And then she looks at Juneau's face and catches a glimpse of that weird contact lens, and her eyes get a little wider. Finally I grab the cash and slap down enough for the total, jam the rest back into the pouch, and push Juneau out of the store in front of me.

"What's wrong with you?" I hiss as soon as we're outside. "You freaked that woman out so much she might call the manager."

"What are you talking about?" Juneau asks, as innocent as a kindergartner.

"Flashing all that money around. Where'd you get it anyway?"

"That's none of your business," she says, frowning.

"Can't you just try to act normal?" I ask.

"What is your definition of normal?" she asks seriously.

I'm about to say, *Well, it wouldn't be pulling a fat wad of cash out of a leather pouch at Walmart and then staring with your freaky contact lens at the bills as if you're hoping the green's not going to rub off,* but I opt for, "Nothing," and beeline to the car. I pile the bags into the trunk and return the shopping cart to its corral. By the time I get back, Juneau's feeding the birdseed to the raven, who's eating it out of her hand like they've been best buds for their entire lives.

I get ready to start the car and then pause. "You have to take out that weird-ass contact lens. Not only did it freak out the checkout lady, but the woman in the breakfast place said that your mentor and his thugs are using it to hunt you down."

She sits there looking like she doesn't know what I'm talking about. Then, putting her finger under her right eye, she says, "You mean my starburst?"

"If that's what you call it, then yes."

"I can't take it out," she says simply.

"What do you mean?"

Blank stare.

"You're not telling me you have a gold iris shaped like a star . . .

naturally?" I don't bother to downplay my sarcasm.

"Yes, actually," she replies. "All the children in my village do. It comes from being close to the Yara."

I nod, unwilling to bite if she's luring me into asking what the hell she's talking about. "So you can't take it out?"

She shakes her head and the sun glints off the gold flecks in her mutant eye, and for a second it strikes me that it's actually not that weird-looking once you're used to it, maybe because her other eye is kind of a nice honey color and doesn't contrast too much.

"Can you wink with that eye?" I ask. She winks. "Can you hold it shut whenever we're in public?" I prod, and she looks at me strangely, and then her eyes narrow and her face closes down like it does when she's mad at me, which seems to be more and more often since she found the raven and realized her mentor is playing for the Dark Side of the Force. Like it's my fault she trusted him.

"Is it essential that we waste time talking about my eye, or can we go now?" she says stiffly.

I try to speak like she does. "Considering the fact that we're being trailed by a dangerous hippie bird hypnotist and two thugs, I don't mind continuing the eye conversation later." Turning the key in the ignition, I head out of the parking lot and toward signs for Highway 47.

As we leave town, I have an idea and pull over in front of a drugstore. "Stay here," I order, and duck out so fast she doesn't have a chance to stop me. Two minutes later I'm back in the car. Juneau's sitting there staring quizzically at me as I pull onto the road and drive toward the edge of town. I let her stare, and we sit in silence until we're way out in the country, driving past a sea of yellow flowers toward a horizon of low purple mountains.

Juneau's fidgeting like crazy, and the longer she tries to fight the urge to ask me what I bought, the happier it makes me feel. She's been freaking me out so much for the last eighteen hours or so, it's kind of nice to finally be getting under her skin. I glance at the clock. Almost an hour passes in complete silence. I'm kicking myself for not thinking to ask to use the phone in the drugstore. But the thought of people chasing us has driven almost everything else from my mind, including the reason I'm driving her. Also, it's so much fun watching Juneau squirm, I don't mind putting off contacting my father a little longer.

Finally I reach forward to turn on the radio. Before I can touch the button, she blurts out, "What'd you get?"

"Well, Juneau, I'm glad you asked," I say in my Dad voice. I hand her the small plastic bag from the floor in front of my seat. She opens it and pulls out a pair of black sunglasses. She stares at them, confused for a moment.

"It's to help you look like a normal person," I say.

"Thanks a lot," she replies, but she cracks a little pleased smile.

"No problem." I grin. "You have to peel this label off before you put them on," I say, and reach toward the glasses. My hand brushes hers, and something electric passes between us. Juneau looks at me, surprised. I return my hand to the steering wheel and focus on the road and try to ignore the tingling in my fingers.

27

JUNEAU

WE'RE PASSING OVER THE LINE FROM WASHINGton into Oregon when Poe starts shifting around in the backseat. He flaps his wings a couple of times, and then goes into full-fledged panic, banging against the window, shedding feathers, and squawking like someone's squeezing him.

Miles throws his arm up to shelter his face, and the car swerves wildly. The giant wheels of a truck we were passing come inches from my window and I yell, "Miles! Truck!"

Cursing, he yanks the wheel and we veer away from the truck just as it lets out an earsplitting honk.

"Is anyone behind us?" Miles shouts.

"No," I yell back, and he crouches down, ducking out of reach of the flailing wings to steer over to the side of the road. I crawl into the backseat with Poe and wrestle with him until I get ahold of him, folding his wings in and pulling him firmly against my chest. His heart flutters wildly against my fingertips. I try to still his panic by closing my eyes and slowing my own heartbeat, but it has no effect on him. No longer able to struggle, his eyes roll in panic.

Something is trying to pull him out of the car. I concentrate and attempt to tap into the Yara, but I am getting absolutely nothing. *Please,* I think. I pull my opal out from under my shirt and press it tightly against the bird. Nothing. A minute passes, and Poe starts to struggle again and there . . . finally it comes, my lips and fingers tingling as I make the connection. "Thank you," I whisper, as my mind is filled with Poe's emotions. Fear. Possession. After a second, I recognize what he's feeling from something we studied in our wildlife lessons with Kenai's dad. Ravens have an ability to remember where they have hidden food. And Poe has the overwhelming feeling that another bird has found his cache. He is desperate to fly there and protect his food.

I can just guess who is messing with his little bird mind, and try to picture where it is that Poe wants to go. I see the same clearing that I saw before—the place Whit released Poe with the note for me. He must have lost my trail and gone back to where he started to wait for the bird's return and get a clear picture of where I am. A flare of anger ignites in my chest.

I still don't understand what Whit is doing, but I am the last of my clan running free, and he wants to help the bad guys capture me too. *Over my dead body,* I think, and wonder if it will actually get to that point if I resist. I don't plan on letting him find me to test that question.

Poe feels my anger, and our fragile connection is broken. He flaps to break free from my grasp, so I pick up the T-shirt he was sitting on and wrap it around him, like I've seen the clan mothers do with their flailing babies. Once he is swaddled and can't move an inch, he gives up. He shudders once, and then his wild eyes close and he seems to sleep. I place him on the floor, tucking Miles's other dirty clothes around him like a nest.

The car has stopped and Miles is staring at me, eyes wide, lips pressed tightly together. I crawl out of the back and into the front, strapping myself in. "He's okay now," I say, but instead of putting the car in gear, Miles turns it off.

"Why was the bird having a panic attack?" he asks, his voice a note higher than normal.

"Whit was trying to get him to come back and tell him where we are," I say, and then, seeing a twitch in Miles's right eyebrow, correct myself. "I mean, Whit was going to read his memory to see where we had gone."

Miles nods, his eyebrow still twitching. "So you used my shirt as a straitjacket."

"It's called swaddling," I said. "It's to calm him."

"Because that's what you do when you're 'close to the Yara,'" Miles says, ending in a spooky voice; then his lips form that sarcastic smile that makes me want to punch him.

"No, that's what you do when your baby's freaking out. So, Poe's a raven—I inter-species extrapolated. And it worked. What would you have done?"

"Rolled down the window," Miles says. "Let the bird go before it shits all over my backseat." He gestures to two white splats on the upholstery and looks mildly upset.

I roll my eyes and pull out the atlas. "We need to get off this main road. When Whit realizes that Poe's not coming back, he will come after us. And if we were headed in the right direction—toward my clan—this would be one of the obvious routes we would take." I trace our path on the map and find a junction where two small roads veer off and away from the highway, one meandering past a lake before it joins back up with the larger road near Idaho.

There's a road sign within view, and I compare it to the map and calculate how far we are from the turnoff. "We'll keep driving another sixty miles and then exit," I say, and then wait.

Miles sighs and turns the key in the ignition. I'm going to have to tell him more. I need him to understand what's happening or else . . . *Or else what?* a voice says in my mind. Or else he might leave me. *And I still need him,* I think, cursing the fact that, for some reason, I need this boy to help rescue my clan.

28

MILES

"GIVE ME BACK MY WATCH, YOU FLEA-RIDDEN winged rodent!" I am chasing a raven around a clearing in the woods in the middle of nowhere Oregon as a brainwashed teenage ex–cult member meditates by the campfire. It seems that crazy spreads, because I have finally lost it. I'm at the end of my rope.

"It's shiny," Juneau calls, shaking herself out of her trance. "Ravens like shiny things."

"Why did you even let him out of the car if there's a chance of him flying back to Whit?"

"He's not acting paranoid anymore. Whit stopped trying to get him, so he's safe now."

I stop chasing the bird and walk over to stand in front of Juneau. "Where. Are. We. Going," I say, my teeth clenched so tightly, I have to bite the words out.

"Like I said, I'm trying to figure that out," she says calmly.

I stare at her, my eyes wide. "Three days, Juneau. We're on day three of our demented road trip now. If you don't tell me right now where we're going, then I am out of here. Gone. And I will leave you and the bird here and go back to California and you'll have to find someone else to drive you. Someone who doesn't mind sleeping on the ground and being forced to eat innocent wildlife on a daily basis by an insane hippie."

"Innocent wildlife?" Juneau says, confused.

"The roasted lizard we ate last night. Which, along with the bunny we ate on the mountain, makes two innocent wild animals that I consumed within twenty-four hours. What next? Bambi? Why don't we eat something non-innocent and annoying? In which case, I vote for the bird."

"If you don't want Poe to pick up your things, you shouldn't leave them sitting out," she rebuts.

"I didn't! It was in my bag!" I growl, and spin to see my bag sitting on the ground beside the tent, its contents strewn all over the ground. "I'm going to kill you!" I yell, and make a lunge for the bird, who flaps away and alights on a branch too high for me to reach.

"Go ahead. Leave us, then," Juneau calls. She turns and walks away from our campsite, out of the clearing onto the pebble beach lining the lakefront. Sitting down on a flat boulder, she pulls her knees to her chin and looks out across the water. I sigh, and my anger fizzles out when I remember what she looked like last night in the tent.

She looked her age—a rare occurrence. She looked defenseless, even though her hand remained inches away from her loaded crossbow all night. She looked sad.

She spoke in her sleep again, but this time I think she was talking about me. "I know. I can't trust him," she said a couple of times. And then she whispered, "Who else have I got?"

Right then, for the first time, I felt bad about what I'm doing. I mean, now that it's clear I can't talk her into going to California with me, all I'm trying to do is stay with her long enough to get a phone call through to Dad. There's no way I'm driving her on her crazy mission. I've decided that as soon as we get to a town, I'm making the call.

But she believes I'm going to help her. She believes her family has been kidnapped and that we're on a quest to save them. She believes she has some kind of superpowers.

Okay, she's not all there, but that doesn't mean I have the right to trick her and pretend that I'm her friend when I'm just going to hand her over to Dad. Not that I have in any way pretended to be her friend, I think. To stay on the moral high ground of this situation, I just have to be careful not to befriend her. She knows I'm helping her for a reason—she said it herself. So there's nothing wrong with what I'm doing unless I lie. Or trick her in any way. So far, so good.

But as for the imaginary superpowers: All day today, she's been trying to do things. Talk to the bird. Press her necklace against the ground and talk to it. Skip rocks and watch the ripples on the surface of the water, lips moving as she does. Each experiment ends with her giving this frustrated, teeth-clenched growl before she goes off to try something else.

She didn't even offer to make lunch today, so I heated up some pork and beans, which wasn't actually as bad as I thought it would be. I left her a bowl of it, but she fed it to the bird. And now it's almost night, and it doesn't look like dinner's going to happen unless I do something about it.

I hesitate for a moment, hoping she'll spontaneously remember mealtime and fix us something from the supplies she bought. I concentrate really hard. *Dinner, Juneau. Remember dinner.* Hell, if she can read the raven's brain, maybe she can read mine too.

Of course it doesn't work. I settle for the direct approach and walk down to the waterfront and settle next to her on the rock. She doesn't move, just sits with her head resting on her knees, looking out over the water.

"You okay?" I ask after a minute.

"No," she replies.

"Is it because I called you insane?"

She balances her chin on her knees and pivots her head back and forth to say no. "That's nothing new. We've already established the fact that you think I'm unbalanced. Which, coming from you, I consider as a compliment." Her mouth turns up slightly on one side.

Something about her expression makes my heart do a little surge of happiness. What's wrong with me? I'm definitely catching her crazy.

She sighs and looks serious again. "I'm staying here until I get a sign telling me where to go next. But I'm not keeping you captive, you know. You can leave at any time."

"Despite my threats, I wouldn't leave you in the middle of the wilderness alone," I protest.

"Because I wouldn't make it out alive without your advanced survival skills," she says, trying not to laugh. "Okay. Thanks for saying you won't leave me stranded. But you could drop me off in the next town," she continues.

I don't say anything.

"Frankie was right. You need me, don't you?" she asks. I feel cornered and shrug. She doesn't press me on it and looks back at the water.

"If you didn't like the lizards, why did you eat three of them?" she mumbles, and I can't help but laugh. This wins me a small smile from her, and she rocks back and forth for a second before sighing and looking tired.

"You haven't eaten," I say. "And though you've hardly said a word to me all day, I can't help but notice you've been carrying on full-fledged conversations with all sorts of inanimate objects. And when they don't talk back, you look like you want to kick the shit out of them."

"Sounds crazy, right?" she asks.

I nod.

"Sounds crazy . . . looks crazy. Why don't you just settle for your insanity diagnosis and let me be?"

"Because you look like you're having a meltdown. And friends don't let friends do meltdowns." I say it even though I know she won't get the reference. She never does.

"So you're my friend?" she says skeptically.

Oh, crap. What have I done? I shrug and look out at the water. "Well, I wouldn't say best buds, exactly, but I don't hate your guts. At least not at this precise moment."

She almost cracks a smile, and there my heart goes again, turning a flip in my chest. *No, Miles. Do not go there,* I urge myself.

She's talking. "Tell me something about you. It doesn't have to be important."

I lean over and pick up a stone from the ground beside the boulder. I roll it around in my fingers, feeling its smoothness, watching the colors change in its quartz-like interior as I turn it back and forth in the blue air of twilight. And then I throw it as far as I can into the water and wait for the plop before turning to her and saying, "I got kicked out of high school with just a couple months left until graduation."

"For what?" she asks.

"Cheating on a test," I say, "among other things."

"What other things?"

"Bringing alcohol and pot to school."

"Pot?"

"Drugs."

"Oh." She hesitates and then asks, "So why'd you cheat? Didn't you study?"

"That's the thing. I didn't need to cheat. I studied—I knew all the answers. I don't know why I did it." I try to remember and can't. It was unimportant. Trivial. I'd done it a million times. "Probably just to see if I could get away with it. For the thrill."

"And you think I'm weird?" she says. I shrug and pick up another stone.

Juneau rubs her hand over her spiky hair again. Then she exhales deeply, and her body looks like a balloon deflating. "I guess it doesn't matter what I say, because you're not going to believe it anyway." She shuffles her body around so that she's facing me. "In 1984, at the outset of World War III, my parents and some friends of theirs escaped from America to settle in the Alaskan wilderness."

"There was no World War III," I interject.

She gives me a frustrated look. "Are you going to hear me out or what?"

I lean back on my elbows and listen.

29

JUNEAU

WHEN I FINISH, MILES SITS THERE STUNNED, HIS mouth hanging half-open and his eyebrows frozen in the up position. Finally he remembers how to talk. "And now?" he asks.

"And now something's happening to my skills. Since yesterday, I can barely Read. I certainly can't Conjure. I can't even get anything from Poe, and we've already had a connection."

"Can I see some of this stuff you use?" he asks, and it strikes me that while I was speaking, he dropped his sarcastic, incredulous manner and is actually being sincere. He might not believe what I say is true, but he believes I'm telling him what I think is true. I don't have to Read him to know that.

Whit taught me to read body language—to be perceptive about the way people unconsciously show their feelings and thoughts through gestures and facial expressions. For the first time, Miles has let down his guard. He's taken the first step to trusting me.

So I reciprocate. I show him my pack. He watches as I pull out the firepowder, the stones, the herbs and animal furs and bones, and asks me what each one is used for. It's strange—I have the feeling that in showing him, I'm betraying my people . . . disclosing their secrets. Just in case, I keep my explanations intentionally vague.

And I don't pull out the precious stones and gold nuggets. Whit specifically ordered that those always be hidden from outsiders. Though Whit is a traitor, his advice is sound. Frankie warned me not to trust Miles. All I need is City Boy to take off with the car, my money, and my gold, and I am well and truly stranded. I watch as he inspects a pouch of pounded hawthorn root, smelling it and wrinkling his nose.

"You're carrying quite a lot of . . . stuff with you," Miles says finally.

"I know," I say. "Whit has a different use for all these. I don't really need most of them. I use my opal for almost everything except fire-Reading. But when Whit's around, I use them just to make him happy."

"Why would that make him happy?" Miles asks.

I squirm, not comfortable about what I'm going to say. "I Read better than Whit. He's already taught me everything he can about Reading, and I'm picking up the Conjuring on my own. He's the one who discovered the human connection with the Yara and has worked hard to find the different ways to connect for different reasons. I'm starting to feel like maybe he's wrong, and that all these totems just complicate things, but I wouldn't dare tell him that." I fiddle with the rabbit feet and brush the soft amulet against my cheek.

"Whit is the one who came up with all this?" he asks.

"Yes, although a lot of what he found he says he gathered from traditions all over the world, especially eastern—like Buddhism and Hinduism. That was apparently all the rage in America back in the sixties. I read about Catholics using rosaries or icons to focus and Buddhists using prayer beads or mandalas or candles. I think these objects"—I gesture to the pile of stuff—"serve the same purpose for Whit. But I've begun to suspect that the objects themselves aren't important. It seems more like the intent behind their use, the will of the user, makes the difference."

"Then why do you still use the firepowder and your opal?" Miles asks.

"Just because I have my theory doesn't mean I trust it to work," I say. "Those are only things I've been thinking about. But my connection to the Yara seems to be getting weaker and weaker. I wouldn't dare try to change the rules now." I realize that I've been petting my opal comfortingly as I have been talking, and press it against my chest to reassure myself that it is still there, my link to the collective unconscious of the superorganism. The Yara.

I feel the need to change the subject and, reaching back into the pack, pull out the Gaia Movement book. Flipping to the back, I pull out the photo I've carried with me all the way from Denali. "These are my parents," I say, handing it to him.

"Old picture?" he asks, peering at it.

"Before I was born," I confirm.

As he studies it, I notice something different about him. There's a softness that I haven't seen before. And I realize it's because he's let his guard down. He actually looks kind.

Once again I see him through Nome's eyes. "Checking him out," she would say. He is handsome in a refined, pampered way, not earthy and rugged like Kenai. The lines of his face—his cheekbones, his chin, his aquiline nose—are as strong and defined as if they were carved from sculpting clay with a fettling knife.

He glances back and forth between me and the picture, comparing my face to those of my parents. And as his lake-green eyes flit over my features, something in me stirs. It feels like the tug in my chest that happened every time I stepped out of my yurt in the morning and witnessed the beauty of Mount Denali towering over our village. Even though I had grown up there and had seen the same view every day, I never failed to be overwhelmed by its splendor.

That's it, I think. *That's the familiar tug inside me. Miles is beautiful.* Without thinking, I raise my hand to my chest and press it with my palm like I did every morning, pushing the emotion back in so it wouldn't spill out.

A leader must be strong. Must not let emotion affect action, I remind myself. I was soon to become clan Sage. I had responsibilities.

I have responsibilities. The realization startles me from my reverie. My goal is to find and save my people. I rise to my feet. I can't allow myself to be sidetracked from the most important thing in my life.

The safety of my clan depends on my doing everything I can to find them. Not spending time chatting with a teenage boy who was kicked out of school for something even he admits was idiotic.

Miles takes my standing as a sign that the show-and-tell session is over and rises to his feet. He hands the photo back to me. "You look just like your mom," he says.

"Thanks. Everyone says that we'd look like twins—if she hadn't died when I was five," I reply evenly, tucking the photo back into the book.

Miles hesitates, and then says, "I'm sorry."

"It was a long time ago. I don't actually remember her that well. My dad raised me with the help of the clan, and Whit's been my mentor ever since Mom died."

"So your dad must be what, in his fifties now? He looks pretty young here." He points to the photo.

I laugh. "He's fifty-eight. And he looks the same now as he did in the picture."

"Except that he's probably got gray hair and wrinkles," Miles says.

"No. My dad's one with the Yara. He hasn't aged a day since this picture was taken," I insist.

Miles narrows his eyes. "Yeah, right," he says with a little twist of his lips. And just like that, his wall is back up and I can see that he hasn't believed a word I said. I'm supremely glad I stopped myself from going into more detail about the Yara. From trusting him with my beliefs.

"Are we going to have dinner tonight?" he asks, while it's clear that his real question is, "When are you going to cook for me?"

"Not hungry," I say, and then realize I'm famished. "If you want dinner, you cook. At least that'll guarantee you won't be forced to ingest lizard tonight." I can't help the frost in my voice.

He shakes his head sourly, as if he regrets having listened to me for the last half hour. Grumbling, he heads to the car to rifle through the groceries in the trunk.

It doesn't matter if he thinks I'm lying. I know it's true. Walking around in Seattle, seeing elderly and sick people, made me feel I had been living in a utopia in Alaska. After the Rite completes our union with the Yara, no one experiences aging. No one dies, unless it's in an accident like my mother's or the elder who was killed by the bear. Here in this outside world, everyone is disconnected from the Yara. They can become old, get sick, and die.

I wonder if our special relationship with the Yara has anything to do with the disappearance of my clan. If someone wants what we have. But how would they have even known about us? We've been in hiding for decades.

Whit, I think. Everything comes back to him. It's still too hard to imagine that he engineered the capture of my clan. But maybe he talked about us when he was out in the world. Maybe he unwittingly betrayed us.

30

MILES

"SO TELL ME, WHAT'S THE LAST READING OR CONJURING or whatever that you successfully did?" I take a bite of the crispy potato that I, yes I, Miles Blackwell, cooked wrapped in aluminum foil in the campfire. In fact, I cooked tonight's whole meal.

All right, so the first can of beef stew exploded. How was I supposed to know you can't cook food in the can? Luckily, we had a few backups, so I opened them and heated them up in a pan.

"Why does it matter?" Juneau asks, blowing on the piece of steaming beef speared on her fork. "You won't believe a word of it anyway."

"True," I respond, holding my spoon up for emphasis. "However, in debate team, I was often tapped to play devil's advocate.

So I don't mind suspending disbelief if it's going to, one, get you out of your lethal mood and, two, let us leave this creepy waterfront. It's starting to remind me of the Jason-infested lake in *Friday the 13th*." I glance over the fire to see Juneau's familiar expression of incomprehension, and my heart falls. "Why do I even try with the cultural references?" I moan.

"I don't know, why do you?" she snaps. And then says, "Reading Poe's emotions in the car yesterday."

"That was the last time you felt like you 'read'?" I clarify, making an effort to keep up with her conversation hopping.

"Yes, although it took me a long time to connect," she states. "I'm used to it being immediate."

"Then when was the last time it was immediate?" I ask.

"When I Read the fire at Mount Rainier."

"Okay," I say. "So what's happened between then and now?"

She looks at me blankly and shakes her head.

I think. "How about Whit?" I ask. "When the bird didn't come back to him, do you think he could have blocked you from connecting to the Yara?" I try my best not to let a sarcastic inflection creep into my words. If she thinks I'm making fun of her, she'll clam right up and this conversation will be over. Along with my effort to soften her up so that we can leave.

She sets her bowl on the ground and shakes her head pensively. "That would be like blocking me from breathing the air around me. 'No one can come between human beings and the Yara except the disbelief of humans themselves.' That's a direct quote from Whit," I say.

I'm feeling sorry for her again. She really believes this crap. I have an overwhelming urge to hold her hand and tell her that it's okay. That she's been brainwashed, and the longer she's away from the hippie cult, the more normal she'll get.

"Well then, maybe you're blocking your own connection to the Yara," I offer, feeling slightly proud of myself for making sense out of her cult gibberish. "Maybe now that you're away from the influence of Whit and your dad, you're beginning to doubt the things they taught you. Which would totally make sense, seeing that they lied about World War III and all." I am only trying to draw logical conclusions from her completely illogical beliefs, but she looks like I just slapped her.

"Or maybe it's not that at all," I offer weakly. "Maybe the farther you get from your land, the less of a connection with the Yara you have?"

She closes her eyes and shakes her head in a how-could-you-possibly-know-anything-about-it gesture. "The Yara isn't just in Alaska. It's everywhere."

She stands and, wrapping her arms around her waist, paces slowly beside the fire. "What you said about doubting," she says finally. "That does make sense. It was after I found out that Whit was working with the people who abducted my clan that my Reading was affected. His blatant spying on me confirmed my suspicions of him . . . if I needed further confirmation." She rubs her fingers distractedly across her forehead. "I guess I can pin it to that instant that I definitely lost all trust in him. And yes, I suppose I'm questioning what he taught me as well."

"Did they have children's books in your commune?" I ask. Juneau looks at me like I've grown another head. "I swear this is relevant," I promise.

"Yes, we had a small collection of children's books."

"Did you have *Peter Pan*?" I ask.

She furrows her brow, trying to guess what I'm getting at.

"What you're saying is kind of like Wendy and her brothers flying with fairy dust. They had to believe it or they couldn't fly."

She nods pensively but still has that hurt look on her face. "You might be right," she admits. She sighs loudly and turns to head for the woods. Looking back at me, she says, "Thanks for dinner. I'm going to go for a walk and think about things." The bird sees her going and flaps over to land on her shoulder like a freaking trained monkey.

As for me, I sit watching the fire and think about how she seems like a really nice person. How I'm actually starting to like her. Why else would I have put off calling Dad whenever I've had access to a phone? Because, for once, I feel like I'm enjoying myself. Having fun.

It's just sad how messed up Juneau was raised. Like a cult member. Totally brainwashed. Totally delusional. It almost makes me want to help her. If saving my own skin wasn't of utmost importance, I would be tempted to try.

31

JUNEAU

I WALK INTO THE WOODS HOLDING POE ON MY arm, feeling as disoriented as if I had stepped through a door into an alternate universe. For the second time in a month. I'm losing my faith, so I'm losing my skills—that must be the answer. And if that happens, there's no way I'm going to be able to save my clan, much less find them. But with all the lies I've been fed, how can I believe anything I've been taught? How do I separate truth from fiction?

Poe flies off and perches far above in a tree as I head straight for a clump of giant holly bushes, letting them scratch my arms as I pass. The pricks from their spines reassure me that I'm not sleepwalking.

I get to the water's edge and begin circling the lake.

I need to figure out what, if anything, I have left. I pull my opal from under my shirt, loop it over my head, and press it to the ground. "Dad," I say, and focus on Reading his emotions. A chorus of crickets launches into their night song on the far side of the lake, and a thick fog levitates inches above the water's surface. I wait. Somewhere out in the lake, a fish jumps, splashing as it breaks the water's surface. I wait. Nothing happens.

I loop the cord back over my head and tuck my opal under my shirt. Then, squatting, I place my bare hand against the moist, cold earth and try again. I get nothing. Not even the slightest tingle of connection.

The sky is pitch-black and the temperature has dropped. I continue my walk around the lake, rubbing my hands up and down my arms to warm myself, but I resolve not to return to camp until I figure this out.

I ran through my entire repertoire of Reading skills today, and none worked except the simplest stone-throw Readings. In which I confirmed things that I already knew: like my father was still far away and Whit was still trying to reach me.

If Miles's off-the-cuff theory has any bit of truth to it, then it's a vicious cycle—the more I disbelieve in the Yara, the less it will work. I can't just pick and choose what to believe.

Yes, you can! I reassure myself. Surely not everything my clan told me was false. I have seen the Yara work. I have manipulated it myself.

But I also know that much of what I was taught was lies.

I feel my belief flicker like a flame in wind. *I know the Yara exists,* I insist, and imagine myself cupping my hands around the flame to protect it.

I whistle toward the woods and click my tongue, and Poe flaps down from a nearby tree to stand next to me on the pebble beach. Crouching, I comb my fingers over his ebony feathers, formulate what I'm going to do in my mind, touch my opal, and try to connect to the Yara.

I believe, I think, and I try my hardest to push all doubts, all feelings of betrayal, as far from me as possible. Nothing happens. Not even a tingle.

I exhale deeply and imagine my tiny flame of faith expanding to the size of a forest fire, and after a second I feel the slightest of buzzes in my fingertips. *Yes!* I think excitedly, and try to center myself.

I look at Poe and then picture my father in my mind. *Poe, can you find my father for me?* I think. I imagine the desert setting and try to pass the image to Poe.

Poe stares at me and then shuffles away and starts pecking at some pebbles as if to say he couldn't care less. Okay, I'll try something easier then. I grasp my opal and place my hand on Poe once more, this time picturing Miles in my mind. *Where is he?* I think. *Take me to Miles.*

Poe cocks his head to one side, as if saying, *You know as well as I do where Miles is.* But he fluffs his wings and takes off, heading toward the camp. Adrenaline percolates through my veins, and I set off at a run, following Poe through the woods. When we get to the clearing, Poe circles the car once and then lands on the roof. He squawks and, his job complete, begins picking something from his wing with his beak.

Panting, I lean over and, looking into the car window, see that Miles has fallen asleep in the passenger's seat with a book on his chest and the overhead light on. I ignore the fluttering in my chest as I peer in at him: his lips are slightly parted and his chest rises and falls with his shallow breaths.

I need to focus. My Conjuring worked. My powers are linked to my faith—that much is clear. And I am progressively losing my faith, not in the Yara, but in Whit and what he taught me. I have to start at square one and test what I think is true. And until I can figure out for myself what I really believe, I will need to gather every last thread of faith I still have in order to continue using my gift.

But what if my problem is much worse? What if my doubt slams down like iron bars and locks me out of my powers for good? If there's even the slightest chance of that, I have a lot to do before it happens.

32

MILES

I AWAKE WHEN THE COOL AIR OF THE EVENING smacks me in the face. Juneau is offering me her arm. "You're going to have a crick in your neck and be no good for driving if you sleep like that," she says. She shuffles me out of the car and over to the tent, where I groggily lie down on my side.

Juneau leaves and then returns with a mug of steaming liquid. "I made some tea. This will help you sleep better." It tastes like licorice and marshmallow, and I drain the whole thing before lying back down.

"I'm sorry if it seemed like I didn't believe you," I say sleepily. "It's just a lot to hear all at once. But I definitely wasn't making fun of you. I'm only trying to help."

Her lips curl at the edges and she looks almost embarrassed. "I know. I could tell," she says, and takes my hand in hers.

The touch of our skin sets off a reaction in me. I am immediately awake . . . 100 percent present. And it feels like a whirlwind of thorns is whipping around in my chest, stinging me all over from the inside. That makes it sound painful. It isn't. It's the kind of itching sensation that makes you want to do something crazy. That spurs you forward to act on an idea you didn't even know was in your head.

Or maybe I did know it, but have pushed it away because Juneau was my ticket to redemption with my dad and I didn't want to mess that up. Now that she's told me her story, I'm certain there's been some kind of mix-up. No matter what Dad says, she's no spy. Okay, she's been raised to believe some pretty weird things, but that's clearly not her fault. And for her to have gone through what she has, Juneau must be incredibly strong. And brave.

I realize all this just as I notice that, for once, she's dropped her defenses. Her tawny eyes brush my face with compassion, and I have an overwhelming urge to pull her to me, take her in my arms, and kiss her.

33

JUNEAU

I SHOULDN'T HAVE HELD HIS HAND. IT DID SOMEthing to him. It did something to both of us. It set off this kind of lightning storm all over my body. The electricity generated when our skin touched was like the tingle I feel when I connect with the Yara. Multiplied by a thousand.

I was just trying to reassure him. To get him to trust me. Saying I might have overdone it would be an understatement. Because one second I was holding his hand, seeing him once again like Nome would—I couldn't help it. He looked so sleepy and defenseless . . . and, to be honest, utterly gorgeous.

And the next second his hand is behind my head and he's eased me down on top of him and we're kissing . . . kissing like crazy. My whole body's buzzing, and all I want is to keep pressing my chest against his and lacing my legs through his and winding my fingers through his beautiful curly hair and feeling his lips brush mine for the rest of the night. But I can't. I can't do this. I have to . . .

"Stop," I say, and push myself up onto my hands and knees, perching above him. Miles reaches up for me, yearning written all over his face, but I shake my head. "No," I say, and pivot so that I'm sitting next to him in the tent.

His expression is a mixture of regret, confusion, and disappointment.

"I'm sorry, I can't," I say.

"No, that's totally okay," he says, raising his hands to his forehead and squeezing his eyes closed. We're both breathing heavily, and my heart is hammering a million miles an hour. I scramble to the mouth of the tent, push through the flap, and then peer in at him once I'm safely out.

"Are you all right?" he asks.

I nod and zip the tent flap up behind me, shutting him in from the night.

I walk over to the fire and flop down in front of it. This is too much. Too much at once. I run my tongue over my burning lips and think of Miles's mouth on mine, and my body flares with heat.

Miles wasn't my first kiss. But kissing Kenai was different. He was a friend, and Nome and I had talked him into trying it out. It's not like we had a large selection of potential kissing partners in our clan. Besides, Kenai was the only boy I could kiss without it meaning anything. It was kind of nice, in a friendly, warm-hug kind of way. But it was nothing like the searing heat of kissing Miles.

Stop thinking about it, I urge myself. I have to stay in control. Miles is nothing more to me than a means to an end. I can't get attached to him. I ready myself for what I'm about to do.

I cast all thoughts of Miles and his soft mouth and his strong arms out of my mind. There's no way I can slow my heart rate if I let myself remember the kiss. I think of what I need to ask. This might be my last chance.

If we are being chased, every moment is precious. I need better instructions to find my clan than a general direction of southeast and a desert setting. And I need to know not only how to elude Whit, but if he manages to catch me, how I can fight him. And win.

I unzip the tent flap and look at Miles's motionless form. The special tea I made has done its work. He is deep asleep and will not awake. I almost falter—this is strictly forbidden. No one would consider Reading another human being without their agreement. I remind myself I am doing this for the good of my clan. For the protection of my people.

I duck down into the tent and sit cross-legged by Miles's side, taking his hand in mine and cupping my opal in the other. He doesn't stir and keeps breathing deeply. My heartbeat slows to match his. *I do still believe that the Yara exists,* I think, summoning all my positive thoughts and funneling them into our joined hands. I shudder as we connect to the Yara. Miles's eyelids fly open. They are unseeing and stare hollowly at the tent above.

"Miles," I say. "You are my oracle."

His head moves slightly as he nods, a thick wave of hair tumbling off his forehead. "Yes, Juneau. I am your oracle."

34

MILES

"HOLY CRAP, I FEEL LIKE I SLEPT ON A PILE OF rocks," I say, crawling out of the tent and pressing my thumbs hard against my temples as the sunlight burns my eyes.

"Breakfast," says Juneau, and shakes a box of Cap'n Crunch at me from where she sits next to the impeccably clean fire pit. I glance around the clearing. Everything's been packed up, and the trunk of the car is open with our supplies stowed neatly inside.

"Does this mean we're leaving?"

"Yep," she confirms, and hand-feeds a piece of cereal to the bird, who stands obediently next to her like the freeloading flea-bag he is.

I sit a few feet away and pour myself a mug of orange juice and take a sip. I glance at Juneau, and she looks away. There's an elephant in the campsite, and it's called last night's kiss. But if Juneau's not going to say anything about it, I'm certainly not going to bring it up. I can't help looking at her lips, berry red though she's not wearing any makeup, and I feel a hunger that has nothing to do with my empty stomach.

"No more sleeping on the ground," I moan, setting my mug down and massaging my forehead. "I don't care if you insist on being out in nature, we're staying in a hotel tonight."

Juneau looks at me funny, then reaches over and pulls a tiny pouch out of her pack. She shakes a couple of pills into her hand and passes them to me. "What are these? Hippie moon-beam pills?" I ask without thinking, and then freeze. "Sorry. Bad habit." I'm determined not to bait her today.

"They're a miracle pill introduced to me by the owner of the Seattle guesthouse where I stayed," she says with a wry smile. "She called them . . . Advil."

I laugh and pop them into my mouth, washing them down with a swig of juice. Juneau pours me a bowl of cereal, plops a spoon in it, and pushes it over to me. "Wow, what'd I do to deserve such service?" I ask.

An odd expression flashes across her face—is it guilt?—but she quickly rearranges her lips into a smile. Something seems wrong. *But what hasn't felt wrong in the last four days?* I remind myself.

She holds up the cereal box and points to the mustachioed cartoon character in the blue hat. "This is seriously good stuff, but this"—she points to a family-sized box of frosted strawberry Pop-Tarts—"is the best thing I have ever put in my mouth."

I laugh. "Is it your desert island food?"

"What's that mean?" she asks.

"It's a game. If you were stuck on a desert island and could only have one food, what would it be?"

She doesn't even hesitate. "I could eat Pop-Tarts for breakfast, lunch, and dinner for the rest of my life. No problem," she says. A small grin breaks through the habitual stern-face. And there she is again. The normal teenage girl I kissed last night. Who I really want to kiss again. Who I wish wouldn't keep hiding behind a facade of grown-upness and responsibility. Talk about split personality . . . Juneau could be the poster girl.

I pick up my bowl and inspect its contents closely. I don't think I've ever had Cap'n Crunch before. My mom raised me on a diet of unsweetened granola sprinkled liberally with nasty wheat germ. Thinking of her makes my stomach twist, and I force her from my mind.

Sugared cereal, I think, pulling my thoughts back to the here and now. I munch tentatively on the 100 percent artificial puffed squares. And my taste buds melt in ecstasy. Juneau's right; these are so good.

"Yummy," I say with my mouth full, and she gives me a full-on beam. Happy Juneau. About as rare as a triple rainbow.

She gets up. "You finish breakfast and I'll do the tent."

By the time I've washed my dishes in the lake, Juneau and the bird are sitting in the car, waiting for me. "Are we in a rush?" I ask as I settle behind the steering wheel.

"We're in a permanent rush until I find my clan," she says.

We reach the main road, and I turn right to head to the

highway. Juneau is studying the map. "Just stay on the smaller road," she says after we've driven a couple of minutes. "We don't want to join up with Highway 84."

"We don't?" I ask. "Why not?"

"Trust me," she says. We drive in silence for about fifteen minutes. The bird is standing up in the backseat, looking out the window, enjoying the scenery like it thinks it's the family dog. "There!" Juneau says, pointing to a sign that says SPRAY.

"That's the name of a town?" I ask incredulously.

She shrugs. "That's where we're going."

"It's a hundred twenty-two miles away," I say. "That's going to take a couple of hours."

She nods, as if she was expecting that.

"Might I point out the fact that Spray is southwest of us, not southeast?" I ask.

"I know that," she responds. "I've got the map."

"May I also point out that we are on day four of this road trip, and we are still pretty damn far from the Wild West?"

"Just start driving, we're on a schedule," she says.

"We're on a schedule now that we've spent an entire day just sitting around?"

"We weren't just sitting around," she responds defensively. "I was waiting for a sign. For confirmation of what to do next."

"And you got your sign?" I ask.

"Yes. I got a few."

"Hey, good for you!" I say, and mean it. Looks like my pep talk worked and she's back into delusional magical mode. I feel a slight pang of guilt at egging her on, but if it makes her happy and I don't have to sleep on the ground another night, I can deal.

"Yeah, but who knows if those are the last signs I ever get," she says, looking out her window with her head propped against the headrest.

"May I ask what they were?"

"One is that Whit is still searching for me and he's not far behind us. He knows where my clan is, and if you and I are heading in the right direction, we have to be careful not to cross paths with him. It's going to be close."

"Double-crossing medicine man and his cronies are gaining on us. Joy," I say as we reach the turnoff for Spray. I take it and we begin heading southwest. Toward California. Toward home. I have to call my dad.

As if reading my mind, Juneau asks, "Aren't your parents going to be worried about you?"

It's the first time she's asked anything about me besides the vague "tell me something about yourself." It's the first hint that she is the least bit interested in me. So why does that spark a tiny flame of hope inside me? Maybe because all I've been able to think about this morning are her golden-honey eyes, inches away from my own, and those warm, soft lips.

"My mom left Dad and me last year, so she's not doing any worrying," I find myself revealing.

"I'm sorry to hear that," she says, and puts her hand on mine. Warmth spreads from where her fingers touch my skin. I try to ignore my body's reaction to this girl, but it's getting increasingly difficult.

Juneau looks at me inquisitively like she's wondering whether I'm going to cry, but those rivers have dried, and it's only the furrows they carved in my heart that are left. "What happened?" she asks when she sees I'm not going to break down.

"She's sick. Severe depression. She tried to kill herself last year, and when she didn't succeed, she said we would be better off without her. And then she left."

Juneau sits there looking horrified and firms her grip on my hand. "Do you know where she is?" she asks.

"Yeah, Dad tracked her down. She's living with her aunt outside New York City."

"Oh, Miles. I don't even know what to say." She looks shaken up. Really upset.

"It's okay," I say, feeling like I'm comforting her instead of vice versa. "I mean, I miss her, but you get used to someone being gone after a while." I'm a big fat liar. And it doesn't look like Juneau's buying it.

"I just can't imagine it," she says. "I've never known anyone to get sick."

"Yeah, well, mental illness is just the same as any other illness. At least that's what people keep telling me. It happens all the time."

Juneau just looks at me funny, like she feels sorry for me. My gaze drops to her lips, causing my heartbeat to stutter, and I quickly turn my focus back to the road.

"What about your dad?" she asks.

"What about him?" I ask, and realize how defensive it sounds once it's out of my mouth.

"Won't he be worrying?"

"Well, he knows I was in Seattle," I say carefully. "I really should check in with him so he doesn't freak out."

Juneau bites her lip.

"What?" I ask.

"Frankie was really clear about me not letting you use the phone while I was with you," she says.

Well, Frankie stumbled upon a grain of truth, I think, and wonder what I'm going to tell my dad once I do talk to him. I mean, I can't just hand Juneau over to him. Not now that I'm sure she's not the person he thinks she is.

"Can I ask you something?" I say, pulling my hand away from hers so I can take some sharp bends in the road. A hawk takes off in flight from the ground near us, carrying its unlucky prey—looks like a mouse—in its claws.

"Sure," she says.

"All that money you were flashing around in Walmart . . . where did you get it?"

A flash of suspicion crosses her features, but then she shrugs as if it can't hurt to tell me. "I traded a gold nugget for cash."

"So you're not actually . . . working for anyone?" I ask, and it comes out all wrong. But she doesn't seem to notice and shakes her head.

"The only job I've ever had is hunting for food. I'm one of the best shots in our clan. Oh, and apprentice clan Sage, of course. Which I have a feeling is over now that Whit is out to get me."

She tries to say it flippantly, but besides the one smile I got at breakfast and just now when I talked about Mom, she's been colder toward me today. Maybe it was the kiss, but I have a feeling it's something else. She seems remote. Something has changed in her.

She picks up a battered old notebook and pen that I keep stashed in the passenger-side door. "Can I use this?" she asks, and begins scribbling something.

"What are you writing?" I ask.

"A note," she says.

I thank my lucky stars for the kazillionth time that she's not a big talker like most of the girls I know in L.A. and turn on the radio. We drive without talking for the next two hours, the bird napping in the backseat and Juneau looking out her window, glancing up occasionally to see how far we've gone.

When we're a mile away from our destination, she sits up and pays attention until finally we arrive at the town limit. "Stop there," Juneau says, pointing to a sign reading ENTERING SPRAY, POPULATION 160.

Tearing the page from her notebook, she folds it up, tears a hole in one end, and laces a piece of string through it. "Okay, Poe. This is the end of the line for you," she says, getting out of the car and scooping the bird out of the backseat. It squawks belligerently, as if it understands what she was saying and prefers to stay in the warm car and be chauffeured across the Pacific Northwest.

She holds it to her as she ties the note around its foot. "Miles, could you tear two blank pages from the notebook and fold one over the front license plate and the other over the back?" I don't even bother asking why and do what she says, hoping that none of the 160 townspeople decides to leave Spray just as I am doing something that looks extremely iffy, if not downright illegal.

Juneau waits until I am done and then carries the bird toward the sign. She makes sure he looks directly at it, and then bows her head and whispers something to it. Standing for a moment with her eyes closed and the raven squeezed close to her chest, she throws it up into the air. It dips for a second, and then flaps upward, circling overhead.

"Get back in the car," Juneau says, "and start driving into town, slowly."

"Can I take the paper off—" I begin, but she cuts me off.

"Just drive, Miles."

"Your word is my command, O dark mistress of bird wrangling," I mumble, and press the gas, rolling into town as slowly as possible. In the rearview mirror I see the bird finish its circling and head back in the direction we came from.

"Stop," Juneau orders before we reach the first building. She jumps out, takes the paper off the license plates, and then hops back in. She pulls the atlas to her lap and traces on it with her finger. "We're going to drive south out of town, and then take 26 east until we get back to the main highway we were on."

I glance at where she's pointing. "So we're going toward Idaho? Which means we're backtracking," I comment.

"Not quite—we'll end up a half hour south of where we camped," she says, and raises her chin like she thinks I'm going to contest her choice. Instead, I shrug and drive through the small town, stopping for gas at the far end of the main street before continuing on Juneau's chosen route.

I don't need to ask. I saw her note. And it explained everything.

So, traitor, you want to play?

The game is on.

35

JUNEAU

TWO HOURS SOUTHWEST. NOW TWO HOURS southeast. A pretty big detour just to throw Whit off our trail. But I need him to think that I'm mis-Reading. That I don't know where my clan is. Of course, there's the chance he knows exactly what I'm doing.

I hesitated before sending the note with Poe. But even without it, Whit would still see me releasing Poe through the bird's memory. See Miles and me getting back into the car. He would know I released Poe on purpose: he would already be suspicious. So the note only served the purpose of making me feel better. I can't help a satisfied smile from possessing my face. The feelings of anger and betrayal are still on a low simmer inside me, but the fear has evaporated. It's me against Whit, and I am ready to fight.

I glance at Miles, and though it's against my better judgment, I feel the overwhelming temptation to reach over and put my hand on his. Not out of anything romantic, I tell myself, just for reassurance. After what happened last night, I don't want to give him any ideas. I can't get close to him. I won't be distracted from my quest. *He is only here to help me get to my destination,* I insist, but my gaze strays back to his hand.

My face blazes as I remember our grappling match in the tent, and I suddenly realize that the boy who kissed me is sitting just a couple of feet away, watching me and . . . waiting for an answer. "I'm sorry, what?" I stammer.

"So next stop is Idaho?" he asks.

"I think so," I say.

Miles is silent for a moment and then says, carefully, "You're asking me to drive more than two hundred miles east and you're not sure?" He avoids looking at me. Stares straight ahead at the road.

"Yes."

"Okay," he says slowly. "Was it fire this time?"

"Was what fire?" I ask, confused.

"Did you read a fire? Or was it the raven? Or what?"

I watch him to see if he's being sarcastic. He's not. He's just trying to get me to talk. "I'd rather not discuss it," I say finally.

"Juneau, you can tell me. I'm not going to laugh at you," he says.

Frankie said I have to tell him the truth. But in this case, I just can't. "You wouldn't understand anyway," I snap, hoping that will shut him up.

It does. He bites his lip and reaches over to turn the radio up. Good. That conversation's over.

I turn my thoughts back to the three prophecies I received last night. The one about Whit was clear enough. But when my next step was revealed, it might as well have been spoken in Chinese. I didn't understand a word of it.

Prophecies are usually cryptic, but I don't even know how to approach decrypting this one. I pick up Miles's notebook, jot the words down from memory, and study them one by one.

Finally, Miles turns down the radio and asks, "Do we have time to stop for lunch?" His voice is back to normal—he's gotten over the insult I used to shut him up. Good.

I close the notebook and tuck it under my seat. My head hurts from thinking so hard, and the puzzle remains unsolved. "Let's just make sandwiches," I suggest.

We pull into a tiny town called Unity and dig Cokes, chips, and sandwich stuff out of the trunk. "We can eat in the car," I say, but Miles frowns and gestures toward a lone picnic table sitting nearby under a tree. "Can we sit outside and eat? I'm getting sick of the car."

My instincts say to keep going. But Miles looks tired. Discouraged.

"Hopefully they fell for our ruse in Spray and are headed toward the Pacific Ocean now," I concede. "I don't see why we can't stop for fifteen minutes."

Relief floods his face. We spread the food out on a table, and he begins to eat standing up. "My butt fell asleep back near

Canyon City," he explains, brushing crumbs from his mouth as he bounces on his toes.

"How long do we have until we hook up to the main highway?" I ask.

Miles jogs to the car and comes back with the atlas and a pencil. "Another hour and a half and we meet back up with 84 at the border of Idaho," he says, making a dot on where we are and tracing lightly to the edge of Oregon.

We're reconnecting with the road we started on. But Frankie's directions were vague—go southeast—and I have no idea what comes next. *Damn cryptic prophecy,* I think.

And then I'm struck by an idea. I touch Miles's arm. "Will you try something with me? I'm going to say a sentence, and you tell me the first thing that comes to your mind."

Miles furrows his brow. "Okay," he says hesitantly.

I pronounce the words of the prophecy carefully: "Follow the serpent toward the city by the water that cannot be drunk."

Miles looks confused. "That means absolutely nothing to me," he says. "What is it?"

"It's our directions," I admit.

"This was one of the signs you got last night?"

"Yes," I say uncomfortably. *Don't tell him any more,* I think. I take a swig of root beer and let the bubbles fizz on my tongue before swallowing.

"You heard those actual words?" He sounds incredulous.

I nod. *DON'T TELL HIM,* my inner voice is now shouting. *I have to tell him,* I think. If I don't follow the rules in the prophecies, I might as well give up now.

He scratches his head and looks suspicious. "How'd you manage that?"

"I used an oracle," I say.

He huffs in amusement. "Did you convince Poe to talk?"

I take another sip of root beer and shake my head. I feel guilt rolling off me in waves and am surprised that Miles can't sense it. I look away from him, and by the time I look back a dark cloud has stretched across his face.

"You didn't," he says.

I nod meekly, but reminding myself that rules don't count in a state of war, I lift my chin and watch as he gathers together his memories of last night, flips through them, and then arrives at the answer. "What was in that tea you gave me in the tent?" His voice is flat. Dead.

"Something we grow in Alaska that's a bit like brugmansia."

"What the hell is brugmansia?" he says, and his face is crimson. His eyes dark.

"Angel's trumpets," I respond, knowing full well he has no idea what that means either.

"WHAT DOES IT DO?" Miles's words are like four small daggers stabbing my skull. My hand rises to my forehead. *Don't think of him as a boy. He is your driver. Your oracle. That is all.* I force my hand back down to my side and raise my chin. I had to use him—I had no other choice.

"It's a narcotic, but when diluted enough, like it was last night, it can be used as a sedative," I say.

"You drugged me." Miles is breathless. As if someone has socked him in the stomach. Pain is scrawled across his face.

I steel myself. I am in the right. "I did what needed to be done."

"Couldn't you have asked me first?" Miles says. He looks like he's still trying to make sense out of what I've just said. Like he doesn't believe it. Like I'm playing a joke on him.

"You wouldn't have said yes," I respond, crossing my arms. And making my voice as flat as I can, I say, "Why would you, when you haven't believed a word I've said so far?"

Miles stands there staring at me in disbelief, his hands shaking with emotion. "That is because YOU ARE DELUSIONAL!" he yells. "I'm not saying it's your fault. You've been brainwashed. But, Juneau, for God's sake, there is no Yara. You don't have special magical abilities."

His face is a lightning storm. "But what *is* your fault is the fact that last night you gave me some kind of homemade drug without my knowledge. All for your crazy fantasy. Was there an aphrodisiac in there too? Because I would rather have kissed that fleabag raven than a freak like you. I can't go along with this any longer. That's it!" he says, and with a swift motion, stabs the pencil into the atlas hard enough to break it in half. Then, turning, he stalks toward the car.

His words sweep over me like an errant wind, hitting me square in the face before flowing over and around me and disappearing.

Unimportant. Because I am staring at the map and the violent slash of graphite marking where the Snake River transects Idaho directly north of the Great Salt Lake.

I scoop up the atlas and make a dash for the car.

36

MILES

I AM ON AUTOPILOT. STANDING THERE IN FRONT of her as she told me how she drugged me and used me as her voodoo doll, I felt like I had been stabbed. But it only took one look at her self-righteous expression and I cauterized my wound with a blowtorch. Up until now, I still had a half-baked plan of talking Juneau into going to California with me. One that I had almost talked myself out of. What would Dad want with this delusional teenager?

But now my mind is made up. I don't care why he wants her. I'm going to deliver.

I let her navigate us down every side road across lower Idaho in order to avoid the highway skirting the Snake River. She shouts out directions over the noise of the radio, which I crank up until it drowns out any other sound.

Seven hours we drive, until the blue haze of dusk settles around us and the trees look like silhouettes cut from black construction paper. A neon sign ahead announces EL DORADO MOTEL AND BAR. I turn the radio off. "We're staying here," I say, and Juneau doesn't argue.

I pull into a parking lot empty except for two semis and a pickup truck and take a space in front of the office. A skinny man with a comb-over the color of squirt-jar mustard takes my credit card and gives me the keys for rooms 3 and 5. No way in hell am I sleeping in the same room as her.

I pace back out to the car, where Juneau's pulled her pack out of the trunk and stands watching a couple of truckers eating dinner in the adjacent building through the bar's plate-glass windows. "Your room," I say, and hand her one of the keys without looking her in the face.

I pull my own suitcase out of the trunk and slam it shut, and ignore Juneau, who's still standing there next to the car as if she doesn't know how to find the hotel room with the big "3" on the door. I'm not about to offer my services. Letting myself into room 5, I toss my suitcase onto the flowered bedspread and pick up the telephone receiver, trying to ignore the overpowering smell of vanilla-scented room freshener. No dial tone. Of course.

I stamp out, pulling the door closed behind me, and make my way back to the office, where Mustardhead is watching a rodeo on an ancient black-and-white TV. "The phone in my room doesn't work," I say.

"Pay phone behind the bar," he says, tipping his head slightly toward the far corner of the parking lot.

I find the pay phone and look at it for a second, unsure what to do. I don't even know how much a pay phone costs. I remember something I saw in an old TV show and, picking up the receiver, press 0. "Collect call to Murray Blackwell," I say, and give the operator Dad's number.

"Blackwell," comes my dad's voice, and the operator tells him I'm on the line. Dad acts civil until she hangs up, and then comes the explosion. "Where the hell are you, Miles? I instructed you to come straight home. That was four days ago. If I wasn't worried about getting you in worse trouble than you're already in, I would have called the state troopers. What are you doing? Partying it up in Seattle?"

"I'm in Idaho. And I've got her, Dad." I look through the glass at the truckers seated at the counter. They're both watching me, like I'm more interesting than the music videos blaring from the TV above the bar. I turn my back to them and hunch over to get some semblance of privacy.

"You've got who, Miles?" my dad asks testily.

"I've got the girl. The Alaskan. She broke my phone. That's why I haven't been able to call."

There is silence on the other end of the line, which is very atypical for my dad. He's usually all freak-out and immediate action, so this throws me off. "I know it's her, Dad. She's got the star thing in her eye. Dark hair, although it's cut short now. She's around five foot five and says her name's Juneau. She lived in this apocalyptic hippie cult out in the Alaskan wilderness."

Dad clears his throat. "Has she mentioned Amrit?"

"What's Amrit?"

"Amrit's a drug I'm trying to acquire," he says impatiently.

"No. See, that's the thing. I know she matches your description, but she can't be the one you want. If you're looking for an industrial spy, she's definitely not involved in something like that."

"What makes you think that?" Dad asks, but there's something in his voice. It's the tone of voice he uses when he's teaching me a lesson. His crafty voice, making me figure a problem out for myself. Like . . . *Of course she doesn't work for a drug company, but tell me why.*

My dad is waiting for an answer. I want to tell him that she's not a spy because she's a brainwashed cult member, but I'm not going to go into the whole Yara crap. It'll just provoke him. I sigh. "She's not working with a pharm company, Dad. Or involved in any espionage. She's like wilderness survival girl just trying to find her dad. If you want someone to kill and cook a rabbit for you, or tell you what time it is by looking at the sun, she's your girl. Otherwise . . ."

"Miles, tell me exactly where you are." My father had put his business voice on. Succinct. To the point. No arguing.

"The El Dorado Motel, somewhere in southern Idaho not far from Utah."

"Good. You stay right there. My men are still in Seattle. They can be there before sunrise. Make sure you keep her there. Don't let her get away."

"Go ahead and send your guys, Dad. But she's not going to get away. It's not like I'm holding her hostage or anything. She can't even drive. I swear she'll be here in the morning."

"Okay, just hold on, Miles. I'm going to get my men on the other line. Don't hang up."

It's started to get chilly, and I wish I had worn my jacket. I look up at the moon, just beginning to emerge above the tree line. Juneau could probably look at that and not only tell me what time it is, but what the weather will be like tomorrow. The magic stuff is a load of shit, but it's likely that she could survive if she was stranded on the moon. She's brave, determined, and . . . fierce. I'd give anything to have even half her know-how. Why'd she have to go and ruin it all with the Yara crap? I feel a twinge of guilt twist in my gut but remind myself that last night she not only fed me some homemade drugs but diverted my attention from what she was doing by kissing me, and I push the feeling aside.

I hear a rapping on the glass, and I swing around to see one of the truckers standing inches away from me on the other side of the window. He does a charades thing where he acts like he's driving a car, manipulating an invisible steering wheel with his hands.

I shrug at him and think, *Stupid drunk redneck,* and then notice that he's pointing toward the parking lot. His buddy behind him is cracking up, pointing in the same direction.

I look toward where they're gesturing and see my car backing up slowly, as the brakes pump on, off, on, off. The automatic overhead light is still on inside the car, and I see Juneau's face illuminated as she pops the headlights on and throws the gear into drive. For a split second our eyes meet, and her stricken expression tells me she must have overheard the entire phone conversation. She witnessed my betrayal.

With motor revving, wheels spinning, and gravel spraying, she swerves wildly out of the parking lot onto the two-lane road and screeches off in a dust cloud of fury.

37

JUNEAU

I AM NUMB WITH SHOCK. MILES BETRAYED ME. I shouldn't be surprised. Frankie said he needed me. But I never imagined it was to hand me over to his father, who is for some reason searching for me. What's that even mean, "working with a farm company"? That must be why Miles asked if I worked for anyone.

I want to run over every conversation we've had in my memory. Pick them all apart. But I need to concentrate on driving. I've watched how Miles handles the car for the last four days, and, although backing up was a bit jerky, I'm going forward just fine. I test the pull of the steering wheel to see how much movement it takes to turn the wheels and then press the right-hand pedal down to the ground. I need to get as far away from here as fast as

I can because now I am running from not just one pursuer but two. Miles's father's "guys" are apparently on their way, and Whit is still out there. And if Miles calls the police to report me stealing his car, there will be even more people for me to escape from.

For a brief moment, I consider stopping and hiding somewhere close to the motel. It would be like hunting deer. As long as you're motionless and downwind, the animal won't see you even if you're standing right in front of them. That might work for Miles's father's men, but if I stay still, Whit will find me easily enough.

Miles knows we were headed to Salt Lake City. He knows I'll follow the prophecy. So I just need to get there before him.

I am hungry and tired and boiling with anger, but there's a thrill working its way through me as I realize that I am behind the wheel of a car, moving faster than I ever did on the sledge with the huskies. I imagine the car around me disappearing, and me seated in the air shooting forward at—I check the speed—eighty miles an hour.

I let go of the wheel with one hand and ease it over toward the door. I touch the window control and immediately feel the rush of cold wind through my hair. Mountain-pure, cold wind whipping my face, blowing away that kicked-in-the-stomach feeling I had when I walked up behind Miles and heard what he was saying on the phone.

Which must have been how he felt when he discovered how you used him. The thought comes unwelcome, but I ignore it. Let it flow with the wind. I don't know what I believe anymore. What's right and what's wrong. For me, there are no more rules. I will do anything I need to rescue my clan, no matter who it hurts.

I drive down the two-lane road over the border of Idaho into Utah. Though I'm tempted by every sign that points to junctions with the highway, I am determined to stay on the small roads. Miles-as-oracle told me that Whit knew where the clan was. And that he was on my tail. And that our paths would cross again at some point. I want to get as close to my clan as possible before that happens.

I follow the dual yellow beam of my headlights, which from time to time reflect from eyes of animals along the side of the road. My thoughts flash back to Miles, and I feel a sharp sting of regret remembering the look on his face when he realized what I had done. I push that thought away, but another takes its place. The empty look on his face when he told me about his mother's mental illness and abandonment.

I don't understand how mankind can watch their loved ones get sick, when following the Yara ensures health and longevity. I remember asking my father how men could willfully destroy the earth and destroy themselves. How something as precious as life could be treated with such disdain.

"The answer was right there in front of them," my father said. "But they chose to be blind. They chose temporary ease over long-term stability." And now that I am out in the very world he was talking about, seeing the effects of not being one with nature, I understand what he meant.

I used all my free time in Seattle reading about current events, catching up with what happened to the world since the 1983 EB left off. The world is as my parents had described its condition leading up to the war. That part was true. Whole species of animals becoming extinct. Natural disasters becoming commonplace. Diseases running rampant . . . diseases that could be avoided in a healthy setting, following the Yara, treating nature as it should be treated and receiving the reward. Why, when offered practical immortality, would man turn his back on it?

Then it hits me. Miles acted so weird when I insisted that my father hadn't aged that I didn't press the point. He treated his mother's illness as normal. He thinks of disease and death as unavoidable. Reading and Conjuring seem like magic tricks to him. They don't know. . . .

From the way my parents and Whit described the world, it sounded like a choice mankind had made—when presented with the Yara, they rejected it. But what if they had never known about it at all?

In that case, our "escape" from the nonexistent World War III was like abandoning ship when things were at their most dire. But why would the elders do that? Why couldn't they live among "nonbelievers" and try to change things for the better with their knowledge?

Why not work from inside the machine to change it instead of running away and waiting for end times to destroy it so they could rebuild it pure and new? It just doesn't make sense. I know deep down that my father and the elders are good people, even if they lied to us. So why would they sit by on the sidelines and watch the earth destroy itself? It almost seems like they hold a secret they don't want anyone to know.

The gas-pump light on the dashboard flashes red. The dial underneath it is on the *E*. "*E* for empty," I remember Miles quipping as he pulled over to get gas. I wonder how far I can drive before the car stops working.

The only buildings in sight are barns set way off the road. I drive for another fifteen minutes, keeping my eye on the gas needle, and begin to worry that I won't make it to a gas station in time and will be stranded in the middle of the Utah wilderness. I have no doubt that I could survive until I made it to a town. But if I strike out on foot, I will be a sitting duck for my pursuers—especially Whit, who could find me in mere hours.

I see yet another sign for the main highway, and this time I follow it. My heart is in my throat as I turn onto the entrance ramp. I've been so worried about running across Whit that when I don't see the big green vehicle from my Reading of Poe the moment I pull onto the highway, I feel a surge of relief. And I feel even better when I see a sign indicating that there is a gas station ahead.

In five minutes I'm pulling off into a Shell station lit up from the inside, and the only person there is the girl behind the cash register. I have watched Miles fill the car with gas enough times to figure it out myself, and in no time I am standing at the counter, handing the cashier a hundred-dollar bill. I left the sunglasses Miles bought me in the car, so I stare downward to hide my eyes, but the girl behind the register doesn't even look at me.

I'm feeling so jittery that when a car turns into the station, I'm ready to make a dash for the bathrooms. But when I see that it's a small red car and a woman in a cowboy hat steps out, I breathe easy and walk back to Miles's car.

I don't want to stay here, out in the open, any longer than I need to, but I've been driving for two hours and was already starving when Miles and I arrived at the motel. One minute is all I need to dig through the trunk and pull out a couple of apples, a bag of walnuts, and a bottle of water. I toss them into the passenger side and go back to close the trunk when I hear a familiar squawk. I look up to see a black shape hurtling down into the fluorescent-lit station toward me.

Poe lands on the ground and ruffles his feathers once before squawking again. There's only one reason that Poe would search me out, and that is if Whit directed him to. Panicking, I pick up the bird and close my eyes. I feel nothing. No connection.

It is only then that I see the tiny flashing light coming from Poe. I lift him above my head to get a better look and see a metal ring clamped around his leg with something electronic attached to it. It must be a device used to locate the bird. Whit sent Poe to find me and will follow this machine's signals straight to me.

I try to crush the metallic tag between my fingers. No use. I remember the way I broke Miles's phone—the fire that I Conjured to melt the insides—and try to repeat it. Nothing happens. My heart seizes with despair. I am no longer connected to the Yara. I feel naked. Powerless.

The sound of screeching tires comes from the highway. I turn to see an army-green Jeep with three passengers swerve across the highway from the left lane in order to catch the exit to the gas station.

I take a split second to assess my strength against theirs. I have no doubt Whit's companions are armed. It's three against one, and I have only a crossbow and a knife. The odds are against me.

I drop Poe, scoop up my pack from where I had set it on the ground next to the car, and leaping over the gas station's cement barrier, run at full speed into the pitch-black night.

38

MILES

DAD'S SECURITY DETAIL TAKES A PRIVATE JET TO Twin Falls and arrives at the hotel in less than two hours. They introduce themselves as Redding and Portman but don't need to say much more—I see them standing around security-guarding every time I visit Dad's office. "Do you have any idea where she was headed?" Portman asks me, leaning over the seat as we speed away from the El Dorado.

I pause. "She was heading toward Salt Lake City," I admit, feeling a pang of guilt when I think of the expression on Juneau's face as she drove off in my car. Is this just another betrayal? No, I decide. I'm helping her. Once she talks to Dad, this manhunt will be called off and he'll go after the people who actually do have the information he needs.

While Redding drives, Portman flips between trucker CB

ham radio stations and the police scanner. We're on the road less than fifteen minutes when a blue BMW is identified as abandoned at an interstate highway gas station about an hour away in the direction of Salt Lake. The plate number matches my own.

39

JUNEAU

MY EYES HAVEN'T ADJUSTED TO THE DARKNESS. I am running blind through low scrub, with my pack thrown over one shoulder and my hands stretched in front of me in case I run into anything. But there is nothing to run into, just knee-high grasses slapping my jeans with a hissing swish, and occasional bushes crackling under my shoes.

I don't dare look back. I'm certain they saw me under the bright lights of the Shell station, and this pastureland offers nowhere to hide. I see a dark wall rising slowly to meet me, and after a few minutes realize that I'm headed toward a tree line.

I hear shouts behind me and am glad for the waist-high barrier around the gas station's parking lot. If it weren't for that, Whit and his men could have driven off-road right after me. But from the sounds of it, they decided to follow on foot. The trees get closer, and my vision is clearer now that the fluorescent glare has worn off.

As I reach the first of the trees, I allow myself a split second to look back, and see two bulky forms lumbering across the pasture, vaguely in my direction, flashlight gleams bobbing up and down as they run. They haven't seen me, or they would be headed directly my way. I take off through the trees, leaping over broken branches and bushes, headed in no particular direction besides away from them.

The trees turn out not to be woods, but rather clumps of evergreens separated by stretches of barren grassland. There is no good cover—I am exposed.

And then it happens: I step into some kind of hole, and my trapped foot remains stationary while the rest of me keeps going. I am blinded by a white blaze of pain.

Crouching, I use my fingers to pull the dirt away from my foot until it is free. Although I can barely see, I can feel that the hole is a big one. *Fox or badger den,* I think. Making a split-second decision, I grope around until my fingers touch a fallen branch, and I use it to dig out the tunnel. Driven by fear, I uncover the empty animal den in less than a minute and, dragging my injured foot behind me, gather the nearest sticks and branches.

I throw my pack in the three-foot hole and then lower myself down into it, lying on my side with my pack at my stomach, curling up fetal-style around it. Reaching up to my pile of evergreen branches, I sweep the stack over and around me until I—and the hole—am completely covered. And then I wait.

Now that I am motionless, my ankle throbs with pain. I want to touch it, to feel if something is broken, but I'm afraid that any movement will shift the branches and uncover my hiding spot. I bite my lip until I taste blood. Every crackle of leaves, every creaking branch is amplified in my ears as I listen for my pursuers. And what seems a mere moment after I am hidden, they arrive. One is close by—I hear the plodding of heavy boots. From a distance I hear the other one yell, "There's no one out here. Like I said, she went the other way."

The nearby footsteps stop, then shuffle around as the man sweeps the area with his flashlight. A ray of it pierces down through the pine needles into my den. But I am hidden well enough that he sees nothing, because his footsteps get fainter as he moves farther away.

I wonder where Whit is. Probably back at the car, letting his henchmen do his dirty work. Where did he even meet these people? What happened to the peace-loving dependable man I've known my whole life? For what possible reason would he have my entire clan kidnapped and imprisoned? And why can't he just leave it at that? Why does he need me?

Acid rage burns inside my chest. I want to scream but clench my fists instead, so hard that my fingernails dig painfully into my palms.

I stay in the hole for as long as I can. Finally, when I get to the point where I am so chilled and in pain that I'd prefer capture to staying another minute in the ground, I lift my hand and sweep my cover away.

I sit up. Look around. No one is here but me and a surprised-looking squirrel, who begins chittering wildly as I lift myself up—scolding me for scaring him. I brush off the dirt and leaves and test my foot. It is painful, but I can put a tiny bit of pressure on it. I press gingerly around my ankle. The flesh is swollen, but not enormous like Nome's when she got it caught in the emergency shelter's trapdoor. "A light sprain," Esther, our clan doctor, had said. But Nome couldn't walk on hers, and I am at least able to hobble my way through the grasslands.

My eyes have adjusted so well to the darkness that I easily locate a large branch on the ground and strip its limbs, trimming it to armpit height with the knife from my pack, rounding off the top so that it doesn't poke me. I try out my crutch and find I can put enough weight on the stick to walk at a reasonable pace.

I look ahead and see a mountain range emerge abruptly out of the pastureland in the near distance, just a few miles away. *I can hide there until I'm sure they've finished looking for me,* I think, and set off in the direction of the towering peaks.

40

MILES

IT LOOKS LIKE JUNEAU GOT DESPERATE ENOUGH for gas to venture off the tiny side roads to the interstate. But why would she abandon my car? The only explanation I can fathom is that Whit caught up with her while she was getting gas. Either he captured her, or she took off on foot to get away from him.

A nagging thought claws at my heart. Everyone she knows has betrayed her. Her mentor, her parents, and now me. I can't imagine how it would feel to be completely on your own, with no one you can trust. She opened up to me. Told me all about her bizarre past. And what did I do? Turned her over to my dad.

But . . . (1) it's not like he's going to do anything bad to her. He's a businessman, not a thug.

And (2) she freaking used me last night. She tricked me into kissing her and drugged me. All for her hocus-pocus Yara delusions. I wonder what I even said to her while I was "under the influence." Something about Whit following her and catching her. And another tidbit about serpents and city near unpotable water. Which she handily interpreted as the Snake River and Salt Lake City.

That was kind of clever, actually, I think. She is a smart girl. She just has her crazy alternate universe mixed up with reality, which is kind of sad.

What's wrong with me? I get kicked out of school just before graduation, I botch up my one chance to earn some respect from my dad, and I'm falling for a lunatic. I wish I could just wipe the slate clean and start back at square one. If I hadn't cheated on the test, I would be graduating and getting ready for my freshman year at Yale.

I have to prove myself. I know how Juneau thinks better than these play-it-by-the-rule subservient goons of Dad's do. As soon as I can get away from them, I'll continue the search for her on my own.

I ride the rest of the way in silence, trying not to think about her honey-colored eyes.

41

JUNEAU

I'VE PACED MYSELF AT A FAST HOBBLE ACROSS THE pastureland and stay as close as I can to the clumps of trees so that I'm not an easily spottable lone figure wading through the seas of knee-high grass. I see up ahead that at the base of the mountain there is a curtain of trees. Hiding will be easier once I am among them.

I look up at the position of the moon and find the constellations. It's around midnight.

Setting my sights on a small stream that flows out of the wooded mountainside, I do my hop-limp-hop toward the water. When I reach it, I follow it just past the tree line, and, once hidden among the evergreens, slump to the ground and scoop several handfuls of water to my lips. It is ice-cold and delicious. Filling my canteen, I allow myself a few minutes to recover but know I can't stay here for long.

I lie back, nesting my head in a pillow of leaves, and close my eyes. I am deep-breathing, trying to restore myself enough to be able to trek for a few hours, when I hear the crunching of boots on twigs. I shoot up into a sitting position, grab my bag, rifle through it, and in three seconds am on one knee, pointing my crossbow in the direction of the light that bobs toward me through the woods.

How did Whit's men manage to get so far in front of me? I didn't see anyone else on the pastureland leading up to the mountain. I kneel there, one eye closed, the other peering through my crossbow's metal sight, when I hear a woman's voice.

"Don't shoot. I'm totally harmless."

I keep my finger on the trigger, ready to fire, and watch the flashlight approach until the person stands five feet away. The light points straight into my eyes, "Yep, it's you," she says, and then angles the light up at her own face. "See? I'm just a woman. Not an ax murderer."

I grab my improvised crutch and use it to push myself up into a standing position as the stranger approaches, but keep the crossbow pointed in her direction.

"Looks like you've hurt your foot," she says, staring at the crutch. "Well, we better get you back to my house. Would it be easier if you put an arm around my shoulder?"

"Who—who are you?" I stammer.

"My mom named me Tallulah Mae, but you can call me Tallie."

I stare at her. Who is this woman who just appeared out of nowhere? I don't think she's with Whit—I never saw any women with him in the Readings. And from the way that she waits, arms crossed, for me to say something, I can tell her attitude is impatient rather than menacing. She throws off her hood and a cascade of elbow-length red curly hair springs free. "See. A normal, unthreatening, thirtysomething woman. Not a serial killer bone in my body, I swear." And she gives this grin that wipes any lingering doubt from my mind.

"There are some men after me," I say, half whispering, and dart an anxious look over my shoulder toward the pastureland.

"Yeah, I kind of figured that," she says. "It's okay. I'm ninety-nine percent sure they won't follow us, and my house is just five minutes upslope. Now come on, let's get you indoors." And she drapes my arm around her shoulder and helps me hobble much more quickly than I could on my own.

As we follow the stream uphill, I don't see anything slightly resembling a house or any sign of civilization. And then, all of a sudden, we are approaching a large log cabin. "Wow, I didn't even see that coming!" I exclaim.

"Camouflage," she says proudly. "I've planted trees strategically around the place so that even if lights are on, you can't see them from the base of the mountain."

We come around a clump of bushes and I get a full view. It stops me in my tracks. "Your house is built over the stream?" I gasp.

The main section of the log cabin is two stories high, but

there's a windowed room—like a closed-in balcony just as wide as the house—that stretches over the rushing water and is supported by stilt-like wood columns on the far bank.

"Yep. You'd think it was just whimsy, but in fact it's terribly practical to have running water so close." Smiling, she opens the door and helps me totter through. Her jade-green eyes sparkle, and the smile on her bowed lips is genuine and friendly.

"Let's see about this foot now. I'm going to be really careful," she says, and eases my tennis shoe off my hurt foot. I wince as a lightning bolt of pain passes through my ankle, but the shoe is off and now Tallie's peeling back the sock. "Well, now. It looks like you might have a sprain here," she says, touching the swollen skin lightly. "But if you were able to put a tiny bit of weight on it, which you did, then it must not be too bad. Let's get you over to the couch and ice it."

She leads me into the space, which I see is one big sparsely furnished room lit brightly by a half-dozen oil-burning lamps.

She eyes me merrily. "Don't usually like guests. But you're a special exception."

"Why's that?" I ask. I hobble my way across the room and lower myself onto the couch, swinging around to prop my hurt foot on the cushions.

"Because I was expecting you," she says matter-of-factly, staring straight at my right eye.

"But why?" I ask. "And how did you know where to find me?"

"Do we have to share all our secrets right away?" she asks, and pulls a metal box from a corner cupboard. She starts rummaging through it. "Let's see. Ace bandage might come in handy. Skin's not broken, so we don't need disinfectant. Ah, here," she says, and pulls out a plastic pouch the size of a paperback book and begins squishing it in her hands. She presses it against my ankle, and I gasp in surprise.

"It's ice-cold!" I say, and put my hand on the first-aid box to see if it's some kind of refrigerator. But no—the metal is room temperature.

"You've never seen an ice pack?" Tallie says with a grin.

I shake my head.

"Okaaaaay," she drawls. "I thought you were supposed to be from the future."

"What?" I ask, mystified.

"Oh, nothing," she says. "By the way, I told you my name. I still don't know yours."

I sit staring at her. What is going on? Who is this stranger who claims to have been expecting me? If she's not with Whit, how did she know I was coming? Her body language suggests friendly, not dangerous. But I'm still wary.

"You don't have to tell me. I'll just pick a name. Hmm . . ." She leans her head to one side, considering. "How about Frederica? Fred for short?"

I can't help myself. I laugh. "I'm Juneau," I admit.

Tallie nods approvingly. "Suits you better than Fred. Goddess or city in Alaska?"

"Alaska," I say, wondering how many times I'm going to have to clarify that. In my clan no one questioned our names. The children were all named after Alaskan towns. It bound us to the past. "You are your own little cities of the Promised Land," my father used to say. "The hope for the future of the earth." My chest constricts as I remember this—just one brick in the wall of lies they built to keep us from discovering the real world. *I still don't understand,* I think, and exhale deeply before noticing that Tallie is watching me with a concerned look on her face.

"Are you tired? Hungry?"

"Both," I respond.

"Let me see what I can get together," she says, and heads toward a door on the river side of the house. As she opens it, I hear flowing water. I turn and lean over the couch to see that the room over the river is the kitchen, with a sink and counters, cupboards, and a wall full of knives and utensils. Tallie opens a trapdoor in the floor and winds a crank beside it, pulling up a metal cage filled with food.

She turns her head to me, and with a quirky smile says, "Best refrigerator a girl could ask for."

My mouth drops open. "That is ingenious!" I say.

"Why, thank you very much," she says, flipping her hair back over her shoulder as she leans in to pick some things out of the cage. "You're not vegan, are you? Vegetarian?" she calls.

"No," I yell back. *Vegetarian?* I think, smiling to myself. If only she could see me skinning and gutting a caribou.

After a few minutes Tallie returns with a tray. "How about a couple of cheeses, some homemade bread, and cured ham?" she asks.

My mouth is watering, but I just stare at it and search her face once more.

She puts the tray down with an amused expression and pops a piece of cheese in her mouth. "See? Not poisoned. Not even spoiled."

I relax. "Sorry. I'm not in the most trusting mood lately. Honestly, this looks like the best meal in the world." I spread some butter on the bread, lay a piece of ham on it, and raise it to my mouth, but then freeze at the sound of a knock on the front window. "Oh no!" I whisper, dropping my food in panic. But Tallie is up in a second and walking toward the sound.

"Don't worry, Juneau. It's just a raven. It's probably hungry."

"Don't let him in!" I yell, and rise to my feet before crumpling back down to the couch, gasping with pain and holding my ankle. But it's too late. She opens the window to place a piece of bread on the sill, and he squeezes past her and into the house.

"Well, aren't you cheeky?" she says, putting her hands on her hips.

"Tallie, you have to get him out of here," I urge. "He has some kind of location device hooked to his leg."

"What in the world are you talking about?" she says, and putting both hands out, traps Poe on the ground and rolls him over. "There's nothing on his legs."

The flashing red light is gone. I breathe a sigh of relief, but my stomach still churns with anxiety. "Come here, Poe," I say. Tallie releases him, and he hops over to me.

"So you know this bird, like, personally?" she asks, one eyebrow raised.

I pick Poe up and comb through his feathers, but there is nothing attached to him: no note, no tiny machine. Someone must have removed the bracelet. But why?

"He's going to have to stay in here. We can't let him go now that he's seen where we are," I say, pulling him onto my stomach. I pet him like a cat, and he nestles his head against my arm.

Tallie stares at me with knitted brow, finger posed pensively on her lips. "People often call me strange. But your bird paranoia problem"—she gestures with her chin toward Poe—"takes the cake."

"It's not—" I begin.

"Shh," she urges, shaking her head. She closes the window, flicks the lock closed, and lowers the wicks of the oil lamps, dimming the room's light to a warm flickering glow that reminds me of nighttime in my yurt. "You eat. As for me, I'm usually in bed by now, but I'll wait until you're done." She walks over to the bedroom corner and pulls some clothes out of a dresser drawer. "I never have guests, so I have no use for walls. Which means if you're overly modest, you might want to turn around, 'cause I'm about to get naked."

I focus on eating, giving her privacy, and in a few minutes she walks back wearing flannel pajamas. She catches me smiling and says, "Like I said. No guests. I wear what I like."

I swallow my bread and nod toward a rifle resting in a rack over the door. "Is that for hunting?"

She shakes her head. "I'm too squeamish to kill anything unless it's about to kill me. It's more for protection."

"From what?" I ask.

"Oh you know. The usual," she grins. "As you noticed, I'm living a bit off the grid," she explains. "No one knows I'm here."

"Why?" I ask. "Are you running from the law or something?"

"You're the guest, so I get to grill you first. But I'm not even going to do that until tomorrow morning. You done with the food tray?"

"Yes. Thanks," I say as she clears it away. She pulls the throw blanket off the back of the couch and drapes it over me.

"You sleep now. The door and windows are locked, although I have a feeling that if the people after you were headed this way, we would have already heard from them. But, as to not take any chances, I'll take this to bed with me." She grabs the rifle from off the wall and lays it on the ground next to her.

I pull my crossbow over from where it's propped on my bag and place it next to the couch. It's cold comfort, and less powerful than Tallie's shotgun, but I feel safer knowing it's by my side.

42

MILES

IT TAKES A LITTLE TALKING TO CONVINCE THE state police to let me take my "stolen" car without pressing charges or filing a missing persons report. Portman, who happens to be in the same war veterans' association as one of the patrolmen, finally persuades them that it was all just a teenage love spat, during which my girlfriend drove off with my car and then was picked up by friends. The gas station cashier claims she had her headphones on and didn't notice a thing.

"You better get home to your father now," Redding tells me as they pull away. He looks resigned, as if he knows I'm not going to obey him. And he's right. Getting home to Dad is the last thing on my to-do list, unless I do it with Juneau in tow.

I turn the keys in the ignition and watch the gas dial swing up to full. So Juneau must have filled the tank before she ran off. I walk up to the station and knock on the bulletproof glass. The girl behind the window ignores me, so I knock again. She looks up. I flash her my most charming smile. She slips her headphones off and pops her gum at me.

"Sorry about that," she says. "I thought you were those cops again."

"Yeah, that car's actually mine. My girlfriend drove off with it while we were having an argument." I decide to stick with Portman's story. It worked on the cops. "I know you told the police you didn't see anything, but is there anything at all that you remember that could help me out? It's late, and I'm worried about her."

The girl smiles widely and says, "I actually just said that because I didn't want to have to make an official statement." She goes on to tell me that she saw everything, including two guys returning a half hour later without the girl and yelling at each other for a while before driving away.

"What direction did they go?" I ask.

"South toward Salt Lake City," she responds.

"Thank you so much," I say. She shrugs and slides her headphones back on.

So it happened as I had hoped. Whit's guys didn't succeed in finding Juneau, yet she hasn't come back for my car. That means she's still out there somewhere. I step over a knee-high concrete wall into the pasture and look around. Trees in the distance, with mountains even farther past them. She could be anywhere. And the point has already been established that my wilderness survival skills are laughably lame next to hers.

Unless she wants me to find her, like she did in Seattle, I have no hope. And after she overheard my phone conversation with Dad, that's just not going to happen. I rub my face sleepily with the palm of my hand. I know she's heading for Salt Lake City, but unless she hitchhikes, there's no way she'll make it there tonight. *I'll just have to hope she's too scared to hitch a ride with strangers,* I think, and then laugh at the irony.

I climb in my car and start driving southward, ready to stop at the first hotel I see.

43

JUNEAU

I AWAKE TO THE SMELL OF BACON AND THE SOUND of eggs popping and spitting on the stovetop. And even though I am completely disoriented, I can't stop a smile from blooming on my lips. I sit up and am staring Poe straight in the beak. He squawks and flaps his wings.

"He hasn't moved all night, watching over you like your own avian bodyguard," comes a voice from across the room. And—snap—I remember where I am.

"Good morning, Tallie," I say.

She adds a log from the woodpile to the stove. "Breakfast?" she asks.

"Yes, please," I respond, and she sets a tray on the low table in front of the couch: eggs, bacon, toast, and orange juice.

"Are you a coffee or tea person?" she asks. Her pajamas have disappeared, and she is dressed in jeans and a lumberjack shirt, with her fiery hair tamed and tied in a knot behind her head.

"Chicory, actually," I answer.

She makes a face like she bit into a sour berry. "Ugh. Nasty stuff. My ex-mother-in-law used to drink chicory. Tea it is, then." And in a minute she's back.

She pulls the armchair up to the table and pours two mugs of tea.

I swallow a bite of toast and ask, "You don't have animals, do you?"

"I don't like pets," she says, eyeing Poe. "I have enough work around here without having to worry about codependent furry things."

"No, I mean where do you get the bacon and eggs?"

"Oh. There's a general store ten miles away. I hike in twice a week and do handyman jobs for them in exchange for the supplies I can't forage for myself. I'm self-contained, self-sustained, and I don't have to pay taxes that go to nice people getting killed in senseless wars."

"Now I understand why you make yourself invisible," I say.

"Yeah, I'm a conscientious objector to just about everything," she says with a grin. "No electricity, no phone or internet, no car. And, contrary to what you're witnessing right now, I'm normally pretty antisocial."

I wash down a piece of honey-smeared toast with a gulp of strong tea and ask, "How did you find me? You said you were expecting me."

"Oh, that," she says, and lifts her eyebrows mysteriously. "I threw the bones."

I pause, a forkful of eggs lifted halfway to my mouth. "You threw the bones?"

She opens a drawer in the table between us and takes out a rust-red leather pouch, and then, loosening its drawstrings, spills a handful of dried, bleached animal bones onto the table. "My great-grandma Lula-Mae's possum bones, passed to her daughter, who passed them to my mom, who passed them to me. Along with double-X chromosomes, all the women in my family possess the Sight. That's them over there," she says, nodding to a table in the corner that holds framed photographs. "I call them my goddesses."

She begins arranging the bones in a circular pattern on the table. "I throw Lula-Mae's bones every morning, to keep in practice. Outside on the ground, mind you. Not here on the table. They have to touch earth. Yesterday they looked sort of like this." A few of the bones cross each other in places, and others are lined up parallel. "I won't go into all the boring details, but it told me a visitor was coming around midnight, and that this wasn't a hunter, as usual, but someone being hunted."

She points to the two skeletal hands, which are sitting one next to the other, thumb bones touching. "This told me that my visitor would be like me. 'Touched' like my women. Are you psychic? Or into divination?"

"Kind of," I admit.

She studies me carefully, like the bones in my face are just as readable as those of the long-dead possum spread before us. Seemingly satisfied, she looks back down and resumes her explanation.

"It also told me that we both have something to teach the other." She picks up her mug and watches me over the raised rim as she takes a sip. I don't know what to say, so I keep my mouth shut.

"But the way the tailbones fell"—she points at a few disjointed bones—"it suggests that you have an important mission. That people's lives or destinies may lie in your hands." Her face is all seriousness now, and she waits for my response.

I swallow hard and meet her eyes. "My father and clan have been kidnapped and are being held against their will somewhere. I am trying to find them. To rescue them." She holds my gaze before leaning back, staring at a point behind me on the wall and rubbing her chin thoughtfully.

Something occurs to me. "Why did you ask me if I was from the future?"

She snaps back into the here and now. "Hmm? Oh. The end of the tail sticking out of the circle. It's sticking out of time, or out of the world. So I figured that I should be on the lookout for either a UFO landing in my front yard, or some kind of time machine bringing you here from the future." She laughs.

"Well, you could definitely say I'm from another world," I allow.

"Yes, I figured you were the one when I saw you through my telescope." She nods toward an expensive-looking model standing next to the window, pointed down the mountain. "And then

I confirmed it when I shone the light in your eye and saw that gold sun-looking iris. Looked pretty alien to me. What is it? A genetic mutation?"

My mouth dropped open. "You're the first person who hasn't thought it was a contact lens."

"Well, you didn't take it out last night. And it doesn't really match the renouncing-your-femininity theme you're rocking."

"I was trying to disguise myself as a boy to avoid my pursuers," I admit.

"Looks like that didn't work out very well for you," she says, amused. "You need to lose the Gap Boy look, by the way, if you want to maintain that disguise. It makes you lumpy, not boyish. Anyway that's my story. I want to hear yours, but let's see how that ankle's doing first."

I pull the blanket off my lap and prop my bare foot on the side of the table. Tallie whistles. "That's not as bad as it looked last night. A little more rest, and you should be up and about in a day or so."

"Couldn't we just wrap it tightly? I really need to go. Like I said, I'm looking for my clan, and although I think that they're safe for the moment, who knows what will happen?" My voice rises slightly as I explain, and I'm suddenly fighting tears. I pick up my mug and take a big swig of tea, swallow, exhale, and feel better.

"Do you know where they are?" Tallie asks.

"I know what the place looks like. And I know it's southeast of here. And still pretty far."

Tallie nods and thinks on it. "Well, you're not going to be much use to anyone if you're hobbling around on one foot. And whoever's chasing you will probably be hanging around the area for a while before they give up, so it's better you stay hidden for the day."

She begins scooping up the possum bones and placing them carefully into the pouch. "And then there's Beauregard here, who says we have something to teach each other."

"Beauregard?" I ask, incredulous.

"Lula-Mae named the possum after her first husband. Don't even ask."

I mask a laugh as Tallie continues. "Have you learned anything from me that's going to help you save your folks?"

I shake my head.

"Okay, well, it's your turn. Tell all. Or at least all that you feel like telling."

I hesitate, not because I don't trust her but because I don't know where to start. My story still feels so fresh and painful after spilling it to Miles—after seeing him brush it off as fantasy. My stomach twists when I think of him. It's not like I ever really trusted him. But I entrusted him with my story. And he betrayed me. *You betrayed him, too,* I remind myself.

Tallie sees my indecision and leans over to pat my hand. "You know what? I find late morning the perfect time for fishing. I'm going to go catch us our lunch, and you can have some time to yourself."

And when she returns a few hours later with a stringful of river trout, I'm ready to talk.

"So now your power is gone," Tallie concludes when I'm finished. We've just eaten lunch, and our lips are both stained from blackberries. She scoops the last spoonful of purple cream out of the bowl into her mouth.

I nod. "I tried the most basic of Readings last night and it didn't work."

She places the empty bowl back down on the table. "Try something now. Try your firepowder. Does it work with a candle?"

I shake my head. "No, it needs to be a substantial blaze with open air around it."

"It's not really cold enough to merit a fire, but I'll build us one anyway." And she sets to work piling up kindling and logs, and soon a good fire is crackling in the hearth. While she works, I pull everything from my bag and set it out. It has been so long since I've seen it all arranged outside my pack that I discover a few things I had forgotten were there.

"Tell me what things are for," Tallie says, placing a hand on my arm. I feel my skin tingle. A little quickening of warmth. Of kinship. Like I felt with Nome and Kenai. And whether or not that feeling is from the Yara, it's a feeling that I trust.

"Telling you what one thing is for is like telling you that basil can only be used with tomato sauce. All these can be mixed to facilitate different Readings, and a few for Conjurings."

I feel like I am back with Whit, teaching the clan children the basics of Reading the Yara as he looks on and makes suggestions or additions.

Tallie's watching me, so I begin. "The concept behind Reading is that everything in nature is alive in a certain fashion. So everything has its own version of what it sees or experiences: either past memories, what is happening in the present, or, since we think time is flexible, a 'memory' of what will have happened in the future. Every living thing is connected through the Yara. So Reading is just reaching out to the right element in nature that can give you the information you want to know. Some things, Whit has established as being consistently reliable for transmitting their knowledge, and those things can be accessed by using a certain object that he's matched with it."

"In a way it's like Beauregard. He's my tool for reading the future," Tallie says.

"I have a feeling it might be all part of the same thing," I confess. "You use the bones to connect with the Yara—or whatever your women called it—just like I can use an animal skull to Read where to hunt our next kill."

Tallie smiles and nudges me. "Sisters in sign reading. I knew you'd be special. I'm shutting up now. You go ahead." She runs her finger over an uncut amethyst.

"The precious stones act as a conduit for pretty much anything," I explain. I pull my opal from under my shirt. "Most of our clanspeople wear one on them at all times to facilitate Reading, although the adults usually leave the Reading to the kids.

We're better at it than they are."

"And you're the most talented of all?" Tallie asks with a raised eyebrow.

"Um, yeah, actually," I say, feeling a little embarrassed. "My father says that my mother and I were prodigies, like any math or musical prodigy, but our gift was in using the Yara. My mother would have been the next clan Sage if she hadn't died."

"I'm sorry," says Tallie softly.

I nod. "It's been a long time. Anyway, because of my 'talent,' I was chosen to be the next clan Sage."

"Figures," she says with a wry smile.

"Why?"

"Because my goddesses wouldn't bring just anyone to teach me the ways of Yara. They'd only bring me the best."

I laugh, and continue taking her through the stones, herbs, ground-up minerals, and bones, skin, and fur, including the rabbit feet, and explain their different purposes.

"And Whit's the one who came up with all this?" she asks when I finish.

"He says he 'culled the world's wisdom' for it. This is Whit's firepowder," I say, pointing to the rapidly dwindling supply in my bag. "It's a mix of ground mica, gypsum, and a couple of other minerals local to Alaska. Besides skipping stones, fire is the earliest thing children Read because it's one of the easiest."

I hand the pouch to Tallie and then shuffle over next to where she's plopped down in front of the fire, being careful not to flex my ankle. "You do it first," Tallie says, looking as excited as a kid at a magic show.

"Like I said, nothing is working for me right now. But this is how I would do it." I take a pinch and throw it into the flames, where it pops and sparkles silver for a second. "You need to relax. Slow your heartbeat. Slow your breathing. And then focus on the person you want to see. You can even say their name if it helps. And then you open yourself up and let the Yara make that connection for you."

"Where am I supposed to be looking?" Tallie asks. She's arranged herself in a lotus position and has rested her wrists on her knees, palms facing up like Whit does when leading the elders in their daily yoga session. This makes me smile.

"Look just above the fire and a tiny bit to one side. And then try to see patterns in the top of the flames and the shimmering of the heat above them."

"Does the person have to be alive?" she asks, not daring to tear her eyes away from the fire.

"Yes—you use fire-Reading for seeing things in the present."

"Says who?" she asks petulantly.

"Whit," I respond.

She pauses. "Okay," she says, "Yara, show me that lying cheat Nick Chowder, may his pecker shrivel to the size of a cheese puff and rot in hell." She stares hard at the fire, squinting at it like she's daring it to comply. I can't help but laugh, but try to hide it so as not to distract her.

"What?" she says, finally turning from the fire with an irked expression. "Why are you laughing at me?"

"I wouldn't try to start with someone whose guts you hate," I say. "Your emotions are supposed to be calm. Like meditation."

"Then you do it," she challenges.

"I told you, I'm not—"

"No, just pretend like you're doing it, so I can copy you."

I straighten my back and exhale deeply, closing my eyes. "Dad," I whisper, and then let my eyelids slowly open as I stare above the fire. I watch the flames lick the air. Watch the negative space above them, pointing downward in flickering Vs, and wait, without hoping, for the tingle of the Yara connection. After a while, I break my gaze and look at her.

"Did it work?" she asks. I shake my head.

She sighs, and then gets up and grabs me a couch pillow to put under my foot. Digging through a cupboard, she takes out a plastic-lined box and scoops something out. "Clay from the riverbed," she says, and comes back to sprawl beside me in front of the fire. "I think better when my hands are working." She rolls it around between her palms.

"So when you were telling me your life story there, you ended up with your theory that you've lost your powers because you've lost faith in the Yara. But since you've been explaining to me how it all functions, I've noticed just how much you do seem to believe in it. Your face kind of lights up when you talk about it.

"However, with all that postapocalyptic crap that your elders were feeding you and the other kids, I don't blame you for doubting everything you ever learned. But you can't throw out the baby with the bathwater, as they say. This is an important time for you, Juneau. You have other people to think about. You have a whole clan that's depending on you. So you owe them to think a little bit harder about this."

The clay is now squished into an oblong shape, and her thumbs are kneading it like she's giving it a massage. "What I've just heard is that this one man came up with the whole idea of the Yara—"

"Whit based it on the Gaia philosophy," I interject.

"Yeah, yeah, whatever," she says, and pats the top of the clay with the ball of her hand with little slapping noises until it's flat. "He gathered the info. He made sense out of it. He mined other belief systems for what would go with it. And sounds like he did a pretty good job synthesizing it all to make it something that is a powerful tool for you and your people. But that doesn't mean he knows everything."

I consider what she's said. "You know what I've been thinking about, Tallie? How all the totems Whit uses for Reading and Conjuring, even though he claims they're all necessary, they seem to detract from the pure connection between me and the Yara. Why do I have to go through something—whether a stone or the rabbits' feet? I should be able to go directly to the Yara to ask what I want. All the bells and whistles might be extraneous."

"Doubt everything, Juneau. Doubt everything at least once. What you decide to keep, you'll be able to be confident of. And what you decide to ditch, you will replace with what your instincts tell you is true. You've been living in a crystal tower that just had the foundations knocked out from under it. Which sucks. But now it's up to you to decide whether you're going to wallow around in the wreckage or rebuild something sturdier. Nothing better than making something with your own hands," she says, gesturing around at the house she built. "Or, in your case, with your own mind."

She smiles at me. "Now that I'm done with my lecture, here is your reward for listening." She hands me the ball of clay, and suddenly I'm looking at a miniature version of myself. High cheekbones, full-moon eyes, and spiky hair made by pinching the clay dozens of times. She's even made the starburst in my right eye.

"Hey, you're really good," I say.

She shrugs but looks pleased. "When I'm not building log cabins, I'm an amateur sculptor."

"Thank you," I say.

"No, thank you," she responds. "I think we just now fulfilled Beauregard's prophecy. You taught me something, or attempted to. . . . I'm going to keep working on the fire-Reading thing until I make it work. And in exchange, I gave you something to mull over, drawn from my own hard-earned life experience. I'd say we're pretty even."

44

MILES

I AWAKE TO THE SOUND OF THE CLEANING LADY unlocking my door. "Checkout was a half hour ago," she says, and stands there with her fist on her hip like she's kicking me out.

"Uh, could I have five minutes to get up and get dressed?" I ask. She makes a puffing noise and backs out, but leaves the door cracked open. I glance over at the glowing red numbers of the alarm clock on the bedside table. Eleven thirty a.m. My first night in what feels like forever in a real bed instead of on the hard ground, and I want to sleep all day.

And then I remember why I'm here and leap out of bed, pulling yesterday's jeans and T-shirt on and running out to the car. I was so tired last night I didn't even bother to bring my suitcase in with me.

Okay, Miles, think. Redding and Portman will already be in

Salt Lake City by now. Whit and his men . . . who knows where they are? And Juneau? She could be anywhere between that service station and Salt Lake City. It's useless to try to search for her in between, when I know that the city is her goal. She'll turn up there sooner or later.

I pop the trunk, fish out the cereal and a bottle of cranberry juice. Juneau had never seen it before, so of course she had to buy a six-pack, and I remember her excitement with a smile. For the next three hours I eat dry Cap'n Crunch out of the box and take swigs of Ocean Spray (which do not mix well) as I drive to Salt Lake City.

But once I'm in the city, I have no clue of where to even start looking for her. I try to think like she does. She had talked about that prophecy of the serpent and the city by the undrinkable water and seemed to think that she would find the next piece of the puzzle once she arrived. But what would she look for? Where would she go to find a sign?

I drive around the downtown area, looking for anything that catches my eye. Temple Square. Capitol Hill. The shopping district. All I can think is that modernity freaks her out, so she would probably head to a park or the lakefront. My stomach's growling, so I park the car and go into a sandwich shop and order some food. I'll eat next to the waterfront. When I give the cashier my credit card, it comes back as declined.

"Try it again," I say, and end up having to pay with cash. I've got twenty bucks left in my wallet, so I head to an ATM. It eats my card. When I go into the bank, the teller tells me that my card has been reported as stolen. And then I know.

"What the hell, Dad!" I yell into the pay phone.

"Watch your language, young man," he growls. "I told you to come directly home. What are you doing in Salt Lake City?"

"How do you even know where I am?" I yell.

"My assistant, Sam, is tracking your card use."

"He reported it as stolen!"

"I'll have him rectify that as soon as you reassure me that you are on your way to L.A. and I will see you here tomorrow."

"I'm not coming home. I'm staying here until I find the girl."

"If you do, Miles Blackwell, you can forget about Yale. I have my men on this, and I don't want you messing it up."

"But, Dad," I begin. The phone line clicks as my dad hangs up.

I head back to the car, flipping through my wallet as I walk. Twenty bucks to my name and my dad's Shell card, which can only buy me gas. I'm not leaving. I'm not going home, but where am I going to stay? I'm not Juneau—I can't survive off the land. What am I going to do until I find her—snare pigeons with my phone charger and cook them over a campfire in the public park?

I press the button to unlock my car, accidentally popping the trunk open. Walking around to slam it shut, I see something I had completely forgotten was back there: the tent and camping supplies.

I glance around at the stunning mountain scenery surrounding the city and smile. I can't afford a hotel room, but I can sure as hell camp.

45

JUNEAU

BY NIGHTTIME I'M DESPERATE TO LEAVE. BEING cut off from all communication with my clan makes me feel so out of control, I can barely sit still.

Tallie helps me limp outside, draws a circle on the ground with a stick, and tells me to throw Beauregard's bones while thinking about my father. This reminds me so much of contacting the Yara that it makes me wonder once again if there is more than one way—Whit's way—to Read and Conjure. And that Tallie's just using a different method and vocabulary to get the same results from the same source. Although the thought is destabilizing, it also appeals to me. I take the dried old bones in both hands and toss them inside the circle.

Tallie squats down and studies them. She runs her finger along a series of small bones lying perpendicular to one another.

"I don't know why, Juneau, but it looks like your quest ends here, right now, at my house."

"What?" I ask, aghast.

"You've deviated from the path you're supposed to take, here." She points to a bone in the series. "This one is off-kilter, and if you don't put it straight, you won't go any farther."

She looks at me. "If you had to divide your journey into major steps, maybe into important Readings, how would it go?"

I think. "Well, first I fire-Read and saw Whit near the ocean. Then, once in Anchorage, my oracle directed me to Seattle. Which is where this old man told me how to find Miles, and said I had to be honest with him, but not to trust him. And . . . oh."

"What?" Tallie asks, hand on her hip.

"He said that Miles was the one to take me far," I say in a small voice.

"Looks like he hasn't taken you far enough," she says. "You're going to have to tuck your tail and go find him. Convince him to keep going with you."

"But his dad is out to get me for some strange reason." Something strikes me for the first time. "What if Miles's dad is actually working with Whit and his men? What if Miles's dad is the one who kidnapped my clan?"

Tallie shrugs. "Whatever the case, it looks like you've got your work cut out. You have to, one, find the boy; two, convince him to forgive you for drugging him and stealing his car; and three, persuade him not to hand you over to his dad."

I gape at her. "But without my ability to Read, how in the

world am I supposed to find him?"

"Well, that'll be a good incentive to get your abilities back. If Whit sent that bird to find you, do you think you could send it to find Miles?" she asks.

I nod. "I've tried that before, with a much smaller distance, and it worked."

"Well then, that's your next step. As soon as you're ready, you let me know. I can hike over to the general store. Mikey over there'll let me borrow his pickup truck, and I can get within a half-mile of here if I go back-road. Then I'll take you to wherever the bird tells you to go. How's that?"

"I'll do my best" is all I say. Although the last twenty-four hours with Tallie have raised my spirits, I'm still awash in a sea of doubt. What we talked about this afternoon was like a wake-up call. I know there is some truth in what I've been taught. But it's going to take time to sift through it all and decide what I truly believe. What makes sense. And I don't have time to spare.

As if reading my mind, Tallie says, "If you're anything like me, it's going to take years to sort everything out in your head." She drapes an arm around my shoulders. "But one thing at a time. Just focus right now on the thing you need. We'll try to find your Miles tomorrow."

Tallie gathers up the bones and places them gently back into their pouch. And then, leaving me outside with Poe on a special security leash she devised, she goes inside. Through a cabin window, I see her settle into the armchair with a book.

She knows what she believes and has built a life around it. I'm jealous of the simplicity of the path she's chosen and, for a second, wish I was back in our village in Alaska, where the only goal was survival, and I was sure of what I believed. I almost wouldn't mind being lied to . . . if I never discovered the lie in the first place. Live oblivious of the deception.

Life is easier in black and white. It's the ambiguity of a world defined in grays that has stripped me of my confidence and left me powerless.

46

MILES

I SPEND THE REST OF THAT DAY AND ALL THE next wandering around Salt Lake City. Anytime I'm not scanning the city's most popular spots for her, I'm in the library, using their computers to research the stories she told me.

It turns out that her Whittier Graves made headlines in the '70s. He was part of a group of scientists who were deeply involved in the Gaia Movement. They were all about the protection of the planet: preserving endangered species, curbing climate change, disarming nuclear weapons, and the like. Several articles refer to the fact that Whit and some colleagues disappeared during a research trip in South America. And that's it. After 1984 there is no more mention of him.

I bet he planted the rumor about South America before going to Alaska just to throw everyone off their trail. A bunch of tree-hugging hippies seceding from society doesn't seem so far out. But the whole WWIII thing sounds more like those cults who move to another country and drink poisoned Kool-Aid. It's all about mind control. Brainwashing. Juneau's story is making more and more sense to me.

47

JUNEAU

I SPEND THAT NIGHT RESTING MY ANKLE AND thinking about things. Showing Tallie all the amulets and totems we use for Reading and Conjuring had sparked something in my mind. As had Tallie's advice to doubt everything and think for myself.

I think that Whit got some things wrong. I don't need a crutch to Read or Conjure. I don't need something material to link me with the Yara. I am a living being who is close to the Yara—I should be able to access it directly. Myself. And for once, I take my opal necklace off when I sleep. Okay, it was within reaching distance of me on the floor, but I felt it was a step. I was going to be stronger, and that strength would come from me.

The next morning when I awake, Tallie is gone. Breakfast is laid out on the table, with a note next to it saying, "Off to find wheels." I eat and dress, then wait outside with Poe until we see a red pickup truck pull up to the clearing at the bottom of the mountain in the distance.

I scramble out the door, and though I'm trying to be careful with my ankle, practically run down the side of the mountain. Tallie meets me halfway. She eyes my sack, which has been packed since the previous night, and then my face, red with exertion and drawn with my impatience to get started.

She plants her fists on her hips. "You sure you don't want to hang out just a few more days?"

"Um, I, uh . . . ," I start saying before I realize that she's making fun of me. "I'm one hundred percent sure, even though you've been the best host."

"Then let's go," says Tallie, taking my pack from me and swinging it into the back of the truck. "Let's get you back on your path."

48

MILES

THE FIRST NIGHT IT TOOK ME A WHILE TO PITCH the tent. After that effort, along with my exhaustion from walking around all day, I didn't even mind the hard ground. I was asleep by the time my head hit the inflatable pillow.

Tonight, however, I have the tent up nearly as fast as Juneau did. After that resounding success, I decide to push my luck and attempt building a fire for the first time. Not because it's cold—it's a bit chilly, but not enough to merit the fire—I just want to see if I can.

To tell the truth, Juneau made me feel inept about all this outdoors stuff. But in L.A. why would I ever need to build a fire? I'm sure there are a million things that I know how to do that she doesn't. I mean, she'd never driven a car. Before she stole mine, that is. I'll bet she's never used a computer. Although something tells me she'd probably pick that up quickly too.

It's obvious that she's smart. I wonder how long it will take her to get used to living in the real world. And I wonder just where it is that her dad and clan are. Although the rest of her story has panned out so far, kidnapping a whole commune seems a bit extreme. Then again, it would be pretty twisted if they had all picked up and left without her.

I build a little fort out of twigs and then add some bigger pieces of wood that I've gathered, like I saw Juneau do. And I'm about to try to light the pile when I hear a car coming down the dirt road. I freeze. No one's come anywhere near my campsite, so far as I know, and I'm afraid some park rangers or police are going to arrest me for staying here since it isn't an official campground. (I had seen signs for some of those, but they all cost money, and I'm seeing how long I can stretch my last five bucks.)

My first reflex is to hide, but if it's the cops, they'll just run my license plate and maybe even call my dad, since it's his name on the registration. Before the vehicle comes into view, a large black shape flies straight at me, and I duck as it glides within inches of my head.

I spin to discover the bird—okay, Poe—perched with its head tipped to one side like it finds my startled expression hilarious. And then a red pickup truck pulls up to the end of the dirt road next to my car. I can't tell who's inside until they turn the headlights off, and then I see Juneau step out of the passenger side and walk slowly toward me. She's limping slightly, and the serious expression on her face, combined with the fact that the driver isn't getting out of the truck, tips me off to the fact that she wants to talk with me alone.

"Welcome to my campsite," I say, gesturing with pride toward the pitched tent and fire-in-the-making. Juneau doesn't even look at it. She's staring directly into my eyes as she walks toward me, and for a second I'm afraid that she's going to come right up and punch me. But she stops two steps away and stands, hands at her side, chin lifted in that proud way she does that usually precedes her saying something awful.

"I'm not here because I want to be," she says. "I'm here because I have to be. I need you to keep traveling with me."

"I thought maybe you had come to apologize," I say.

"For what?" she asks, putting her hands on her hips indignantly.

"For drugging me and then forcing me to talk while I was in a drug-haze."

"What about the fact that you were going to hand me over to your father?" she asks, and her voice is tinged with anger.

"I would like to explain that to you," I say, and taking her hand, pull her closer. Her skin is warm, and I find my gaze pulled down to her mouth before skipping back up to her eyes. I lick my lips and try to focus. "Juneau . . . the reason I'm still here and not already back in L.A. is that I want to take you to my father so that he can see you're not the person he's looking for."

"I'm not going anywhere that will keep me from finding my family," she begins, slipping her hand out from mine. But then, seeing how earnest I am, she concedes. "Okay. Explain."

"My dad owns a pharmaceutical company," I begin. "There's this new drug he wants to get his hands on—I mean, buy. But the guy he was doing business with disappeared. He heard that for some reason you were the key to getting the formula."

"Me?" she asks, astonished.

"My description was a seventeen-year-old girl from Alaska, around five foot five, with long black hair and eye jewelry in the form of a star."

"That sounds like me," she admits. "But I don't know anything about a drug. My people don't even use medicine. All we had was a first-aid tent for cuts and broken bones."

I know she's telling the truth. Her confused reaction isn't feigned. "I told him he had made a mistake, but he wouldn't believe me. He sent some men to find you—the guys who were following you in Seattle. I saw them driving around yesterday. They're here in Salt Lake City keeping a lookout for you now."

"So if you know I'm not the one he's looking for, why are you so eager to prove it to your dad?"

"I've been in his bad books since I got kicked out of school. I think the fact that I went to such lengths to find you, and prove that his sources were wrong about you, would redeem me. But I'm not going to force you to go with me if you don't want to. And I'm not going to turn you over to his men, either."

She waits, thinking before she answers. "Miles, I will go with you to see your father if you go first with me to find my clan. I can't find them without you."

"Why? What do I have to do with it? Did I say that while I was fortune-telling?" I can't help a note of bitterness from creeping into my words.

"No," she says, and her mouth quirks up in a smile. "What would you say if I told you it was revealed to me by some hundred-year-old possum bones?"

"I'd say it sounds just like you. And that's fine: I'm ready to accept anything you tell me, as long as you don't do anything to me without my knowledge. And as long as you don't steal my car."

Her grin is huge until she reins it in, opting for a closed-lipped smile. She holds out her hand.

"And that would be my cue," comes a voice from the truck. A woman with a mane of red curly hair steps out of the cab and walks toward us. "I'm Tallie," she says.

"Miles," I respond, and she takes the hand that Juneau's just let go of and shakes it heartily.

"Enchanted," she says, and turns to Juneau. "So you're good?" she asks, and something passes between them that tells me they've done some major talking. Juneau nods at her. "Thanks for everything," she says.

Tallie hands Juneau her pack. "If you ever need me, you know where to find me," she says. "Just make sure you keep it a secret."

Juneau smiles. "Of course."

They hug briefly, and Tallie heads back to the pickup and drives off into the night. Juneau and I stand there, neither knowing what to say.

"You look . . . different," I say finally.

She looks down. "These are Tallie's clothes. She forced me to wear them."

"She forced you?"

"She hid my boy clothes and said I could either wear hers or go naked," Juneau says, looking embarrassed.

It's not like she's wearing a dress. She just has on a pair of black jeans and a red V-neck shirt. But for once they actually fit. Juneau's not skinny, and you wouldn't exactly say muscular. But something in between. She's so much shorter than me that I could easily pick her up. Of course, I refrain since I don't feel like being punched.

"You look nice," I say.

She grins. "You don't look bad yourself," she says, and her eyes stray to the fire I was building, "but that's the worst-looking campfire I've ever seen." I laugh and the tension is broken. Juneau goes over to rearrange the kindling while the bird flies over to the tent and makes himself at home.

Something is nagging at the edge of my consciousness. It's a good feeling, but I can't quite place it. And then suddenly I do. It's a feeling of being where I'm supposed to be. A feeling of knowing that I'm in the right place at the right time. With the right person.

I watch Juneau light the fire, and the flames shine through her hair. It looks so soft that I want to go touch it. Run my fingers through the short tufts, that for once seem like she's done something to them besides running a towel over her head. Tallie must have insisted on doing her hair as well.

"Do you want something to eat?" I ask.

"No, Tallie and I ate in the truck," she responds.

"So how did you find me? Messenger raven?" Though I'm joking, I realize that until this moment, I hadn't questioned the fact that this girl found me in the middle of nowhere. Probably because she took it for granted—it just seemed natural to her that (1) I was in Salt Lake City waiting for her, and (2) she could locate a lone boy in the middle of the mountains.

"We're going to need to talk about that, Miles," she says, sitting down next to the fire and rifling through her pack. "I know you don't believe anything I have to say about the Yara, Reading, Conjuring, and all that, but—"

I hold my hands up. "Listen, I think it's better if we avoid that whole subject."

She doesn't look at me. Just puts her face in her hands and squeezes her temples. "Okay," she says finally. "What do you want to talk about then?"

"You were limping. Did you get hurt?" I ask.

She nods. "Whit and his men found me at the gas station—the place I left your car, which I'm glad to see that you found."

I nod. I'm not even ready to talk about her grand theft auto adventure.

She continues. "I had to run off. Stepped in a hole in the ground and hurt my ankle."

"And how'd you find . . . what's her name, Tallie?"

Juneau nods. "Tallie actually found me. She has a house in the mountains, and I stayed there for the last couple of days."

"How about the search for your clan?" I ask. "Do you know what you want to do next?"

"Well, I have a clue. Something else you told me when I Read you—I mean . . . when you were my oracle."

I let my breath out all at once and feel tired.

"What?" Juneau insists, and there's a challenge in her narrowed eyes.

"Maybe it would be better if we just made a plan. Besides the 'Readings,' do you have any solid indications of where your people could be? I mean, for example, is there a place they could have gone if they needed to leave your village urgently? Not suggesting that they would leave you on purpose, or anything."

But she sees in my eyes that that's exactly what I'm suggesting, and her face flushes pink. "Like I told you, they were kidnapped by men in helicopters," she says, her voice low.

"But, Juneau," I say, "you heard a helicopter and found your clan missing. I think you should be open to other possibilities."

She stands, and I can see in the light of the fire that she is trembling. "Miles, we are not going to be able to do this if you don't believe me."

I stay seated. "Juneau, I *can't* believe you. I'm sorry, but what you are talking about is magic. And magic is not real. And there's no way you're going to convince me otherwise unless you show me something I can see with my own eyes."

Her face is scarlet, her hands squeezed into angry fists. "I broke your phone, you know," she says, and her look is menacing. "You saw me do that."

"iPhones break all the time. So that has a rational explanation."

"What about Poe?" she asks.

"What about him? He's probably been fed by humans before and is so lazy he prefers following you around so he doesn't have to catch his own food."

"That doesn't make sense," she says. "I used him to find you just now. I showed him an image of you in my mind and asked the Yara to have him locate you."

"Okay, that's weird, but I'm sure it can be explained." I feel a twinge of guilt for forcing her to this point, but it has to be done. She has to accept reality.

"Don't ask me to prove things to you now. I've just begun to work it all out in my mind." She looks like it cost her every ounce of pride she possesses to admit that to me.

"You claim you were able to conjure Poe into finding me," I say.

"That was really difficult. It took all afternoon."

I shrug, as if to say, *See?* "Well, go ahead. Do something." I feel like a shit for insisting, but I stand my ground.

Her eyes widen in dismay, and she gives me a look like the one thing in the world she wants to do is slap the smug smile right off my face. Turning, she limps over to her bag, digs around in it, pulls out the rabbit feet, holds them in her hand, and closes her eyes. She's concentrating so hard that she looks like she's about to explode.

I wait. "Is something supposed to be happening?" I ask after a moment.

Her eyes fly open, and I know that if she could shoot a laser at me out of her starburst thingy, she'd be doing it right now. "It's probably the rabbits' feet," I hear myself saying, though I know I should keep my mouth shut. "Maybe the magic in them doesn't travel well."

She glowers at me, pure unadulterated hatred blazing her eyes, and then she pitches the rabbit feet forcefully into the fire, where they ignite in a puff of blue flame.

"Holy crap!" I say as she advances toward me, arms folded across her chest. "I didn't mean you had to go all *Firestarter* and destroy your charm. I was just suggesting . . ."

My voice trails off as I begin to scramble backward. Forget the conciliatory Juneau of ten minutes ago, ready to make a deal so I'll keep driving her. This girl is an irate goddess. A Fury. Five foot five inches, and she's going to rip my head off.

"I'm sorry!" I blurt out, because I am—for all sorts of reasons. Sorry I tried to impress my dad by finding her. Sorry I've been making fun of a brainwashed girl for a delusion she can't help. Sorry I egged her on just to make my point. "Honest, Juneau, I'm so sor—" I begin to repeat, but the words freeze on my lips.

Because Juneau has come to a stop three feet away from me.

She gazes down at me, arms loose, fingertips grazing her thighs. And disappears.

It takes me about three seconds flat to throw my things together, toss them in the car, and leap behind the steering wheel. I turn the key in the ignition, throw the gear into reverse, and then . . . the car stalls with a wheezing cough of the motor. Juneau appears, illuminated like a slasher-film killer in the harsh glare of the headlights. One hand rests on the car hood and the other on her waist, as she regards me with an icy glare.

I try to start the car again. Nothing. Juneau walks over to the passenger side, opens the door, gets in, and slams the door behind her. "Believe me now?" she says. She peers out at the bird, who flaps anxiously around like it's afraid we're going to leave him.

"Now you've fried my car" is all I can say. I'm in shock. The door handle is poking my back, and I realize that I've backed as far away from her as I can.

"You were leaving me," she retorts, meeting my eyes. She looks angry. Hurt. But there's something else there that wasn't there before. Something hard and cold that runs a hot needle of fear through my chest.

I break our gaze and breathe deeply. "You freaking disappeared," I say.

"Did it scare you?" she asks, a flicker of curiosity in her tone.

"Yes, it scared me," I admit. "You could have warned me."

"I've been telling you the truth this whole time," she says bitterly.

"Yeah, well, would you believe me if I told you I could fly? Or, I don't know . . . turn blue when I eat blueberries?" Fear has pumped my voice up an octave, and I can feel myself sweating.

Juneau looks at me strangely for a moment and then bursts out laughing. The scary gleam in her eye is gone, and I'm so relieved I put my head down on the steering wheel and try to calm the drum-machine staccato of my heart.

Finally I look up and see her sitting with her head leaned back against the headrest and eyes closed. "You did it," I say in awe. "You did magic."

"Conjured," she corrects me.

"Whatever."

49

JUNEAU

I SIT DOWN IN FRONT OF THE FIRE, SUDDENLY exhausted. I can barely believe it. I Conjured and did it without an amulet. And it didn't feel anything like the Reading and Conjuring I've done before.

I have always experienced a tingling sensation as I connected with the Yara. The adults who lived in a world of electricity before the war—before they secluded themselves from society—described the sensation of the Yara connection as feeling like a tiny electrical shock.

But when I Conjured a physical metamorphosis without use of the rabbit feet, I wasn't just connecting to the Yara. I wasn't merely tuning into the wavelength of all living things. I plugged myself directly in. Melded with it. I felt like every molecule of my being merged with the energy of the universe. This was no tiny shock. It was more like a lightning bolt.

I know I've finally done something right. Something true. And even though I have only done one Conjuring unaided by an amulet, I'm suddenly sure that my theory was right: all the stones, powders, and herbs Whit taught me to use are truly just props. Crutches. Like a stepladder to get to a height that I just leapt to without assistance.

I hear the car door shut and footsteps walk in my direction. Miles stands near me—but not too near—and lowers himself to sit facing the fire.

"I don't know what to say," he murmurs.

"You don't have to say anything. I just needed you to believe me."

He nods and wraps his arms around himself. After a moment he says, "So all those other things you told me about . . ."

"Everything I've told you has been true," I say. "When Frankie told me I had to be honest with you, I took that seriously. Which is why I'm here. You are the one who has to take me far."

Miles nods again and watches the fire. "What would happen if you tried on your own?" he asks, not looking at me.

"I'm guessing I probably wouldn't get the next sign that I need," I say. "Or I would make a vital mistake."

He tips his head and looks at me out of the corners of his eyes. There's something about his expression that tugs inside me. He looks . . . not scared but vulnerable. I realize that he prefers to be in control of the situation, and now I've put him in a position where he has no control at all. And no idea what to expect.

"Miles, it's not like I have magical powers or anything. I'm just more skilled than the rest of my clan."

He nods, pensive. "Okay, new subject: how are we going to go anywhere if the car is fried?"

"I think I can reverse it in the morning."

He looks back toward the fire. This conversation is difficult for him, I can tell. He closes his eyes, breathes deeply, and turns to look at me. "So what's the next step?"

"It's another prophecy you gave me. I haven't figured it out yet." I reach out to take his hand, but he pulls it away.

"Sorry. I'm too weirded out."

"So it was better when you thought I was insane?"

"Almost. Because at least there's an explanation for that. I thought you were delusional when you said you used me as your oracle. Did I really tell you things that turned out to be true?"

I nod. "At least I think so," I say. "Otherwise we're in the wrong place to figure out the next prophecy. And it wasn't exactly you who told me. You were just my channel to nature's collective unconscious."

"Please don't say that again," he says, eyebrows knit in concern. "Thinking of myself as a channel to anything is extremely freaky."

I stop myself from trying to touch him again. I want to comfort him. To tell him it's no big deal. But that would be wrong. It is a really big deal to him. And I need to give him time to process it. To give him space.

"I'm going to go to bed," I say. He glances up at me, and I read the look on his face like it's in flashing neon. "Don't worry. I'm not going to touch you," I say. "I won't ever do anything to you again . . . without your consent."

He nods and looks back at the fire.

I turn away from him, exhale, and walk toward the tent. I hope I won't need to.

50

MILES

I CRAWL INTO MY CORNER OF THE TENT, ALTHOUGH I'm sure I won't sleep tonight. I lie on my side and watch Juneau. She has the crossbow within hand's reach and sleeps on her side, curled in toward it. She looks like a totally normal girl, but she is anything but normal.

She says it's not magic. *Right,* I think, my chest constricting with fear as I remember the look on her face the second she disappeared. Not magic? Bullshit.

Suddenly, and randomly, I have this flashback to history class, when we learned about how afraid the Native Americans were when they saw the European explorers' rifles for the first time, calling them magical "fire sticks." Right now I feel like them: just because I don't understand the Yara doesn't mean it can't have a logical explanation. If I ever understand the mechanics of what she's doing, maybe I'll be able to accept it as merely a tool, the way she seems to.

It is in pondering these things that sleep tugs me like a current and pulls me under.

I awake to an empty tent. Pushing the flap outward, I see Juneau sitting with her back toward me. In her lifted hand she holds a small rock. And just below it is an egg-sized stone, which is floating in midair about a foot off the ground. Though I feel like retreating—closing the flap and hiding out in the tent—I push through and stand.

Hearing me, Juneau turns. "Good morning," she says, and then looks back to her floating rock as if it is nothing out of the ordinary. It slowly lowers until it's an inch off the ground, and then drops the rest of the distance with a soft thud.

I look around at the campsite. Something is missing, and for a moment I don't know what it is. "The bird," I say finally. "Where's Poe?"

"Gone," she says. "He was gone when I got up at dawn and hasn't come back."

"Do you think he went to Whit?" I ask.

"Either that or he got bored hanging around with us," she replies, but the way she presses her lips together shows she doesn't believe he would voluntarily leave.

I lower myself to sit near her by the burned-out campfire. "So what's the deal with the levitating rocks?"

"Practice," she says.

"Why? Seems like after last night's disappearing act, you definitely have your powers back."

"They aren't powers," Juneau insists. "Reading is making my will known to the Yara in order to get an answer. Conjuring is actually affecting the nature of something: making Poe want to find you, camouflaging myself, breaking your phone. But before leaving Alaska, I had barely done any Conjuring. So I'm experimenting."

"Whatever you say," I respond. "But let me ask you . . . why didn't you ever show me anything before, when you saw I didn't believe you?"

"Because you don't toy with the Yara. You only use it as a tool. For a purpose. At least, that's what Whit taught me. He would have thought it was being frivolous to use it just to prove myself."

"And your purpose in levitating a rock?" I ask skeptically.

"Maybe I don't care what Whit thinks anymore," she says, and there's the cold look in her eye again.

"You're going renegade?" I ask, daring to give a slight smile.

Juneau laughs. "Yes, actually. That's exactly what I'm doing. Tallie and I talked about it—about finding truth by taking only what you believe from your upbringing, leaving behind what doesn't work for you. So that's what I'm doing with the Yara. Last night I saw that I don't need the crutch of an amulet. That my link to the Yara is stronger without an object interfering with my connection. Now I just have to find out what I can actually do with the connection I have."

"Can I try?" I ask. She hands me the rock, and I hold it above the smooth stone. "What am I supposed to do?"

"I was Conjuring the elements in the stones so that they became magnetic."

I hand the rock back to her without trying. "Okay. I'm officially out-magicked."

"Like I said, it's a whole way of living, of thinking. I'm sure you could do this. It might just take a while."

"And eating Pop-Tarts for breakfast helps you be one with nature," I say, nodding to the empty foil wrappers near her feet.

"Like you said," she laughs, "I'm going renegade."

"Nothing against your balanced nutrition plan, but do you think we could go into town to get a real breakfast?"

Juneau stands. "Tallie and I passed a place on the way here last night."

"Um, I think we're both forgetting something important," I say, rising and brushing leaves off the back of my jeans. "The car. Fried by Invisigirl."

"I fixed it," she says. "At least, I think I did. You might as well try it out."

"What'd you do?" I ask, picturing her using her hands as jumper cables or performing some kind of automotive healing ritual.

"That's a good question. I don't understand the mechanics of a car. The connection through the Yara is a connection to nature's collective unconscious. I considered what force of nature could affect a car's engine, but not ruin it permanently, and decided I'd try humidity. I thought 'Make something important wet,' and the image that popped into my mind was these little cylinders, half-white, half-silver. I could see that electricity or sparks come off one end of them to help make the car go. So last night I asked the Yara to pull all the water in the surrounding air to their surface, and they stopped working."

"Those little cylinder things are called spark plugs," I say.

"Okay," she says, mentally filing away the term. "This morning I pictured them drying out. So it should work."

I shake my head in wonder. "Should I pack up the tent or leave it?" I ask.

"I'm hoping we'll figure out your last prophecy today," she says, spreading the ashes of the fire outward with her tennis shoe. "And if we do, we have to be ready to follow it immediately."

I begin pulling out the tent poles and folding them up. I can't help smiling to myself as I do. This camping thing is definitely more fun with Juneau around.

Ten minutes later, we're in the car. I turn the key in the ignition, and the engine fires right up. I glance over at Juneau and lift an eyebrow, impressed.

"Dry spark plugs," Juneau says, looking proud of herself.

I turn the car around and begin driving down the dirt path toward the main road. "So if you used water on the spark plugs, what did you use to fry my phone?" I ask.

"Fire," she replies. "It's funny you use the word 'fry,' because that's exactly what I pictured. I melted something inside."

"I am guessing you can't reverse that," I say, nodding to my iPhone under the dashboard.

"Nope," she confirms, tapping it with her fingernail. "As

amusing as it is to watch you play with it, you might as well throw it out."

A half hour later we sit in a booth at Ruth's Diner, eating stacks of buttermilk pancakes smothered in strawberries. Juneau's actually drinking a coffee, although she's transformed it into tan-colored sludge by adding almost a whole carton of half-and-half. She grimaces as she takes a swig.

"You don't have to drink coffee," I say. "Some people drink tea for breakfast. I mean, no one I know, but . . ."

"Trying to integrate," she says, one eye narrowed and her nose wrinkled in distaste. But I can tell her mind isn't on our breakfast beverages. Her thoughts are miles away. She sits there, zoned out for a moment, and then shakes her head.

"I just can't stop thinking about how the elders could lie to their own children for all those years."

"Instead of asking how, maybe you should ask why," I say. "I imagine that your elders were good people, and if they lied to you, there must be a reason."

"I've gone over so many scenarios in my mind already," she admits. "Their conviction about the harm that mankind is doing to the earth makes sense. I mean it's well founded. But why not just move us out to the middle of nowhere and tell us that's the reason? Why make up such an elaborate lie?"

"They didn't want you to leave," I suggest. "If they kept you in that small area of the country, they must have had a motive for why they didn't want you to come into contact with the rest of society. Like fear of persecution. Or a secret they felt they had to hide. And both of those could be reasons they would be kidnapped. Although kidnapping dozens of people is kind of extreme."

"The lies they told were pretty extreme too."

"True."

We both fall silent but something is nagging at me—pulling on the corner of my mind. "Okay," I say finally. "Why don't we start with something obvious? Like your 'starburst,' as you call it. Tell me more about that."

"All the children in our clan have them. They show our closeness to the Yara."

"But the elders are supposed to be near the Yara too, and they don't have them, do they?"

"No," she answers. "Their explanation was that we were the first generation of children to be born with complete immersion in the Yara. Children of Gaia—of the earth. They were all practicing it when they arrived in Alaska. And we were brought up knowing nothing else."

"Does that actually make sense to you?" I say, as gently as I can. Because it sounds like a total crock of shit to me.

"Now that I'm explaining it to you, and knowing that the elders lied about other things, no. It doesn't make sense. We just trusted that explanation because . . . why would we question something they told us?"

"If every single child born into the clan has the eye starburst, maybe your parents and their friends were all exposed to something in Alaska. Like radiation, or something in the water. But that's still strange, because why would they lie to you about it? I would think they'd try to figure out what happened and call it what it is: a genetic mutation." I hear the words come out of my mouth and then drop my fork and reach forward to grab her hand. "I mean, a nice genetic mutation, of course, not like you're freakish or anything."

She smiles halfheartedly and puts her other hand on mine to show she's not upset, before pulling her hands back to her lap.

"Is there anything else that is different about you?" I ask, picking up a piece of crispy bacon and biting off a big, greasy chunk.

"I've told you before, but you didn't believe me."

"Well, tell me again. Before, I was an ass. Now . . . well, I'm still an ass, but an ass who is willing to learn."

"Miles, we don't get sick. And we don't age."

I draw in a sharp breath, inhaling a chunk of bacon down my windpipe, and it takes me a couple of minutes and a glass of water to cough it back up and start breathing normally again. "I remember you saying that before," I finally squeak. "But at that point I thought you were schizophrenic. Could you repeat that?"

"We don't get sick. And we don't age."

"What do you mean, you don't age?"

"We grow to adulthood and then just don't get any older."

"And no disease?" I ask.

"No. I mean, people break bones and that kind of thing. It's not like we're supernatural. But we don't get ill."

I hesitate, and Juneau reads the question in my eyes. "My mother died when her sled broke through lake ice," she says, and looks down at the table.

I nod and wish I were sitting in the booth beside her so that I could hug her. From the lonely look on her face, I think she'd let me. "So I'm guessing the elders explained this immunity to disease and death by telling you it's from being close to the Yara," I say.

She doesn't answer.

And suddenly everything falls together in my mind. The realization of what this is all about hits me like a head-on collision. "Juneau," I say, and the urgency in my voice makes her look up at me. "I think we're getting somewhere with the 'Why were they kidnapped?' question. Don't get sick and don't age? Who wouldn't want a piece of that? My dad, for one, obviously."

"But it's not a drug, like you said he was looking for. It's a whole way of being. Of living." Juneau looks upset. Like reality is becoming clear to her as well.

"Living out in nature has nothing to do with health and aging," I prod.

"No? Eating well doesn't make you live longer? Clean air and water and growing and killing your own food doesn't make for better health?" Her voice is defensive, but her expression is pleading. She's still holding on to the "truth" she's been taught.

"Of course it does," I concede. "But, Juneau, one generation of healthy living doesn't wipe out disease, and definitely doesn't make you immortal. That is where your logical thinking stops and brainwashing kicks in."

Her eyes get all glittery, and she looks like she's about to cry. She closes her eyes and clenches her jaw. "I don't feel like talking about it anymore."

"That's okay. That's fine," I say, and fishing for something to change the subject, I say, "Hey. What about the riddle you hadn't figured out? What was it anyway?"

Juneau takes a deep breath and looks grateful for the switch of topic. "Your exact words were, 'You will go to the place you always dreamed of as a child.'"

"And?"

She shakes her head and begins playing with her napkin, folding it over and over into smaller and smaller squares. "It's impossible to figure out. I dreamed of going just about everywhere as a child. Except Salt Lake City, that is."

"Well, if under-the-influence me made the prophecy about the serpent and the lake, it must be a specific place here in Salt Lake City. Why don't we drive around and see if anything jogs your memory?"

"Good idea," Juneau says, and plops her origami napkin in the middle of the lake of maple syrup on her plate before standing to leave.

When we get to the car, she turns to me and in her solemn, grown-up way says, "Hey, Miles?"

"Yes, Juneau?" I respond.

"Thank you. For believing me. For wanting to help." Her lips curve into a smile and her eyes crinkle, and I want to hug her so badly, my arms ache. But she turns and opens her door. As she gets in she looks at me and says, "Just . . . thanks."

51

JUNEAU

WE'VE BEEN DRIVING IN CIRCLES AROUND THE city for the last hour. Miles keeps a sharp eye out for his father's security team, while I look for any place I could have dreamt of going as a child. Nothing is ringing a bell for me. Finally, Miles suggests that we get out of the car and walk. "We could park over by the library that I went to yesterday," he says.

And it clicks. "The library!" I say. "The library's the place I always dreamt of as a child."

"A library?" He looks astonished. "Out of everywhere in the world you could pick as a child, you wanted to go to a library."

"Where would you have picked?" I ask defensively.

"Disneyland," he admits.

I laugh. "Miles, in my childhood Disneyland wasn't an option. We had a hundred and thirty books in our clan. I know, because

I read every single one of them at least five times. I practically memorized *Moby-Dick*. Reading was the only way I was allowed to escape. And I wanted more. In the EB, I mean in our encyclopedia, there was this illustration of the domed reading room at the British Library, with books going up the walls so high that they had ladders to reach them. That was the place I dreamed of going."

"We're going to the British Library?" Miles looks worried.

"No. Oracle-you brought us to Salt Lake City, not to London," I remind him. "Whatever sign we're looking for or Reading I'm supposed to do, it's got to be in the Salt Lake City Library."

"You haven't seen the public library," Miles grumbles. "It's huge. We could spend weeks looking through all the books and find nothing."

We pull up to a massive glass-paned building in the center of town. "See?" says Miles. "How are we going to find anything in that . . . monument if we don't even know what we're looking for?"

"Well, hopefully we'll get a nudge from the Yara," I reply. "Otherwise, we could be looking around for a long time."

We walk into a huge atrium lined with shops and trees and topped with glass several stories up. Sunlight is streaming down, illuminating the entire interior of the building. Miles and I stand there gaping at the enormous, brightly lit foyer.

"Let's sit down," I suggest.

"Um, all right," he says, looking overwhelmed.

We walk over to a table under a potted tree, and the heat from the glass-filtered sun toasts my back as I take in the layout of the building. There are five floors, and it looks like the middle three hold most of the books. Winding staircases take people from one floor to the next. I look through the transparent walls of the ground floor toward the outside and see two big lake-like basins of water hugging the curve of the building.

"That's where we need to start," I say, pointing to the water. Standing, I lead Miles through another doorway and into the building's courtyard.

The water ripples green, reflecting the glass and concrete of the building. "What are you going to do?" Miles asks with the slightest hint of discomfort.

"I'm going to Read the water," I answer. "It's kind of like when I Read fire—I can get images from it, and it's good for finding hidden things."

Miles nods. "I'm just going to take your word for it."

I reach automatically for my opal and then remember that I don't need it. I loop the necklace over my head and hand it to Miles. "Could you hold this for me?" I ask.

"Anything to feel helpful," he says, and tucks it into his back pocket.

The simple fact of separating myself from the opal has made me feel strong. It's lit a flame of confidence in me, and I know without a doubt that I will be able to do this. I reach for the Yara, and my mind connects with it almost instantly, stunning me with its force.

I breathe out and focus on the surface of the water . . . on the reflection of the floors and floors of books, and my attention is caught by a flash of orange. I stare directly at it, and as I do, it is as if a magnifying glass is being held above the water, and the orange grows and becomes a book in a bookcase, its thick spine shining like a beacon in the glistening water.

Without breaking my gaze, I lean down and feel around at my feet until I'm grasping a small, flat stone. Turning slightly to the side, I flick my wrist and skip the stone across the surface of the water. "One, two," I count, and the stone veers off to the left before plunging into the depths of the basin.

I turn to Miles, who is watching me expectantly. "Three skips," I say. "It's on the third floor, left-hand side. A big book with an orange spine. Let's go!"

Miles looks bemused but says, "You're the boss!"

Taking his hand, I dash into the library entry. We sprint up two flights of stairs, and head down the corridor toward the shelves on the left. "Don't run," an elderly man chastises as I speed past, and I slow to a fast walk.

"It's probably near the window," I say, and lead him toward the glass wall. We begin going up and down the aisles, and then there it is, near the window reflected in the water three floors below.

"Over here, Miles," I say, but he's already arrived and is running his finger down a row of books.

"Okay," I say, and read the tag on the shelf aloud. "'Geography and Travel, North America, Southwest.'"

"No way," says Miles, and turns to me with this huge smile on his face. "The water led us to your Wild West!"

I slip the orange book out from its spot. "*Scenic Landscapes of New Mexico*," I read.

Miles runs his finger along the other spines. "The whole shelf's about New Mexico." He looks up at me, incredulous. "Due southeast of Seattle. You were right!"

I smile back. "Looks like we know where we're headed!"

Miles and I huddle over a U.S. road map that we pull from a neighboring shelf, and study the roads between Salt Lake City and New Mexico.

"A few of these smaller roads can get us to the Utah/New Mexico border, so we might as well head that way and I can try to Read again once we're there," I say. I look at the scale on the map and calculate. "It's about eight hundred miles to the farthest part of the state."

"That's about thirteen hours nonstop," Miles says.

"We are thirteen hours away from my father," I say, breathless with excitement. "Thirteen hours from my clan." And just as fast as it arrived, the excitement dissipates, leaving a feeling of despair. They tricked us, I remember for the thousandth time. It doesn't matter now, I remind myself. My goal is to find them and free them. We'll worry about explanations once everyone is safe.

Where will my clan even go if I can free them? I grab the box in my mind labeled "Open later" and shove all those thoughts inside. One step at a time. And the next step is getting out of Salt Lake City and as far away from our pursuers as possible.

We buy sandwiches in one of the ground-floor shops and take

them to the car with us to eat while driving. I can't wait another minute to get started. I have just thrown my pack into the backseat and placed our lunch on the dashboard when a hand grasps my arm. I look up into the face of someone more than twice my size—one of Whit's guards is towering over me. "You're coming with us," he says, and jerks me out of the car.

My brain is in shock, but my body takes over, and all the hours spent practicing brigand raids instinctively kick in. In a heartbeat, I've twisted my arm out of his grasp. Since he's tall, I aim high and kick him hard between the legs. He doubles over and stumbles back a few steps, giving me the time I need to grab my crossbow from the car's floorboard.

I load an arrow and fire, hitting him in the shoulder. I spin to see the Jeep parked around the corner. Whit is behind the wheel, but the second guard is coming toward me. I shoot him, landing an arrow square in his upper arm, and he lets out a howl of pain and stumbles back to the car. He pulls it out with one hand and grabs something in the backseat to stanch the bleeding.

And then I see the impossible happen. The first guard pulls the crossbow bolt out of his shoulder, looks at it curiously, and tosses it into the grass. No blood comes from under the hole it pierced in his shirt. He isn't even wounded, and I shot him from mere feet away.

He grabs my arm and sends my crossbow clattering to the ground. I struggle and kick, but he's much stronger than me and forces me toward the Jeep.

I see Miles standing next to his car, fear painted white across his face. Everything has happened within seconds, and he doesn't know what to do now that the guard has me in his grasp.

"You two will be coming with me," the guard says loudly enough for Miles to hear. "And no more scenes. Just close the door and follow me to my car."

"What makes you think I won't start screaming bloody murder?" I ask. I look around, but there's no one nearby. "Anyone coming out of the library would see you dragging me away and come help."

"Well, the fact that we know where your people are being held might change your mind about trying to draw attention," he grunts.

My eyes widen. So Whit does know where they are. Something deep inside me refused to believe it until now. I turn and see him sitting behind the wheel of the Jeep with his shock of black hair sticking up messily and the sunlight behind him, hiding his features. A blinding surge of hatred sweeps through me, and I know that if, in this moment, I had the chance to hurt him—or even kill him—I would.

"If I come with you, will you let him go?" I ask, gesturing to Miles with my head, since my arm is still in the guy's iron grip.

"I'm going wherever Juneau—" Miles starts to say, but the guard cuts him off.

"You're both getting in my car. Now."

We head toward the Jeep. The other guard is sitting in the backseat, wrapping a tourniquet around his arm and growling through clenched teeth. From behind the wheel, Whit is saying,

"I told you not to take her on." He leans over to open the passenger door from the inside and indicates I'm supposed to get in. "Juneau. Finally," he says.

"You don't want me to sit next to you," I manage to say. I have to force the words out, because Whit's sitting there looking like his same old self. The same man who mentored me for over a decade.

"Why not?" he asks, a fake smile plastered to his lips.

"Because I seriously doubt I'll be able to refrain from scratching your eyes out," I say evenly.

Whit pulls on an expression of false surprise. "No need for histrionics," he says. And then, lowering his voice, he urges, "Get in the Jeep." He glances down at a folded-up piece of paper sitting square in the middle of the passenger seat and raises an eyebrow, looking back up at me. "Get in! Now!" he yells.

All of a sudden, the sickening sound of crunching metal comes from behind the Jeep, and the vehicle lurches forward, its door springing away from me. As everyone swings around to see what happened, I scoop the paper from the seat and stuff it in my pocket.

"Sorry about that," comes a man's voice from the large black car that rear-ended the Jeep. "Let me get my insurance papers."

The guard drops me and heads for the reckless driver. As I turn to see who hit the Jeep, another man jumps out of the black car and heads straight for me. I recognize him. He's one of the guys who was trailing me around Seattle—he must work for Miles's dad. Before I can run, he's grabbed me around the chest and growled, "I've got a gun."

I turn frantically to look for Miles, but he's been pulled away by Whit's guard.

"Miles!" I scream. But my new captor has shoved me into the black car, the driver jumps back behind the wheel, and we take off just as Miles realizes what's happening. Away from Whit and his men. Away from Miles, who I watch running after us until it's clear that he'll never catch us.

Whit's guard is right behind him and, seizing him by the arm again, leads him back to the Jeep. We turn a corner, and they're gone.

52

MILES

THE GUY WHO GRABS ME HAS ARMS THE DIAMETER of a telephone pole. So guess what? I don't even fight. I let him drag me by the shoulder to the Jeep and stuff me in the passenger seat. He hops in the back and we're off.

There's a young guy driving. His hair is like Albert Einstein's if Albert dyed it with black shoe polish. He looks kind of crazy, but in a good way. Like your favorite science teacher at school—brilliant but hanging out in another dimension. He had exchanged a few words with Juneau, but I couldn't hear what they said.

The two guys in the back look like they were made from the same cookie cutter. Neckless boulders of steroid-fueled muscle. Both dressed in khaki, green, and camouflage like they think they're in the middle of a war zone. But the one is giving himself a shot in the arm and bandaging the wound Juneau gave him, and the other is unbuttoning his shirt to inspect the dent Juneau made in his Kevlar vest.

I taste copper in my mouth and realize that I'm scared. And then it occurs to me that I'm not afraid of them. I'm scared for Juneau. I don't think that Portman and Redding will hurt her, but these guys look rough. I wouldn't be surprised if they were wearing weapons strapped under their flak jackets.

We pull up to a fork in the road, and the driver looks both ways. There's no sign of Juneau and her captors. They had too much of a head start: we've lost them. He pulls over onto the sidewalk next to a Dairy Queen and puts the Wrangler in park. "Where'd they take her?" he asks, turning to me.

There's something off about his eyes. Like one of his pupils is slightly facing the wrong way. It freaks me out because I don't know which eye to look at.

"No clue," I respond, and receive a cuff on the side of my head from one of the GI Joes behind me.

"Ow!" I yell, and swing around to stare at him.

"Answer the man's questions," he says in a thick voice, like his tongue's on steroids too.

"I'm being honest. I have no clue who those guys are or where they could be taking Juneau," I lie, looking at Einstein's right eye.

"You're the one I saw camping with her," he says.

What? We didn't see anyone else when we were camping, I think, and then all of a sudden I get it. He used the bird to see us. This must be Whit.

But how can it be? This guy's in his midtwenties. Thirty, max.

As if reading my mind, he says, "I'm Whittier Graves. I've known Juneau since she was a baby. And I need your help to find her. She could be in grave danger."

The men in the back chuckle like Whit's cracked a really good joke, and he glances back at them, exasperated.

"You can't be Whit. Juneau told me about him, and he's some old guy."

"Good guess. Fifty-three. So I suppose Juneau hasn't told you all our secrets."

And then it hits me. The no-aging thing. I believed her, as much as I could, when she told me this morning. But here's the proof, sitting right in front of me. I have no question now that what this guy's got is what my dad is after: whatever's keeping him young.

No wonder he's after Juneau. And no wonder someone invaded her village. An antiaging drug could make its owner a fortune.

I ask myself just what my dad would do to get his hands on it. How far would he go if he could be the richest man on earth? All of a sudden I no longer trust Redding and Portman with Juneau's safety.

53

JUNEAU

WHEN WE'RE FINALLY FORCED TO STOP BECAUSE of traffic, I try to slip up the door lock, but it's frozen in place. "Child safety locks," says the driver, who is bald and wearing sunglasses.

"Who are you?" I ask, knowing exactly who they are but wondering what else I can find out.

"We are your escorts to Blackwell Pharmaceutical. Mr. Blackwell has something he wants to chat with you about."

"So you're just going to kidnap me and drive me to L.A.?" I ask defiantly.

"No," the man in the backseat says. I turn to look at my other captor. He's got a brown crew cut and thick neck, and his clothes look too small. He sees me looking and puts two fingers inside his collar to loosen his tie. "We're not driving you to L.A. You get the special princess treatment." He glares at me as Baldy pulls into the Salt Lake City airport. "We've been looking for you for days," he says, as if I have been hiding expressly to piss them off.

"That's not my fault," I say.

"Well, it doesn't make me like you more," he says.

We pull into an isolated section of the airport with signs for PRIVATE: CHARTER AIRCRAFT, and drive straight up to a tiny plane with BLACKWELL PHARMACEUTICAL painted on the side. My stomach drops, and I feel all the blood leave my face. I'm going up in the air. In an airplane. Oh Gaia.

Baldy clicks the unlock button, and we all get out of the car. "Don't bother running," he says, opening his jacket to show a gun holstered across his chest. *They need me. They're not going to shoot,* I think, and take off running across the pavement. I am immediately tackled from behind.

Baldy slaps handcuffs on my wrists and pulls me writhing to my feet. The heels of my hands are scraped raw, and my elbows and knees sting from my collision with the concrete.

"Got a live one," he chuckles to Necktie, but he's red and panting with exertion.

I take a deep breath and try to look calm. "You guys are going to feel pretty stupid when you take me to Mr. Blackwell and I tell him I don't know anything about a drug formula."

"Not our problem," says Baldy, and puts a hand on my back, steering me toward the plane. There's nothing I can do but go with them. I consider metamorphosis, but that only lasts a few minutes, and there's nowhere out here to hide once I'm visible again.

I grasp for straws . . . I could try to call any animals in the vicinity. I glance around at the barren landscape. Nothing to work with. *I could try to Conjure a strong wind,* I think, but before I can form a plan, I am walking up the stairs toward a man in a pilot uniform who steps aside to let us board.

"Didja get my message?" Baldy asks him.

"Yes. Ready to go," the pilot confirms. I am trying to control my shaking, but my bowels are twisting and I feel like I'm going to be sick. And we haven't even left the ground.

Planes were one of the evils of society that Dennis taught us about. They polluted the air and gobbled fossil fuels. In the Seattle newspapers, I saw the term "carbon footprint." If Dennis had known that term, he would have used it.

I saw pictures of planes in the EB. I know that the pilot sits in the cockpit, in the front of the plane. That the passengers sit behind in rows. But this plane only has six seats, and they look more like overstuffed armchairs, all grouped around tables. I stand there, not knowing what to do, and Necktie points to one of the chairs. "You sit there," he says, and pushes me down into a cream-colored seat that smells like new leather. As soon as the pilot closes and locks the door, Necktie produces the key to my cuffs. "You can't go anywhere now, but you can be a pain in the ass. Tell me you won't, and I'll uncuff you."

"I won't," I say, but only because I haven't yet thought of a plan.

I'm not sure what to do once I'm uncuffed, but I watch Necktie pull seat belts up from the sides of his chair and click them together, and I begin to do the same. And then I remember something and unclick the belt. "I need to go to the bathroom," I say.

"She needs to go to the bathroom," he yells to Baldy, who has stuck his head through the cockpit door and is talking to the pilot. The sound of the plane's roaring engine and spinning propellers is deafening.

"Well then, let her go to the bathroom," Baldy shouts back, shooting him a *what are you, stupid?* look.

"It's back here," Necktie says, and standing again, leads me to a door in the back, stationing himself just beside it, thumbs through his belt loops as he waits.

"Are you going to wait here by the door while I pee?" I ask, raising my chin. Daring him.

He looks offended. "No!" And he sits back down in his seat.

I squeeze into the toilet, find the door lock and pull it over, and then fish in my pocket for the paper that Whit left for me. It's a page torn from a map. Printed across the bottom is ". . . w Mexico." About an inch above Roswell—in the middle of nowhere—is a circle drawn in blue ink. And at the bottom of the page, in handwriting that I know as well as my own, Whit has written, "Things aren't as they seem."

54

MILES

"IS JUNEAU IN DANGER WITH THOSE MEN?" WHIT asks.

I cross my arms defensively and stare at him.

"Are you and the men who took her working for Blackwell Pharmaceutical?" he asks, and something in my expression must be giving it away, because he nods like he's thinking, *I knew it!* One of the guards in the backseat shuffles uncomfortably.

"Since when does Murray Blackwell hire teenagers to do his dirty work?" he prods.

I don't say a word. I just give him my *eat shit and die* look. But it doesn't seem to be working on him because he just gives me an astonished look, like he read my mind and knows exactly who I am. And then I notice that his hand is positioned over the gear-shift so that his fingers are lightly touching my jacket.

"You were Reading me!" I say.

"What on earth are you talking about?" Whit protests, but something in his eyes tells me that's exactly what he was doing.

"Come on, let's get this show on the road," urges Thick-tongue from behind me.

Whit puts the Jeep in gear, and I scrabble to pull up the door lock while yanking on the handle. *It's already unlocked!* I manage to think before I tumble out the door, landing hard on the sidewalk and sending a shock wave of pain through my right shoulder. Rolling to my hands and knees, I leap forward and make a run like mad for the Dairy Queen.

I hear swearing behind me, but don't dare look as I sprint across the parking lot and in through the glass door. I push it closed behind me and see Thick-tongue stop mid-run as Whit yells something at him. The burly guard turns his head and gives me a scorching glare, pointing his thumb and index finger at me like a gun. He shoots. And then he turns and stalks back to the Jeep. They drive off in a screech of rubber, leaving skid marks on the sidewalk.

"May I help you?"

I swing around to see a teenage girl standing behind a cash register. I stick my hand in my pocket and pull out my cash. Juneau paid for our uneaten lunch, so I still have change. "What can I get with a dollar twenty-nine?" I ask.

"Water," she says snippily.

I look back at the street. They're definitely gone, although who knows if they're just turning around to come back for me. I have two choices: hang out drinking water in Dairy Queen in case they come back, or risk it and make the trek back to my car.

"That's okay," I say. "Not thirsty."

She rolls her eyes, and I walk out the door.

A twenty-minute walk later and I'm amazed to see that my keys are still on the ground where I dropped them when Portman and Redding smashed into the Jeep. Our lunch is still sitting in the bag on the dashboard where Juneau had set it. And Juneau's pack is still in the backseat.

I've got this Tabasco-hot anxiety burning in my chest, but it quickly turns into anger as I think of Dad's men snatching Juneau. They better not lay a finger on her. I'm comforted by the knowledge that Dad will treat her well as long as he thinks she can help him. But knowing her, she won't be very helpful. Even if she knows the formula or technique or whatever it is that they use to stay young, there's no way in hell she's going to give it to him.

I think of her face when she's angry and can't help but smile. I wouldn't want to be my dad before a wrathful Juneau. If Portman and Redding are taking her to L.A., like I imagine they are, she's going to be majorly pissed off. Her goal right now is New Mexico, and the longer Dad keeps her from it, the angrier she's going to get.

But my frown returns when I think of my father and how cutthroat he is when he can't get something he wants. He's got a whole corporation, money, and manpower behind him. And what does she have? Her earth magic. I start the car and buckle in. There's going to be a major face-off in L.A., and I need to be there to stop it.

As I pull out of my parking space, something black lands on my car and blocks my view through the windshield. I hit the brakes and see that it's Poe, wings spread wide as he flaps to get my attention. I unbuckle and jump out of the car. "What the hell are you doing here?" I say, and then realize. "You led Whit here, didn't you? You . . . you traitor!" The bird squawks and struts across my hood to look me in the eye.

I know Poe was just an unwitting tool, but I still want to strangle his little feathered neck.

"Why don't you make yourself useful and go find Juneau?" I say. He leans his head to one side, as if considering my question. Then he squawks loudly and flies off to the north—the opposite direction of where Juneau's being taken. I'm obviously not "close enough to the Yara" to use him as a messenger raven.

I climb back into the car. How did I ever get involved in this mess? Oh yeah. Dad. Dad's greed. And a girl who may or may not be holding the secret to a drug for immortality.

I shake my head and try to find a radio station. Country and oldies are all I'm picking up. It's going to be a long drive to L.A.

55

JUNEAU

I FLUSH THE MAP DOWN THE PLANE'S TOILET after memorizing exactly where the circle is drawn. I wash the grit off my scratched hands and pat my bloody knees with a wet wad of toilet paper. And then I make my way out to my chair and strap myself in. Necktie is watching my every move. I trade him a scowl for his leer, and he picks up a magazine so he doesn't have to look at me.

And then we're moving. Baldy comes back and takes the seat across from me, strapping himself in as we begin to taxi down the runway. I want to throw up. I have never left terra firma. *Be strong,* I urge myself. *Don't show any weakness.* I cross my arms over my chest and close my eyes, like I'm settling in for a nap. Squinting with one eye, I see that the men are both engrossed in sports magazines and no longer watching me.

I have been thinking about what I could do to stop the plane. *Does a plane have spark plugs?* I think. But the fear that I would do something that would kill us all keeps me from trying a Conjure with the engine.

I turn to look out the window just as we are lifting off the ground at a slow incline. Parting with earth. Joining the sky. When I think of airplanes, I think of bombs being dropped from them. Missiles travel by air. Nuclear weapons are delivered by air. The mushroom clouds and green haze of radiation that have populated my nightmares since I was a little child explode like an apocalyptic Fourth of July before my eyes, and I can't help but shudder.

I dig my fingernails into my palms and try to calm myself. And suddenly we're in the midst of the clouds, traveling through a fog. No visibility. Just when I think I see something flickering to one side of us and wonder if brigands could have hijacked an army plane, we burst through the cloud and are floating above a sea of soft cotton. And I remember that there was no World War III. That this airplane I am in right now, this destination I am hurtling toward, are all a part of a functioning, modern world.

56

MILES

IT'S A LONG SIX HOURS FROM SALT LAKE CITY TO Vegas. I've given up on the radio and already sang all the songs I knew with the window down. (Somehow my voice doesn't sound as bad that way . . . not that I would dare sing a note if anyone was within hearing distance.) So the only thing I have to do, after finishing my third rendition of "Sweet Home Alabama" (complete with instrumental guitar noises), is think.

And man, my brain is racing around, trying to make sense of what has happened to me over the last week. I try to remember everything that Juneau told me about her past, about Yara, and about her "earth magic," as I've come to think of it. But it's hard to recall most of it, mainly because I was so sure she was spouting crap that I was only half listening.

They don't grow old. They don't get sick. The kids all have

those star things in their eyes. They cut themselves off from the rest of the world three decades ago. They believe in this thing called the Yara, which allows for transfer of knowledge between anything in nature. And which also allows nature to be manipulated.

And . . . there's something her clan's got that powerful people want bad enough to kidnap them and hunt down Juneau.

Everything makes sense now. Juneau's sullenness, her self-protectiveness, her weird reaction to anything modern . . . anything created in the last thirty years. It's got to be hard for her, knowing that the people she always respected have lied to her for her whole life. And now she's risking her own safety to find them.

I think about what I would do if my father were in trouble: how far I would go to rescue him. I can't really imagine it. But with a pang the size of Texas, I know in an instant that if she let me, I would do anything to save my mom. And that certainty helps me understand Juneau's fierceness in her will to reach her goal. She's tough. Determined. But she's just one girl up against at least two powerful factions, including my dad and his multibillion-dollar corporation.

Although I try to stop it, my mind insists on wandering back to the night I kissed her in the tent. I feel my pulse pick up as I remember the softness of her mouth, the surprise and then acknowledgment in her eyes, the weight of her body on mine. I've probably kissed a dozen girls. But none of them were like that kiss.

Juneau is different. She makes me want to be a better person.

My heart falls when I remember the look on her face when I told her the reasons I was kicked out of school. I want to be someone she respects. Admires. But in order for that to happen, I'm going to have to change. To become stronger. As strong as her.

It's 9:00 p.m. when I reach the WELCOME TO LAS VEGAS sign. The only stop I made was for gas and supplies. I used Dad's Shell card to stock up on a square meal of Cokes, Rolos, pretzels, and chips, which was all they had at the service station. And when I tried to collect-call Dad, he didn't pick up the phone. I push aside the heavy feeling in my gut. There's nothing I can do from this far away at night.

I drive down Miracle Mile past all the flashing lights and continue on until I'm out of town. My eyes are closing by themselves when I decide I can't go farther. I pull the car well off the road and am so exhausted that I lie down in the front seat, draping my coat over myself, and within seconds I am dreaming.

Juneau is walking toward me through a snowy winter landscape, an ice-capped mountain behind her. She is wearing furs, and thick black hair hangs halfway down her back. A small box is nestled in the palms of her hands, and out of the open top, light pours out. Golden light, as if daylight were transformed into liquid. It spills in pools around her feet as she walks, but does not touch her. My heart skips around like a mad cricket in my chest. Juneau is no longer angry, defensive, bitter. She is beautiful and serene. She smiles as she nears me and stretches her hands forward as if offering me the box.

The liquid sunlight spills onto my feet and burns me as it

slowly travels upward—up my legs—and climbs, inching toward my torso. The burning becomes severe, and I cry out, but I'm paralyzed and can't move. Now the gold has spread across my chest and has seized me by the neck. I sputter, but I can't inhale: it is strangling me.

Juneau's expression has shifted from serenity to compassion. "Miles," she says, though her lips don't move. "You are one with the Yara."

I am on fire. A golden statue alight, flames licking around me, melting the snow into puddles at my feet, heating Juneau's face and reddening her nose and cheeks. She leans in closer until her lips are touching mine. And as she kisses me I disperse into a million tiny flames, sparks flying up into the cold winter air and diffusing once they hit the starry night sky.

I open my eyes and glance at the dashboard clock. Three a.m. I lie there stunned by dream hangover and fatigue until I finally sit up and buckle myself in. I start the car and continue toward Los Angeles, spending the remaining four hours thinking about Juneau.

57

JUNEAU

LANDING IS TEN TIMES SCARIER THAN TAKEOFF. The ground grows closer and closer and we are going so fast, I am sure as soon as we touch ground the impact will rip off the bottom of the plane. Instead, with a sort of pulling tension, we land smoothly and taxi around large loops of runway as we slow. Finally we stop near a long black car that looks like it could easily fit twenty people inside.

Baldy slaps the handcuffs back on me, and I am shuffled quickly from the recycled air of the plane through the stifling hot oven of the runway and into the pine-scented frigid air inside the car. Although I spent most of the plane trip coming up with escape plans, my curiosity has gotten the best of me. Somehow, Miles's dad knows something about my clan that I don't. Or at least he thinks he does. And I'm determined to find out what he knows.

So I don't give the men any trouble this time and climb willingly into the car. We spend most of the next hour sitting stationary on the road, with hundreds of other cars, inching forward from time to time. Again, I think of Dennis and his mournful tone when he talked about pollution.

At last we reach a downtown area, which has the same forest of glass buildings as the other cities, all perched next to the sea. The car stops outside the tallest of these mirrored buildings. Baldy acts like he is helping me out of the car but actually uses the gesture to get a firm grip on my upper arm as he leads me over the simmering-hot sidewalk through the front doors.

I have seen these skyscrapers from the outside but, besides the Salt Lake City Library, which was small in comparison, have never been in one. I wasn't even tempted to in Seattle. The giant glass plinths look more like tombstones than a space where people would work and live.

We walk through an immense cavern of an entryway into the tiny mirrored space of an elevator. I feel my stomach drop to my toes as we shoot to the highest levels of the building, moving as quickly upward as we would be if we were free-falling downward.

Lights flicker on a wall panel until the very last button, 73, lights up. A bell rings, and the doors open. My head swims, and although a man stands directly in front of us, waiting for us with hands clasped behind his back, all I can focus on is the window behind him. We are so high that the world is a tiny toyscape laid out in miniature as far as the eye can see. My legs refuse to hold me any longer. I sink down to the ground, my hands still cuffed behind me, and use every remaining bit of willpower not to throw up.

"What have you done to her?" the man says, and strong arms lift me and carry me through a door into an office.

"She tried to run," Baldy says as he deposits me onto a white leather couch and unlocks the handcuffs. Necktie runs to a shelf lined with bottles and pours one into a glass.

I lift it to my mouth. Water. Just water. But it tastes so good, and is the only natural thing in the room besides a large treelike plant near the window. *Oh Gaia, the window,* I think, and my stomach churns.

"Leave us," the man says, and Baldy and Necktie make a quick exit, pulling the door softly behind them like it's made of spun sugar. The man scoots a chair close to the couch, and when our eyes meet, I see Miles in thirty years: still-thick but graying hair cut short and carefully combed, aquiline nose, and dark-green eyes.

"Are you okay?" he asks.

"Why did you bring me here?" My throat is clenched so tightly, my words come out in a croak.

"I brought you here because you have some information that I need," he says simply. His expression is solicitous. He doesn't look like what I expected—I thought I'd find a tyrant. Someone willing to use torture to get what he wants. But this is just a middle-aged man in a business suit.

I glance around the room and see, to my horror, that there are no actual walls: We are surrounded by windows. The granite floor is strewn with intricately woven rugs, and tasteful furniture is positioned around the room to make it appear more like a living space than a place of business.

"I can't . . . I can't be this high up," I say, clutching my stomach.

"Let me close the blinds," he responds, and walking to a desk, picks up a little black box and clicks a few buttons on it. The windows automatically begin darkening, while the lights of the room become brighter until we are in an enclosed space and I can no longer see the frightening view outside.

I close my eyes and try to slow my breathing. After a moment, I open them and see that he's sat back down in the chair in front of me. "My name is Murray Blackwell," he says, leaning forward, his hands clasped together. He stares at my starburst. A muscle under his eye twitches, and his jaw clenches and unclenches. "And your name is . . . ," he prods.

"I'm Juneau," I say, and take another sip of the water. I have to decide how much I'm going to talk. His movements are graceful. But the more I watch him, the more I notice something in his eyes—something cold—that doesn't match his body's lithe gestures. He's like a snake, smooth but poisonous.

He is dangerous, I think. I can't trust him, but I'll tell him as much as I need to find out what he's after.

"Juneau . . . ," he says like a question, and waits.

"Yes?" I ask. My brows knit in confusion. I don't recognize

his body language. He could be speaking Swahili for all I understand.

"Juneau what?" he asks.

I stare at him.

"Your last name," he says finally.

I exhale. "Oh! Newhaven," I respond. Everyone in the clan knows one another's last names, but we never use them except in ceremonies, and I've never actually had someone ask mine.

"Juneau Newhaven, you are from . . . ," he asks, and this time I respond automatically.

"Denali, Alaska."

He nods, acknowledging the fact that I'm playing along with his game.

"Good, good," he says. And then leaning farther forward, so his elbows are on his knees, he asks softly, "That means, I suppose, that you know a man by the name of Whittier Graves?"

I gasp, not even trying to hide my surprise.

"Yes, you do know him," he says with a jolly smile, like we're sharing a joke. "Well, I'm glad to hear it. I've been wanting to talk to him for the last few weeks, but it seems like he has disappeared. Along with the rest of your—what did he call it?—your clan."

Facts start pinballing around in my head. This man knows of Whit. He knows about our clan, and where we live. He knows enough about me to have me followed.

Instead of launching my own questions, I wait quietly to hear what other details this man will give away.

"Mr. Graves approached me about a drug he and some

colleagues developed some time ago. He called it Amrit. Does that sound familiar to you?"

I shake my head no.

"I expressed interest in purchasing the formula for Amrit. Even offered to come to Alaska to visit your clan and see how his field study had gone. Mr. Graves refused, insisting on personally bringing me the data. We made an appointment to meet here a month ago. Mr. Graves did not show. As you can imagine, that had me worried."

Mr. Blackwell leans back in his chair and crosses his arms across his chest with a pained expression, like it's difficult for him to tell me this story. But from my study of human facial expressions and body language, I see anger behind his careful words.

And he is watching me as carefully as I watch him: studying my face for any change of expression. Seeking any clues he can gather from my reactions. I relax my facial muscles and, leaning back in the armchair, do the same with the rest of my body. I already gave away the fact that I know Whit. I don't want to accidentally give him anything else.

"I sent some men to Alaska to try to find him. We had a clue of where he was. Traced the calls he made by GPS to a cave near Denali, where they found residue from a recent fire."

I can't help it—my eyes widen, and I suck my breath in. This man tracked us down to our territory. He knew where we were.

Mr. Blackwell raises an eyebrow—he's curious. In my surprise at hearing him describe Whit's cave, I gave something away. The edges of his lips move upward just a millimeter, but he readjusts his poker face and continues.

"A tracker I hired followed a path from the cave to an abandoned village some miles away. Twenty or so yurts. Lots of dead dogs killed by gunshot. A few farm animals, chickens, goats, and pigs, wandering wild in the ruined encampment and the woods nearby."

He comes to a stop and waits for me to say something. I formulate my question carefully.

"Why would you come after me—one of the clan children—if Whit . . . Mr. Graves is the one with the information you need?"

"I was told by a reliable source that you are Mr. Graves's understudy—that he is your mentor. I was told that if I couldn't find him, you may be able to help me. That, in fact, you were indispensable. I don't know if Mr. Graves went directly to one of my competitors, but I certainly won't lose both of you to another drug company."

"How did you know I wasn't with the rest of my clan?"

"A tip from the same credible source," he says, and then sits silently again, waiting.

"Exactly what information are you trying to get?" I ask.

"As I mentioned before—the chemical makeup of the drug Amrit," he says. "The formula for the drug."

"See, that is what confuses me—what I haven't understood since I overheard Miles talking to you. My clan doesn't make drugs! We don't use any kind of medicine besides first aid!" I say, trying to steady the anger in my voice. "I have no idea what you're talking about."

"Oh, but I think you do," Mr. Blackwell shoots back. "Tell me something. Are there others in your clan with the same iris deformation you have?"

Through all the rage and frustration and betrayal, I am beginning to feel something new. A genuine interest as to what the hell is going on.

"All the children have the starburst," I respond, raising my chin to show him that he can't bully me into telling him anything I don't want.

He nods, considering what I've said. "A drug as strong as Amrit is capable of producing this severe of a genetic abnormality . . . maybe 'mutation' is a nicer way to say it—in the offspring of those who take it. Mr. Graves was very vague with the details, but did mention the necessity to develop the drug further in order to avoid severe aftereffects. I see now what he means."

"Our starbursts are from being close to—" I stop myself before I tell him anything about the Yara.

"Being close to what?" he prods. "A nuclear testing site? A water source containing biohazardous materials? There are other things capable of causing a genetic mutation like yours, but I don't believe it for a second. I think your parents and their friends took Amrit as a part of a test, and now their children bear its mark."

As I listen to him, something tugs deep inside me. I suddenly think of Tallie and of how she urged me to think of what I learned from my past and weigh it against what I feel is right. And though I don't want to believe a word this man is telling me, something about his theory rings true.

And then everything falls together and then falls apart and I can't think, can't talk, can't move, can't breathe, as the fictional pieces of my past begin flashing before my eyes and re-form themselves into facts.

A loud buzzing rings in my ears, and my vision is gradually reduced until the blackness around me is as dark as a cave. I can't move. I'm no longer here.

I hear Mr. Blackwell's voice, as if from a long ways away. "Ms. Newhaven? Are you okay? Ms. Newhaven?" Someone is patting me—lightly slapping my face. I hear a voice say, "Quickly. Send a doctor to my suite. I have a visitor who is having some sort of attack. A teenage girl. Make it fast."

58

MILES

I PULL INTO MY DRIVEWAY AT 7:00 A.M. DAD'S CAR is there, along with another I don't recognize. I leave all my crap in the car and march through the front door yelling, "I'm home! Where is she?"

I gave up trying to call my dad after Vegas, and knew he wouldn't answer in the middle of the night. But judging from the car outside, he's home, and if he's not awake, I'm ready to do the honors.

No one's in the sitting room, so I stride on through the double doors into the open kitchen area. A wall of windows at the far side of the room overlooks Holmby Hills. My dad sits in a chair, gazing out as he sips a cup of coffee. This in itself should warn me that something's wrong. Dad never relaxes. Never takes in the view. Normally he drinks his coffee while walking out the door and would be halfway to his office by now.

"Dad," I say, and he turns around and looks at me, genuinely surprised.

"Miles. You came home." He stands and moves toward me.

"Yeah, after your cronies snatched Juneau right from under me, I figured I should probably make my way back." I take another step toward him so that we are an arm's length away from each other, staring eye to eye since we're practically the same height.

"What. Have. You. Done. With. Her?" I ask, each word a challenge.

"What does it matter to you?" Dad quips, and setting down his cup, puts his hands in his pockets.

"I care about her," I say. Fuck explanations. Fuck Dad's expression now that he looks like the cat that ate the canary. I'm done tiptoeing around him, hoping he'll approve of me. Wanting him to act like a real dad for once instead of a CEO who happens to have a teenage boy living under his roof. Wishing he'd say something . . . anything . . . about Mom. It's like she never existed. But all that is in the past, because there's someone else I care about now, and he's the only one who can tell me where she is.

"Juneau is in one of the guest bedrooms," he says. "She's being taken care of by a medical assistant." He crosses his arms as if daring me to challenge him.

"What happened?" I yell, taking a step closer to him. "What did you do to her?"

He backs up and puts his hand on my shoulder to keep me from bulldozing into him. "All I did was have a little chat with her. Unfortunately, I seem to have brought up something that distressed her. Greatly. She has been receiving sedatives throughout the night, and a nurse has stayed on call in her room in case she tries to hurt herself."

"Juneau would never hurt herself. All she wants is to save her family."

"So after a few days with her, you think you know her?" he retorts.

"Better than you do, obviously," I say. "When I talk to her, she doesn't have a breakdown."

"Sometimes stating the facts as directly as possible is the best way to make someone respond," he says. "To shake their answer loose."

"Looks like that worked real well for you," I say, narrowing my eyes.

My dad gets a supremely pissed look on his face, and then exhales deeply and shades his eyes with his hand. "Why don't you go talk to her then, Miles? She won't speak to me anymore. She won't even look at me. I have no doubt she has the formula for Amrit stored somewhere in her head. Somewhere she doesn't even know, because she didn't realize what it was. We need to get her comfortable with us. We need her to trust us, so that she will talk."

I hate my dad in this instant. This is the business side of him, willing to negotiate anything to get what he wants. His human side gets turned off until his bid is successful, and then—maybe—he acts like a real, caring person again. Well, you know what? I can do the same.

"What'll you give her back if she talks? Will you pour all your resources into helping her find her family?" I ask.

"Every resource I have," he promises, and looks so sincere that I have to look hard to see that twitch at the corner of his eye that says he's lying.

I pause for a second, searching for what to say. I have to make him think I believe him. "Thank you. That's the only thing she wants. I'll see if I can get her to share any information, Dad. I'm sure she'll talk to me."

"Good boy," Dad says, clapping me on the shoulder. "Any details. Anything at all could be valuable, even if she doesn't realize it. Just . . . well, be careful, son. You can't even imagine how much she is worth to us."

Loathing rolls off me in black waves, but Dad keeps his positive-outlook face on until I leave the room. There are so many things I would like to say to him. To hurt him. But I bite my tongue and walk to the "guest room" to see what, if anything, I can do.

Nothing has changed in my mother's room since she left. She and Dad shared a room until she was hospitalized the first time. He moved out. And then she left. My heart is in my throat. I have avoided coming in here for the last year.

But there, lying in a tiny lump under the covers, crowned with her black spiky hair and a sickly pale face, is Juneau. The nurse is reading a paperback in a chair on the far side of the room, but when she sees me, she stands.

"My father wants me to talk to her," I whisper to the woman.

She nods and lets herself out, leaving the door open. I close it and carefully sit down next to Juneau on the bed. I want to touch her but don't know how she'll react. "Juneau," I say, and her eyes flutter open. "It's me, Miles," I say. "Are you okay?"

She bites her lip and shakes her head no.

"What happened?" I ask. "What was it that my dad said to upset you?"

She closes her eyes and lets out an exhausted sigh. "Your father basically suggested that my starburst—and those of the other children in my clan—is a genetic anomaly. A mutation caused by our parents taking some sort of strong drug. The drug he's looking for. 'Amrit,' he calls it."

"And what do you think about that?" I ask carefully. Her eyes are brimming with tears. She wipes them away with her knuckle and sighs again.

"It makes a lot of sense," she says finally. "Which means it's just more proof of the web of deceit that's been spun around us since we were born. I am the product of deception. My whole life has been a carefully formulated and maintained lie. Your dad inferred that I and the rest of the clan were part of a 'field study' that Whit was running for the drug."

I don't know what to say, so I take her hand and hold it between mine. It's cold, and I rub it between my palms as she continues.

"I had begun figuring out what from my past I thought was true," Juneau says. "But after what your father said yesterday, I don't know what to think. It put me back at square one. I'm totally lost again. Worse than before."

She closes her eyes.

"How are you feeling, physically? Think you're strong enough to walk?"

Juneau's eyes pop open. "Why?"

"Because I have a promise I need to keep," I say. "Something about getting you to the Wild West so you can find your family, if I recall correctly. Even if your dad and the others lied to you, they're still your family. They still need to be found."

A light goes back on behind Juneau's empty eyes, and a smile blooms on her lips. She leans toward me, and I take her in my arms for a hug while she nestles her head against my neck. After a long moment, she pushes back a little so she can look at my face, and traces it with her fingertips, running her fingers lightly over my eyes, nose, and lips.

We're so close that I can feel her warm breath on my face, and then she lifts her head slightly so that our lips meet. And she kisses me. Her skin is so soft, it's like brushing my mouth against flower petals. I taste her and she tastes like the lemon drops that the nurse has set by the bed in a bowl.

This kiss isn't urgent and needy like the last one. It's a slow kiss that promises more to come. Which is exactly what I want: more Juneau. More time.

"We need to get you out of here," I say finally, forcing myself to pull away from her embrace.

"I was hoping you'd say that," she says.

"I am going to tell my father that you were too tired to talk," I say. "That I can try again in a few hours."

I start to get up, and she squeezes my hand to stop me. "Miles?"

I raise an eyebrow, waiting. Keeping a totally straight face, she says, "Even though you make a crappy fire and wouldn't survive more than ten minutes in the wilderness, there isn't anyone I'd rather be with at a time like this. You're my desert island friend." And she grins.

I laugh. "Even though you could probably kill me in fifteen different ways with a table fork, and even though you barbecue bunnies, I like you, too, Juneau. So let's get our butts to New Mexico."

"A very good plan," she says. I stand and lean over the bed and kiss her forehead. She gives me her crooked mouth-closed smile, and I feel a rush of relief. She's going to be okay.

My dad is waiting in the den, wearing his "caring father" expression. "Did she tell you anything?" he asks expectantly.

He probably thinks I can't see through his act. Well, I learned my lying skills from the very best. I rearrange my face to show concern and disappointment. "She was too tired to really talk," I say, and his face falls. "But she did mention that you said something about her eye being a genetic mutation?" Dad nods and, leading me into the kitchen, grabs a bottle of apple juice out of the fridge. He pours us both a glass and takes a swig from his.

"The girl's eye is a mutation, and if all the children in her clan have the same one, as she claims, it means that their parents all did something that would produce that dramatic of an effect in their offspring."

"And you think this has something to do with a drug."

"What I was told, Miles, is that a group of greenie scientists were working on a drug to solve the problem of endangered animals. To help species that were dying out resist disease and extinction. They tried it on themselves and found it had made them immune to every illness they tested. It would have been at least a year—nine months, of course—before they discovered its effect on a developing fetus. And when they knew what they had, they escaped America for somewhere they could live undetected, in seclusion."

"Just to hide their kids' eyes?" I ask doubtfully.

My father sets his glass down on the counter and looks at me intently. "I'm guessing that they didn't initially know what they had. But they stayed when they discovered they had stopped aging."

"So that's what Amrit is," I say, confirming my theory from before—from when I saw Whit with my own eyes. "It's a drug that stops aging."

"If you want to get technical about it, Amrit doesn't completely stop aging. But it slows it down to an imperceptible rate—at least that's what Dr. Graves claims. It's the holy grail, Miles. The fountain of youth. They have figured out how to cheat death."

I just stare at Dad, at the greed on his face, and feel sick. "Not only do I think you're all crazy," I say, "but I think you've been duped."

Dad holds a finger up, like he's scolding me. "Believe it or not, it's true. I've seen the test results. I've seen Mr. Graves himself. I know what's possible with this drug, Miles. And Blackwell

Pharmaceutical will own its patent." He turns and leaves the room.

I'm not going to let this happen. When I hear his office door close, I sneak away to the carport and start cleaning out my car, leaving all the camping gear in the back. We're going to need it. Hopefully soon.

59

JUNEAU

THE BUZZING IN MY EARS HAS FINALLY STOPPED. My vision is normal, but I feel shaky. And the last time I went to the bathroom, the nurse had to come over and help me walk. My legs feel like rubber bands.

No one knows what happened to me. The paramedic said I could have just fainted or had a panic attack. It could have been the stress of the last few days. All I know is that when Mr. Blackwell said what he did about the elders taking a drug and having mutant babies, something snapped in me. Maybe because it made sense. Maybe because I didn't want it to be true. My clan's lies are never-ending. We kids are experiments. The whole thought of it made me sick.

I am left alone with my thoughts and for once don't want to be by myself. It's just me and the realization that what Mr. Blackwell said about a drug is true. I didn't make the connection before, didn't realize that what I thought was a complicated ceremony to unite a person to the Yara could actually be broken down to one essential component. That the singing and dancing and arrangement of the body was just a farce. That the tying of elements to the hands and feet, the nine sips of pure water, the furs and feathers and candles and crystals were all symbols. Like Whit's totems. They were all a sham.

Only a second of the eight-hour ceremony counted for anything, and that was when the concoction of plants and minerals was poured down the initiate's throat. It was a drug. And it had a name: Amrit.

I didn't think I could feel any worse, but this has made me numb with shock. United with the Yara? What a joke. I have a bitter taste in my mouth, and if I weren't sitting in someone's nice bedroom, I would spit.

I hear the sound of a door slamming, and a minute later the roar of a car engine starting up and driving off. Miles bursts into the room. "Dad just got called into the office for something urgent. We've got to get you out of here before he gets back. The closer Dad thinks he's getting to the truth, the more pressure he's going to put on you. You're never going to be able to get away until he gets what he wants, and maybe not even after that."

Miles grabs my shoes from beside the door and hands them to me. "The nurse is watching TV. If we go out the back, she won't see us leave the house, but she can see my car out of the window. And if she sees you outside, she'll definitely phone my dad to let him know. Do you think you could do your disappearing act for the length of time it takes you to walk from the side of the house until you get into the car?"

I nod, although I'm not really sure. I lace up my second shoe and rise unsteadily to my feet. Miles puts an arm around me, and we tiptoe out of the bedroom and down a corridor to a glass door leading out to a flagstone patio. Miles turns the key in the lock and opens the door, careful not to make a noise.

We slip out onto the patio, and I follow Miles around the side of the house. He looks at the car, and then points to the front window. The nurse is sitting facing the window, watching an enormous flat-screen TV that is to one side of it, but with a clear view down the drive.

"I'm going to walk first, open the car door, and hesitate a second before I get in. If you can slip past me in through the driver's-side door and stay invisible until we drive off, the nurse will think it's only me who left."

"Okay, just give me a second," I say, and closing my eyes, I take a deep breath. Suddenly losing my equilibrium, I stumble, and Miles reaches out to grab my shoulder.

"Are you okay?" he asks, his brow knit with worry.

I nod. "Closing eyes—not a good idea," I say. "I don't know if I'm going to be able to connect to the Yara while standing up. I'm still dizzy."

"Okay, how about if you hold on to me while you walk. Would that work?" he asks.

"Let's try," I say, and looping my arm through his, put some of my weight on him. "Put your arm down a little, or it looks like you're holding someone up." Miles puts both of his hands in his front pockets, and I get a good grasp of his arm. "That's perfect," I say. "Now hold still."

I stand, holding Miles's right arm with both hands, and keep my eyes open this time. *Metamorphosis,* I think, and look at the colors around me. Green everywhere. The grass, bushes, and trees make an almost solid verdant backdrop, and I picture a chameleon in my mind, skin changing to meld in with its environment. I feel the Yara flash through my body like a lightning bolt as I change to resemble my surroundings.

"You're green!" says Miles from next to me. "Not just green. Kind of greeny brown, like camouflage."

"Let's go!" I urge, and we set out toward the car. Miles opens the driver's-side door and then drops the keys on the ground. As he bends slowly to pick them up, I slide past him and slither into the passenger's seat, pushing myself as low down under the dashboard as possible, in case my camouflage wears off.

Miles gets in the car, closes the door, and starts the ignition. I watch him smile and wave good-bye to the nurse before putting the car in gear and looping around his driveway and back down the drive.

"Was she watching?" I ask, not daring to move until we are well away. We pull out onto the main road, and Miles floors the gas pedal.

"She waved at me," he says, "and as soon as I waved back, she turned and walked off in the direction of your bedroom. She'll be finding out about now that you're gone. And the call will go straight in to my dad."

I raise myself up off the floor to sit on the passenger seat and strap my seat belt across me. Miles looks over at me and smiles a wide smile. "We did it!" he crows.

I lean my head back against the headrest and exhale a deep sigh of relief. I feel the Conjuring leave me and look down to see my own suntanned skin, jeans, and tennis shoes.

"All right. Dad will have someone following us as soon as he knows you're gone. I won't be able to use any of my credit cards, so I hope you've got money."

"I lost my bag in the scuffle back in Salt Lake City," I say mournfully.

"No, you didn't," he says. "It's back there."

I lean over the seat and see my bag sitting on the floor and almost faint from relief. "Miles, thank you. My whole life is in that bag." I pull it over the seat to rummage through. Everything's still there, except my crossbow, of course, which I dropped when I was seized outside Whit's car. Although I feel defenseless without it, I still have my knife.

"Next stop, New Mexico!" Miles says.

"Woo-hoo!" I yell.

But our excitement disappears seconds later when Miles glances in the rearview mirror and starts swearing. I turn to see what he's looking at. A block away, coming upon us at a frightening speed, is an army-green Jeep.

60

JUNEAU

MILES FLOORS IT. THIS IS HIS NEIGHBORHOOD, and he manages to stay ahead of the Jeep. And then he takes a right, and suddenly we're leaving the suburb and heading toward a desolate landscape dotted with sparse trees and sagebrush.

"Where are we going?" I ask.

"To the desert. I think we can lose them better out here. I know of a place we could hide. A place my friends and I used to go to hang out when we didn't want our parents to find us. It's an old shack."

"But, Miles, out here we're easy prey. There's nothing to hide behind. It's just a matter of who's faster."

"It's the only plan I've got," he says with a worried frown.

For a while, we stay ahead, but the Jeep gains a little with each mile. Finally, when it's only a few yards behind us, the Jeep swerves into the left lane and speeds up until we are almost side by side. Whit is in the passenger's seat, his window down, waving at us to pull over. "Stop!" I can see him yell, but the roaring of the motors drowns his voice.

And then everything happens at once: the guard in the backseat lifts a gun and pulls the trigger before I have time to react. "No!" I scream, just as there is a loud crack of gunfire. Whit turns and wrestles with the guard. The gun goes off again. Miles makes a grunting sound, and our car swerves dangerously to the right. I grab the wheel and straighten us as Miles slumps over toward the window.

"Miles!" I yell. "Are you okay?"

"I think I just got shot," he says. "Take the wheel."

I unfasten both of our seat belts, grab the wheel, and scoot over to knock Miles's foot off the pedals. He slumps down to lean back across the seat, pulling his legs up toward him to make room for me. I am numb. My body has taken over, since my mind can't deal with what just happened.

I glance over at the Jeep and see Whit's white face in the open window. He looks horrified. He hadn't expected his guy to shoot—that much is clear. I feel a wave of nausea hit me and have to concentrate to keep from trembling. It's my second time behind the wheel, and I'm barreling down a desert highway at top speed. *Just stay on the road and keep the pedal down,* I tell myself.

I know I can't outdrive Whit's men. I have to do something. Reach the Yara. I'll never be able to calm myself enough to connect. But those were Whit's rules, I remind myself. And though my heart's beating like a drum against my rib cage and my breathing is erratic, I wipe everything from my mind and focus on the force that runs through everything: me, Miles, the car, the road, and the air around us. This force is mine to use and I, in return, am its tool. I feel the lightning bolt of connection, and suddenly I am clear. Focused.

Both cars have slowed down. It looks like Whit is yelling at the guy in the backseat and not completely focused on the road. I glance at the Jeep and imagine the inside of its motor. I picture the silver-and-white spark plugs that I Read before, and think water, focusing on taking any moisture in this dry landscape and gathering it right there, right between the connection of the plugs and the motor. And all of a sudden the Jeep skids out.

I watch it in the rearview mirror, spinning in circles on the road behind us before flying off the road and landing on its side. That's all I have time to see before we pass over a ridge and out of sight.

Miles moans from beside me. "Miles!" I yell. "How badly are you hurt?"

"I'm alive," he says, "but I think he got me in the chest."

"Miles, I can't take you back to town if that means passing the Jeep. If they're still alive, they might try to shoot us again." I slow the car down enough so that I can think. Now that the strength of the Yara has left me, I feel numb with shock. "Where is this place you wanted to hide?"

"It's just this old shack. Take a right past the Exxon sign, hidden behind a boulder," he says, panting hard. I see an Exxon billboard in the distance and head straight for it, then take the dirt road behind it so fast that the back of the car fishtails. My heart leaps to my throat, but I manage to straighten out and stay on the road.

We are coming up to a massive boulder-like rock formation. A nearly invisible path winds behind it, and right there in the middle of nowhere, but invisible from the main road, stands a shack.

I screech to a stop between the shack and the boulder, hiding the car from anyone who might drive by. Jumping out, I run around to the passenger's side and open it. Miles is lying on his back with his legs bent. There's blood all over the place: I can't even see where it's coming from.

"Oh, Miles," I whisper. Though I'm used to hunting—to seeing blood and gore—I feel powerless.

"Do you think you can walk?" I ask.

"I'll try," he says. His voice is weak. That scares me more than all the blood.

Be calm, I think. *You have to be strong. Now is not the time for emotions.*

"Let's get you inside the cabin," I say. "The Jeep flipped onto its side, but they might be able to get it back on the road."

"When he finds out you're gone, Dad will be after us too," Miles says.

"Don't worry about that," I say, and prop him into a sitting position, pulling his legs to swing them around and out of the car. I loop his arm over my shoulder and heave him up. We half stumble over the pebbled ground toward the ramshackle house,

Miles groaning and pressing his hand to his side. I get him up onto the porch and, seeing that the door is ajar, kick it open. I take a look around. There is nothing inside. No sink. No furniture. No electricity. Just one small room with beer bottles and cigarette packets strewn about.

I help lower Miles to the floor, then rip off my jacket, fold it a couple of times and place it under his head. I run back out to the car and pop the trunk for my bag and the camping gear, in case there's anything in there that will be of use.

It's dark inside the room, so I light some of the camping candles and put them around Miles's body. I don't take the time to unbutton his cotton shirt, I just rip it and let the buttons fly. The T-shirt beneath is so thoroughly soaked in blood I have no idea what color it was originally. I take scissors out of my pack and cut straight up the middle of the shirt through the neckline, and then down through the sleeves, so he is lying bare-chested and the bullet hole in his side, between two ribs, is exposed.

Miles lets out another groan and, wrapping his arms around his chest, writhes in pain.

"Shh, Miles. Try to stay still," I say, and bring a candle closer so I can see his wound. It is a round hole the size of my fingertip, with blood oozing from it. I touch it, pulling the flesh apart enough to see that the bullet is embedded a couple of inches in. I don't know what to do. I glance around the room once more, assessing what I have available to me.

I should call someone to come help us, but there's no phone in this shack. "Miles, you didn't get a new phone, did you?" I ask.

He shakes his head no. I wonder how close the nearest hospital is. I doubt I'd even be able to find it in time. And I could try to flag someone down on the road, but I have no idea if Whit and his men have their Jeep back up and running.

This is up to me, I realize. Miles's life is in my hands. I inspect the bullet hole again, and then, digging through my bag, pull out my bowie knife. I've dug thousands of crossbow arrows out of dead prey, but never a bullet.

Miles starts babbling something about a dream, and I can tell he hasn't got long before he will pass out. Which would probably be a good thing, because this is going to hurt. I could sedate him with some brugmansia but don't have the time it would need to take effect. I've got to do this now. I turn the knife blade inside the candle flame and summon all my courage.

Holding Miles's wound open with my left hand, I insert the knife tip into the hole alongside the bullet and follow it down. Miles lets out a tortured scream, convulses, and then falls unconscious. His movement has made the knife slice slightly to the side. I straighten it and then quickly dig down, wedging the blade tip under the bullet, and pull upward. Once it is partially through the skin, I pull it out the rest of the way with my fingertips. Blood begins to pour out of the hole.

I pull off my long-sleeved shirt, leaving only my tank top, wad it up to press against the wound, and roll him back and forth to pass a shirtsleeve underneath his torso. I tie it off and sit back to inspect my work.

The bullet's out, but he's lost a lot of blood. And although my knife was clean, I know he could get an infection, unlike me and my clan, who heal quickly and cleanly from the occasional accident. His skin has become ashen, and if he wasn't breathing, I would think he was already dead.

My heart beats so hard, I feel it pattering in my throat. What else can I do? And then it occurs to me. There is something I can do. Although I've never performed it alone, I know that I am able. I have a moment of hesitation: will it even work on someone who has not grown up with the Yara? Then I remember—Mother and Father didn't grow up with the Yara, and it worked for them. Whit was going to sell it to the outside world, so he must think it will work on anyone. Besides, I have no other choice but to sit and let Miles die. One look at his bloody form and my decision is made.

I carefully empty my pack until all its contents are spread across the floor, making sure I have everything I need. I begin picking up stones and bunches of herbs and lay them out in lines. I take a packet of mixed plants and minerals and place it next to Miles's head, along with the agate cup and the ceremonial blade.

I put a large moonstone in each of Miles's hands. I arrange the candles in a halo around his head. And I begin the Rite.

I think of what I am doing and wonder how much of it is necessary and how much just for show. Until Miles's dad began going on about the ingestion of medicine before we stopped aging, I hadn't questioned the Rite. No one questioned the Rite. Only Whit and I knew how to do it, I having taken the place of my mother before me. He told me that it had to be performed by a woman, that he was just there for show, but I wonder now why he wasn't able to do it himself.

And although I know now that most of what I've been taught is in effect a smokescreen for the drug, it makes me feel better to perform the preparations for the Rite as I always have. Unfortunately, in Miles's case, I don't have all the time in the world, like I usually do.

Working quickly, I strip off the rest of Miles's clothes, and then, taking two gold nuggets, I bind them to the underside of each foot using strips of cotton cloth. I sing as I work, the song the children sing outside Whit's yurt, where the body will lie during the death-sleep. I sing about death and rebirth. I sing of sleeping and awakening; the winter hibernation of the animals and the renewal of life in spring.

It's not the singing, it's the drug, I remind myself, but Miles deserves this treatment. Even if it's needless ritual, it's meant to symbolically tie the spirit of the person to the Yara. To join their life to nature. To give it more meaning than just living for themselves—after the Rite, they are so integrally entwined with nature that they live for everything and everyone on the planet. I want that for Miles. I think that he would want it himself, if he understood. Even if it's all a sham, it means something to me.

I feel myself descending into the trancelike state I fall into when performing the Rite. My body doesn't matter anymore. I move outside it, watching myself circle Miles three times, crumbling dried herbs above his body and letting them fall like dust to his skin. I join it again to pick up the cup and empty the packet of herbs and minerals into it.

"Miles," I say, and shake him gently. "Miles, are you still here with me?"

He takes a shallow breath and says, "I think so." He tries to open his eyes, blinks a few times, and then stops trying. At least he's conscious again. I must work fast.

Taking the small, curved ceremonial knife, I cut the palm of my hand and let my blood drip onto the greenish powder, and then stir it with the knife's spoon-shaped hilt.

"You have to swallow this," I say, and scoop the blood mixture into his mouth. I pick up the canteen of water and pour it down his throat, washing the concoction down with it. He sputters and coughs, but keeps the powder and liquid down.

"Miles Blackwell, do you hear me?" I say.

"Yes," Miles responds.

"Do you agree to become one with the Yara? To dedicate your life to the earth and the force that binds every living thing to one another?"

"Juneau," breathes Miles. "What the hell are you talking about?"

"Miles, do you agree to trade your life of eighty years for one of many hundred?"

Miles pries one eye open and lets it rest on me. He speaks, but his voice has no force behind it, and I have to lean down to hear him. "If I don't, do I die?" he whispers.

I touch my hand to his chest, and though my body is numb

and my spirit calm from the trance, I feel my eyes cloud with tears. "You might die anyway. But this is my best try," I confess.

"Then I do, Juneau," he says, and his voice is a mere whisper.

I position myself near his head. With my other hand I begin combing his wavy hair with my fingers as I wait for the mixture to take effect—for the death-sleep to come. Miles's breaths become increasingly shallower until he breathes his last breath and becomes still. Tears flood my eyes as I lean over and kiss his still-warm lips. And then I go to sit in the open door of the shack.

I close my eyes as my spirit disconnects from the Yara. I feel myself emerge from the otherworldly haze of my trance. And as I do, the weight of the decision I just made presses down on me, crippling me with fear. What have I done?

The only thing you could do, I tell myself. I open my eyes and look out upon the landscape before me—the flat, barren wasteland with rolling red hills far in the distance.

Besides the desert animals, I am the only living, breathing thing for miles around. I sit in the doorway and wait.

ACKNOWLEDGMENTS

EB ARTICLE FOR EDITOR: "EVERY PUBLISHING HOUSE has manufacturing, marketing, and accounts departments, but the heart of the business lies in the editorial function." Tara Weikum, you have been the heart of my five books. Not only having the vision to imbue them with coherency and life but providing the love needed to make my projects grow.

EB article for agent: "The relationship that exists when one person engages another to act for him—e.g., to do his work, to sell his goods, to manage his business." Stacey Glick, you are an agent extraordinaire, finding the perfect home for Juneau and her clan.

I will now switch to the E(ncyclopedia) P(lum), since the rest of the clan's EB collection seems to have been destroyed by brigands.

EP for beta reader: Claudia Depkin. Also known as she-who-has-more-patience-than-the-gods. (Not that they're renowned for their patience, but you get the idea.) Thank you for having the very first look at everything once again, for asking the right questions, and for prodding me into action.

EP for copy editors: Valerie Shea and Melinda Weigel. Thank you for correcting the SAME errors book after book, for making sense of my French-addled English ("This is not a word."), and for finding the inconsistencies that my ADD brain flings left and right on the page.

EP for assistant editor: Christopher Hernandez, or he-who-always-finds-the-perfect-word. Chris, your suggestions for *After the End* were spot-on. You ask the right questions and concoct the perfect solutions. Thank you!

EP for cover artists and designers: the fine people (Ray Shappell, Alison Donalty, Craig Shields, Howard Huang, and Kelly Delay) responsible for giving *After the End* its awesome cover. Thank you for creating such perfect packaging for Juneau and Miles's story.

EP for mistress-of-the-road-trip: that certain cousin who drives with you from Seattle to Albuquerque just so you can follow your protagonists' route while taking notes on the flora, fauna, and very strange habitants along the way. Diana, wish we could do one of these every year.

EP for Wereboar Sisterhood: a group of writers who, after sharing a den for a week, discovered they were long-lost pack members. Merci, my sisters-in-taxidermy, for all the support, love, and Kleenexes.

EP for Hotel Eldorado: a hotel in the Clichy neighborhood of Paris that was the frequent habitation of Amy Plum when she needed a faraway Batcave in which to conceive the ideas behind *After the End*. Don't look for the one in Idaho, but if you find it, be extra careful when making private phone calls.

EP for loyal readers: you are the reason my job is fun. Thank you for your enduring support and enthusiasm for my stories.

FALL IN LOVE
IN PARIS
DIE FOR ME
Would you risk your life for love?
AMY PLUM
UNTIL I DIE
How do you choose between love and life?
AMY PLUM
IF I SHOULD DIE
AMY PLUM
HARPERTEEN IMPULSE
DIE FOR HER
A Die for Me Novella
AMY PLUM
Don't miss Jules' story in
DIE FOR HER.
Available as an ebook only.